MW01268232

Walking Through The Mist

No Frills
<<<>>>
Buffalo
Buffalo NY

Copyright © 2013 by Sinéad Tyrone

Printed in the United States of America

Tyrone, Sinéad

Walking Through The Mist/ Tyrone- 1st Edition

ISBN: 978-0-9910455-1-8

1. Walking Through The Mist – Fiction.   2. Irish Heritage – Family
No Frills – Fiction.
1.   Title

Cover designed by Beth O.riginals

No Frills Buffalo Press
119 Dorchester
Buffalo, New York 14213
For more information visit Nofrillsbuffalo.com

Walking Through The Mist

Sinéad Tyrone

<<◇>>

To Ann, my mentor, my guide, my "big sister",
and my friend.

1

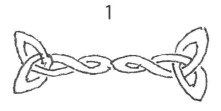

Mack Macready peered around the corner of the backstage curtain to the crowd filling seats at the Riviera Theater near Buffalo, New York, then turned to the band behind him and announced, "Full house again tonight, boys. Give it your best."

"We always do, boss." Patrick Leahy, Macready's Bridge's crack fiddler, picked up a metal chair, turned it to face the back wall, and sat down.

"Prayer time?" Mack asked.

Patrick gave a wide grin. "You know my routine by now."

Mack remembered the rack of amplifiers and wiring that had fallen over the third week into their tour, just missing Niall, and the kitchen fire at their hotel two weeks ago an observant waitress had discovered just before it burst into an uncontrollable inferno. Surely Patrick's prayers had paid off those times. He wondered how many other disasters the band had avoided during the past six weeks due to Patrick's steadfast prayers. Whatever the number, he wouldn't dare risk a break in their protection now. He nodded, "Go ahead."

Patrick's eyes were already closed, his lips moving, "Dear God, please look after Moira this night and tomorrow, as she runs our house without me. Guide and protect her and our twins, Conor and Caitlyn. Help them mind their mam and be good to each other. Please guide Michael, Niall, Aidan and myself as we bring our music to the people gathered here. Let our music bring them as much joy as you give us. Give them and ourselves safe travel after the show." Sensing Mack could still hear him, Patrick finished, "Please tell Mack to let us sleep in tomorrow."

Mack laughed. "You can sleep in all you want. The other boys will be heading out to see Niagara Falls."

"Oh yeah!" Patrick turned his eyes upward once more. "God, cancel that last request."

Mack continued across the backstage. "Something wrong?" he asked as he walked past Michael Sullivan, the group's golden-voiced tenor.

Michael frowned at his mobile phone. "Susannah wants me to go to Barcelona with her when our tour's done."

"I take it you don't want to go."

"I'm not sure." He turned from his phone to Mack. "I'm crazy to hesitate, aren't I?"

"No." Mack saw the conflict in Michael's brown eyes. "You and Susannah run hot and cold, don't you? One minute you're fighting, the next you're head over heels in love. That's hard enough when you're home; it would make for a very unhappy vacation wouldn't it?"

Michael nodded. "It would."

"Try to put it out of your mind for now. The show's almost on us. We can talk about this later if you'd like."

Michael reread the text Susannah had sent, "Join me at my uncle's villa in Barcelona in three weeks. I know you'll be tired; the rest might do you good. Let me know ASAP." Her photo smiled out at him from his mobile phone, golden silky hair fanned by a breeze, green eyes sparkling as she laughed. She was beautiful alright, the kind of beauty that

8

caused people to stop in their tracks, men to dream she was theirs, women to try to capture her style and make it their own. Michael recalled for the hundredth time the thrill as he walked down Dublin streets and into restaurants with Susannah on his arm, knowing that while all eyes were locked on Susannah, they watched him as well, the fellah lucky enough to be with her. He also knew that behind all her beauty lie a spoiled, stubborn spirit. On a good day, Barcelona with Susannah would be heaven. On a bad day, it would be hell. "Oh Suze," Michael spoke to the picture before him, "why do you have to be so hard?"

Niall Donoghue was double-checking the reeds and joints of his uillean pipes when Mack reached him.

"Everything okay?"

"Aye boss." Niall handed his pipes over to the stagehand who would set them by his chair. "Fit as a fiddle, they are."

"If they're fit as a fiddle, we've got a problem!"

They both laughed, then Niall pulled his phone out and handed it to Mack. "One for my mam and dad?"

He stood far enough to the right that the theater's curtains hid him from the crowd but Mack could still capture the crowd and the theater's rich interior behind him. Mack snapped the photo and handed the phone back to Niall. "Tell your folks I said hi."

"Riviera, Buffalo, New York. Tomorrow, Niagara Falls." As he typed his message, Niall pictured his parents checking their computer every morning for the updates he sent. He could still hear their frustration, and occasional laughter, as he taught them how to log on and access their emails. "Ah well," he thought, "it's enough they run their sheep farm well. Electronics isn't a requirement." Before signing off, he added, "Love you, see you soon."

As Niall emailed the picture and message to his parents with his customary good night, Mack moved on to Aidan O'Connell, who paced the backstage with his phone pressed to his ear.

Mack held five fingers up to remind the guitarist how little time he had before the show started. Aidan nodded and returned to his call.

"Da, I've caught you before you turned in."

"You always do!" his father teased across the five hour time distance that separated them.

"I know," Aidan laughed back. "Hey, Da, I was thinking about the home studio."

"You always are."

"So are you. Listen, Mack was telling me there's a place for sale out Gortree Road way." His father's deep inhale stopped him. "What's wrong?"

"I'm rethinking the moving idea," the elder O'Connell confessed. "Jeannie's got such a short time left at school, and all your grandmother's friends are here."

"You're the one who said our house wasn't big enough for a studio, that we should move out to the country," Aidan reminded him.

"I know, and I know it's your dream."

"It was your dream first, remember? Roisin Studios? After mom?"

"You're right. Okay, tell me more about this place."

"Like I was saying, out on Gortree Road, before Lismoghray. The house has three bedrooms, there's a grand old shed large enough for a studio and office, and extra bedroom if we lay it out right."

Aidan caught the dimming and rising of house lights, which warned everyone it was almost show time. "Da, I have to go. Check the place out tomorrow and let me know what you think."

"Can't be tomorrow. We're off to Ballymena for the day to see your gran's old schoolmate, Molly Pearson."

"Oh, that's right." Stories he'd heard of Cathleen and Molly and the adventures they'd had over the years flashed through Aidan's mind. "Day after then?"

"Will do. Oh, your gran asked me to tell you Jeannie saw a magpie today."

"Only one?" Aidan could hear his grandmother's voice recite the saying he and his sister had grown up with, one for sorrow, two for joy, whenever they'd spotted one of the large black and white birds. "Did she make Jeannie go out and find another?"

They both laughed. "I'm sure tomorrow she'll see a dozen of them. It's springtime, they'll be everywhere looking for mates and building nests."

The lights dimmed once more. "Gotta go now! Hugs to Jeannie and Gran for me."

"Okay. Have a good show. And Aidan," Daniel O'Connell uncharacteristically prolonged the pre-show call, "I'm proud of you, boy."

Aidan held the words and the phone a few seconds, then softly answered, "I love you Da. Can't wait to get back home."

Mack chuckled as Aidan turned off and pocketed his phone. "Anyone who thinks Patrick's the family man of the group should see you and your family in action."

"Yeah," Aidan grinned, "a bit much aren't we?"

"Is there a day this entire tour you haven't been on the phone with them?"

Aidan shook his head, "I don't think so." He checked his shoes, which never managed to stay tied. "It's just the four of us, you know? We've only got each other. I think that's what makes us so close."

The Riviera's house lights lowered once more, its gold stage curtains parted, blue, green and white spotlights swept across the stage, and the sold out crowd cheered as Macready's Bridge burst onstage with "The Jolly Beggarman." They followed that with a mix of traditional Irish songs, which roused the crowd who clapped, sang and danced along, and their own compositions, which held the crowd mesmerized. Even though he'd seen the same show a hundred times over, Mack found himself drawn in, as captivated as the audience by the music and the musicians themselves, and considered again how blessed he was to have found each of them.

As Michael's voice floated over "Mary in the Mist," Mack recalled his discovery of the tenor at Merchant's Arch pub in Dublin's Temple Bar district, where Mack had ducked in to escape a downpour. He'd ordered a pint of stout, then followed the packed pub's attention to the singer at the end of the bar. Mack couldn't tell whether the singer's dark-haired, dark-eyed, classic good looks or his rich, strong voice was the larger draw. He only knew, after twenty years' experience managing musicians that this singer could do much better than playing in pubs. The rain outside stopped; Mack stayed on, taken in by the unique voice, power and softness combined, liquid iron.

"Mack Macready," he introduced himself when the singer's set was over. "I enjoyed your music."

"Michael Sullivan. Thanks." They shook hands.

"Do you sing here often?" Mack set a fresh pint in front of Michael.

Michael shook his head. "Just filling in for a mate."

"Are there any other places you sing?"

"Nothing regular, whatever I can pick up after work."

Mack studied Michael, saw passion in his brown eyes, and something else. Pain? Conflict? "What kind of work do you do?"

"I'm a front desk manager at a hotel down the road." Michael saw a mix of surprise and disappointment cross Mack's face, and shrugged. "It pays the rent."

"That's not how you plan to spend the rest of your life is it?"

Mack's words sounded so much like Michael's father's when he'd tried to explain his passion for music, his desire to make that his career, that Michael shivered. "That's not how you plan to spend the rest of your life!" When his father had spoken the words, they had sounded harsh, like his father was spitting his choice, and even Michael himself, out. When Mack spoke the words, they sounded incredulous, as if Michael were throwing gold away.

"I'm twenty-nine. High time I packed my dreams away." Michael gave a resigned smile.

"You've got talent." Mack handed Michael his card. "Let me see what I can do for you."

Patrick's fiddle flew over notes in "Geese in the Bog," the crowd cheered and clapped in time, and Mack heard once again a similar performance in Sligo, at the Swagman Pub where he'd gone to meet a friend for dinner.

"That's some fast hand you've got there," he'd complimented Patrick as the fiddler with flamboyant red hair and flashing smile stepped down from the stage when his set was done.

"It's not in me hands," Patrick corrected with a hearty laugh. "It's the bow and fiddle, they have minds of their own. I just do me best to keep up with them."

"You do a fair job. Where else do you play?"

"Wherever they'll have me when my day at the quarry's done." Patrick replied, nodding in the direction of the cement quarry outside of town, as if it were visible through the pub's solid walls.

They reached a table where a brunette woman and two red haired children sat. "Ah, here they are now, brightest lights in any northern sky."

"Your family, I take it?"

"My wife, Moira, and our twins, Conor and Caitlyn."

"Mack Macready," Mack introduced himself and handed Patrick his card. "Would you be interested if I found a way for you to play that fiddle full time?"

For a moment, Patrick's eyes glowed at the prospect of realizing the dream he'd so long carried in his heart. "All I've ever wanted was to play music," he confessed, "but I've got me wife and kiddies, and bills to pay. Can't just walk away from a steady paying job, now can I?"

"If he thinks he can find you work in music, you should take it." Moira took the card from

14

Patrick's hand and smiled at Mack. "If you come across something, we'd be very much interested."

Mack's third card went to Niall, whose haunting uillean pipes over "Minterburn Spring" entranced the Macready's Bridge audience now as it had when Mack first came across him playing pipes to sheep in a field near Minterburn. Mack had pulled his car over, lowered the window, and listened for nearly ten minutes before Niall stopped.

"Were you looking for something? Can I help?" Niall asked, sure this was another tourist trying to find his way on the countryside's narrow, unmarked roads.

Mack pointed to the uillean pipes in Niall's arms. "I was intrigued by the sound of your music."

Niall felt suddenly embarrassed. "Kind of silly, playing to sheep, isn't it?"

"Not at all. They seem to enjoy it."

Niall gazed out over the flock, white clouds drifting over a green, gorse-lined field, and pointed his pipes towards a house on the other side. "Family farm's over there. There's always work to do on a farm, you know." Niall smiled at Mack. "Sometimes I escape to watch over the sheep, but my folks know it's just to practice the pipes."

"Do you like working on the farm?" Mack asked. "Is that what you think you'll do with your life?"

Sunlight reflected off Niall's bronze, wavy hair as he stared awhile over the flock and field. "Maybe someday. But music's what I'm really after."

"I think I can help you there, if you're interested."

Niall nodded in humble response to the crowd's applause, and Mack thought again how fortunate he was in signing the lad, and Michael, and Patrick, and Aidan who now fingered his guitar and entered "Jeannie's Dream," a song he'd written for his younger sister. That car repair was the best break I've ever had, Mack thought as he watched the hushed audience whose eyes were glued to the charismatic blond with the honey gold voice.

He recalled the day in Derry when his car's water pump burst. He'd had it towed to nearby O'Connell's Garage; Daniel O'Connell was installing a new water pump when Aidan entered.

"Gran sent me to remind you dinner's early tonight." Aidan glanced around the garage and nodded to Mack before asking his dad, "Is this your last job?"

"It is," Daniel called back. "I still have a bit of bookwork though. Tell your gran I'll be home in an hour."

"Da," Aidan started to protest, but Daniel stopped him. "An hour. If you have to eat earlier and leave I'll catch up with you."

Aidan rolled his eyes heavenward and agreed, "Alright. Maybe you can catch a cab with Jack and Rita."

"It sounds like I'm holding you back from something. I'm sorry." Mack apologized after Aidan left.

"The boy's got a gig at Peadar O'Donnell's tonight, his first time playing there. He's a wee bit nervous."

Mack's business instinct kicked in once again. "Oh, what does he do? Sing? Play an instrument?"

"Sings and plays guitar. He's got talent, that one, and dreams to match." Daniel's face shone with pride.

"That good, is he?"

Daniel tightened two screws and stepped away from the car, wiping his hands on a cloth. "If you fancy good music, give yourself a treat when you're done here and head down to O'Donnell's. You'll not be disappointed."

Mack had to pick his way through the throng that spilled out onto the street in front of O'Donnell's that night. Inside Aidan held court, fingers dancing over guitar strings, eyes closed at times as he sang, at times open, scanning the faces around him. He spotted Mack and called out, "I see my dad's dragged you out to hear his boy!" Aidan called over to the bartender, "Gary, get this man a pint." As the bartender complied, Aidan closed his eyes and launched into "Carrickfergus," delivering the song with such heart it seemed his own life was ebbing away.

Mack stayed a full hour, amazed by the depth of Aidan's guitar and vocal abilities, and his knack for charming his audience, teasing and telling stories in between songs.

Aidan took a seat at his family's table when the show was over. Mack squeezed through the crowd to join them.

"I see you followed my advice." Daniel pushed a fresh pint towards Mack. "Hope you found it worth your while."

Mack handed his fourth card over. "I'd like to see what I can do for your boy."

As he drove home that night, an idea slowly formed in Mack's mind. He'd been working to find the right jobs for Michael, Patrick, and Niall; what if, instead of individual spots, they were all meant to join forces with Aidan? Mack called them each and laid out his plan. A week later, all four met with Mack for the first time; two weeks later they had started regular rehearsals. Within two months four individuals had melded into one tight band, with bookings in pubs across Ireland and Northern Ireland. Several months later their debut album was out and now, a year after they'd met and with album sales soaring, they were touring America.

"How did the name Macready's Bridge come about?" they were frequently asked, to which each of the boys gave a different answer.

"It's about the bridge between ages," Patrick, at thirty-eight the oldest next to Mack, would answer.

Michael, the lone protestant amid a trio of Catholics, would say, "It's about a bridge between faiths, being able to respect and work with each other."

Niall would point out, "Two of us are from Northern Ireland, two from Eire. It's the bridge that joins us together."

"It's the bridge between the traditional music we've all grown up with and more current musical styles," Aidan would explain. "We've brought the past into the present and given it hope of a future."

Macready's Bridge's followers knew all four answers were right.

The Riviera theater concert ended as all the others had, with an electrifying version of "Home Boys, Home," Aidan's fingers racing across his guitar to keep up with Patrick's flying fiddle, Niall almost losing his breath as he sought to outpace them, and Michael surprising newcomers with his prowess on the bodhran. They segued into "Cliffs of Moher" and finished with the rousing "Macready's Reel," blue, green and white spotlights flashing across every seat in the theater, the crowd on their feet, ecstatic. When Aidan hopelessly lost pace with Patrick, he threw his hands up, they all broke into laughter, and the concert was over.

"Ye just couldn't do it there, could ye, boy?" Patrick teased as they rested backstage for a moment before packing their instruments away.

Aidan shook his head with the same amazement he had after every show. "Someday I'll catch up with you and blow right past ya!" He nodded to Michael and the bodhran lying near his feet. "And you! Ya nearly broke through the skin of that thing tonight!"

"It was possessed, to be sure," Michael agreed, then turned to Niall. "So, what's the plan for tonight?"

Niall studied his phone's Internet. "Mack's booked us into a hotel at Niagara Falls. There's a casino next to it, a diner nearby, or we could just order food up to our rooms and relax."

"Your choice, Mr. Entertainment Director," Aidan replied, then yawned as the physical demands of performing caught up with him.

"You're not fading away on us already, are you?" Niall teased.

Aidan nodded towards Patrick. "Blame him. He wore me out!"

They agreed on the diner. Over burgers and fries, Mack congratulated them, "Great job, boys. Another good show tonight."

"How many left, boss?" To the waitress refilling Mack's coffee, Aidan asked, "Do you have any hot sauce?" She threw him an odd look and turned away.

Michael stared at Aidan, eyebrows raised. "Hot sauce? For your burger? You get stranger every day."

"Not my burger." The waitress returned with a small bottle, which Aidan opened and poured over his french fries. He pushed his plate towards Michael. "Try one."

Michael grimaced, "Not on your life!"

Patrick shook his head the way he did when Conor and Caitlyn teased each other, and checked his phone's calendar. "Eleven more days and we'll be home."

"Not that you're anxious or anything, right?" Niall nodded towards Patrick. "Tell me, aside from Moira and the kids, what are you most looking forward to back home?"

"Aside from Moira and the kids there is nothing." Visions of Moira and the twins and their seaside cottage danced across Patrick's mind. Eleven more days, and I'll be home with you all, he thought and smiled, then nabbed one of Niall's french fries. "What about you? Looking forward to those sheep of yours?"

They all laughed. "Bet they'll all be lined up to see you!" Aidan raised his glass of cola, the hardest drink the diner had to offer. "Lady-killer be damned! Here's to our own sheep-boy Niall!"

"Sheep don't talk back." Niall studied the layers of meat, cheese, lettuce and tomato stacked between bread and thought, they don't cheat on you either. Mary's face rose before him, vowing she'd wait for him while Macready's Bridge traveled to Scotland, explaining in a letter he received when he'd returned home that she'd moved in with Gary, his best friend, because Gary wasn't away for such long stretches of time. Niall thought of Patrick's Moira, and Michael's Susannah, and Aidan's any-girl-he-wanted, and ached inside that all he did have to look forward to was a flock of smelly sheep.

"What about you?" he asked Michael. "Is Susannah anxious to get you back home? Or are you two still not speaking to each other?"

Michael shrugged. "One week we're fighting, the next she wants me to join her for holidays in Spain. I can't figure her out."

"Spain?   Wow!" Patrick whistled. "Are you going?"

"I don't know."

"What was she mad at you for last week?" Aidan searched back through his memory. "Oh yeah, you wouldn't be home for her father's birthday."

"It was a big event," Michael defended. "He turned sixty, her mother planned a huge party, Susannah was disappointed I couldn't be there."

"She's a tough one." Niall remarked. "I'd much rather deal with my sheep."

"She is stunning, though."

"She is that," Niall and Aidan both agreed with Patrick.

"It's just a trip to Spain," Mack pointed out, "not a marriage proposal. What would the harm be?"

The harm, Michael thought, would be of him falling deeper in love. The pain would be hell if he and Susannah broke up. Trying to dissect all the facets of Susannah with the group would take too much time, though, and it was far too late in the night for that, so he deflected the attention to Aidan. "What is it you can't wait to get home to, as if we didn't already know?"

"Daddy, sister, granny!" Patrick, Michael and Niall spoke in unison, and the whole group laughed.

"Too right!" Then Aidan turned serious. "That and the sea. She's calling me something fierce the past few days."

"You do love her, don't you?" Niall noted the faraway look in Aidan's eyes.

"Aye. I can't wait to get back and breathe her sweet air."

"Bet the first thing you do when we get home is go out and buy that boat you showed us the other day."

Aidan shook his head. "No, Pat, first thing I want is to build the studio my daddy's always dreamed of. I can get a boat anytime."

They all fell silent with thoughts of home. To break the stillness, Michael asked, "What time are we heading over to see the Falls tomorrow?"

Niall turned to Mack. "What time do we have to leave for Albany?"

"We can leave as late as midnight, sleep on the bus, and arrive in Albany in the morning. You've got all of tomorrow free."

"I'm not getting up till noon." Aidan stared at Niall, the perpetual early riser. "You got that?"

Niall stared back through narrowed eyes. "Ten a.m. I've seen the list of fun you have in mind."

"Oh, yeah!" Aidan pulled the Niagara Falls brochure out of his coat pocket. "Look at this! Whirlpool jet boat! Patrick, you're going on this with me, right?"

Patrick glanced at the picture of a large yellow boat powering through a whirl of white waves, life-jacketed riders clinging for life, and shook his head vehemently. "You'll never catch me on that."

"How about this?" Aidan showed him the Whirlpool Aero Car photo. "You'll do this."

Patrick pulled the brochure away from Aidan, turned to a photo of a crowd standing by the Horseshoe Falls, feet firmly planted on the ground. "Here. This is what I'll be doing."

"What about that other boat ride?" Michael asked.

"Maid of the Mist," Mack recalled. "We all want to go on that one."

Patrick turned again to the brochure. "That looks harmless."

Niall nodded towards Aidan. "I can see the wheels spinning. We're not standing on your side of that boat!"

Aidan tried to pull an innocent look, failed, and burst out laughing.

"So, ten a.m., coffee in the lobby, then we head out," Niall suggested.

"I have a bit of work to do in the morning," Mack told them. "If I'm not done by ten you can all go ahead and I'll catch up with you. But don't do that boat ride without me." With that, he picked up the bill, added his share of money to what the boys had laid down, and turned it over to the waitress. "I'm heading for bed," he announced to the band. "The rest of the night is yours."

"I'm heading up too." Michael rose and joined him, with the others close behind. Soon they were each in bed, Mack turning occasionally to find the position that best suited his aching knees and back; Patrick dreaming of Moira, Conor and Caitlyn and their peaceful seaside cottage; Niall dreaming he was home doing farm chores with his parents; Michael sleeping fitfully, visions of Susannah floating through his dreams, beautiful in the same way a volcano was;

23

and Aidan dreaming of the studio he'd build with his dad, of riding in a boat with his sister, and of his granny's stew and homemade bread at the end of the day.

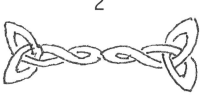

Aidan strolled into the coffee shop, hair still damp from his rushed shower, left shoe untied, staring at his phone with a puzzled look.

"Have any of you tried calling home today?" he asked the others who had already gathered by the pastry display case. "Are there any storms back home, anything that might have knocked power out? I can't get hold of my dad or Jeannie."

"Moira didn't mention any storms when I talked to her, but then, I didn't ask." Patrick saw the concern in Aidan's eyes. "You've been through this with them before; they probably don't have their phones switched on."

"Could be," Aidan agreed. His father's words from the night before echoed in his mind, "Jeannie saw a magpie." He'd always laughed off his grandmother's warning about "one for sorrow". This morning, though, the phrase nagged at the back of his brain. A vision of one of the nuisance birds flew across his mind. He shivered and shook the vision off, and glanced at the menu board. "What's everyone having?"

"Coffee and cheese danish," Niall chose.

Michael selected, "Espresso, and the pecan scone sounds good."

Patrick viewed the menu board again. "I'll have the sausage, egg and cheese sandwich and a piece of that coffee cake there. Oh, and tea."

"Are you sure that's enough?" Niall teased. "Last meal for you, you know. That boat ride's coming up."

Michael pointed to Aidan's left shoe. "Do you want to tie that thing before you have an unfortunate meeting with the floor?"

Upstairs, Mack glanced at his watch, relieved to find it was only ten a.m. In a quick hour's time he'd confirmed their Albany hotel reservations, confirmed ticket sales and backstage arrangements with the Albany venue, and given Larry, the band's bus driver, the go ahead to have the bus given a once over at a local garage. "Just the oil and belts," Larry had suggested, "and those brakes are feeling a bit soft." Larry was sure the bus would be in top shape by dinnertime.

Satisfied he'd covered all the details for the next show, Mack powered his laptop down. If he hurried, he could catch the boys at the coffee shop before they headed out for the Falls. He had just slipped his jacket on when his phone rang. He didn't recognize the Ireland number. Puzzled as to who would be calling, he answered with a formal, "Hello."

"Is this Mack Macready?"

He could not place the caller's voice. "Yes."

"Jack MacLaren here, Aidan O'Connell's neighbor." The strained voice paused. "We've met a couple of times at Aidan's shows."

"I remember." The image of a husky man with white hair rose before Mack. "Was it Aidan you wanted?"

"Yes." Another pause. "I mean, I need to talk to him, but I don't want to catch him alone." Jack inhaled a full, deep breath. "I have some hard news."

Mack sat in the chair by the hotel room's desk. "Why don't you tell me first."

"Almond streusel coffee cake." Aidan pointed to the top row pastry after his third study of the display case. "That's what I want."

Patrick motioned towards the lone empty table in the coffee shop. "Michael, why don't you and Aidan grab that spot. Niall, you can help me get our orders."

They were next in line for service when Patrick's phone rang. He glanced at the phone screen, mouthed "Mack" to Niall, then answered, "What's up, boss?"

"Where are you?"

Patrick thought Mack's voice sounded odd, almost gruff. "Still at the coffee shop," he answered. "Are you coming down?"

"Are you all together?"

"Yeah." Patrick frowned, worried over Mack's somber tone. He'd heard Mack yell, cajole, tease and laugh; he'd never heard his voice so grim.

"I need you all to come up to my room."

"Can we order first? We'll bring something up for you too."

Mack hesitated. Would it hurt if his news was delayed? They could at least have breakfast. What harm could that do? Jack would be waiting for Aidan's call, though, and Mack knew he had to get this over with. "No, Patrick, I'm sorry. I need you all back now."

"Something's wrong." Patrick drew Niall aside and called Michael and Aidan over. "Mack wants to see us right away."

"Did he say why?"

Patrick shook his head and answered Niall, "No, but it must be big. I've never heard him sound so serious."

"Busted!" Michael teased, looking straight at Aidan. "What did you do now?"

"Nothing! Why do you always assume it's me in trouble?"

"Because it usually is!"

Aidan gave Michael's arm a playful punch.

"Let's go see what Mack wants. The sooner we're done, the sooner we can head out to the Falls." Niall turned to the door; the others followed, but Patrick, who'd heard Mack's tone of voice, had a sinking feeling they wouldn't see the Falls at all.

A dozen tasks called Mack now, yet Jack's news had frozen him to the desk chair. Outside, mist from Niagara Falls rose against a clear blue sky. Somewhere the Maid of the Mist chugged into action, escorting passengers as close as possible to the bottom of the Horseshoe Falls. Cars rushed along the streets below; a siren blared in the distance; in the room next door two kids fought for control of the t.v. remote. Mack was aware of all of these, yet as if they were part of another world. His world was consumed with searching for the right way to break Jack's news, news that would devastate Aidan and impact them all.

"That can't be true," he'd insisted to Jack. "It's just too awful to be real. Are you sure there's not some mistake?"

"I'm sure," the older man had replied, and outlined the steps he had taken during the hours that led to his call.

"That must have been hell for you."

"Aye, it was, for me and our Rita." Jack had agreed. "It's Aidan now who'll have the hard part."

Mack couldn't even begin to imagine the nightmare Aidan would face. He was still debating the right way to tell him when he heard the boys' familiar footsteps and voices in the hall, then their knock on the door.

As they entered, Aidan spoke first. Full of humor, as always, blue eyes sparkling, he cracked, "This better be good. I haven't had my Mocha Frappuccino yet."

"You never have a Mocha Frappuccino." Niall shot back with equal humor.

"I was looking forward to my first."

Patrick thought Mack's face looked unusually pale, his eyes dead sober. Something was up alright. The hairs on the back of Patrick's neck rose. Michael glanced at Patrick, questioning. He's seen the same thing, Patrick thought. He shook his head at Michael, shrugged his shoulders, and leaned against the wall by the closet, arms folded, waiting to hear Mack's news.

"I'm sorry to break into your fun, boys," Mack started. "Sit down. Here, Aidan, you sit here." He pulled out the desk chair for Aidan.

"Special chair, eh?" Aidan eyed the rest of them, laughing. "Now I know I'm in trouble!" His mind scanned the catalog of recent days, searching for which infraction he was about to be charged with.

Mack passed his eyes over each of them, stopped at Aidan, held his gaze on the young man, eyes innocent, whole face and demeanor innocent, carefree, nothing but music and fun on his mind. All of that was about to change. He took a deep breath then said, "Aidan, I've had a phone call from your neighbor, Jack MacLaren."

"Jack? What did he want?"

"You need to call him." Mack hesitated. He could let Jack deliver the news, take the coward's way out. But no, the news was his to tell now. "Your family was out near Belfast today?"

Aidan caught the grim look in Mack's eyes. The premonition he'd felt all morning rushed from the back of his mind through his body. "Yeah, out to Ballymena. Why?"

There was no easy way to say the next words. Mack just had to push them out, say them fast, get them over with. He closed his eyes, whispered a quick prayer, opened them again and fixed his eyes on Aidan.

"They were in an accident. A lorry hit their car."

At first Aidan didn't comprehend. Mack's words hung in the air before him, foreign, as if Mack spoke Swahili. "What?"

Mack repeated the words, "Your family was in an accident."

Now his words sank in, but they didn't make sense. "Jack called you to tell you my family was in an accident? Why didn't he call me?" Something was wrong; Aidan couldn't put his finger on it. "Why didn't my dad call instead of Jack?"

Patrick, Michael and Niall glanced at each other, afraid.

Mack sat on the edge of the bed opposite Aidan, eye level with the boy. There was no way around it, not for himself, not for Adian, not for any of them. His next words would change all their worlds. "Aidan, your father was killed in the accident, and your sister and grandmother as well. They were all killed."

Patrick gasped.

Niall whispered, "Oh my God."

Michael stared at Mack, too stunned to speak.

"What?" Aidan demanded. He studied Mack's face, trying to discern the cracks that would reveal Mack's words were untrue. He shook his head, eyes large, unbelieving. "No. That can't be right." The grief on Mack's face was all too real, though. Aidan drew deep breaths, fighting to take in enough air. There had to be a mistake. He'd call his dad, find out the truth. He'd hear his dad laugh over the cruel lie and everything would be alright. He grabbed his phone, punched in a number, and frowned when he got a response, "The number you have dialed is currently unavailable." He punched in another number; it rang several times before reaching voicemail. "Jeannie! Call me right away!" He tried his father's number again, and Jeannie's, and ordered, "Damn it! Answer your phone!" When he started to dial again, Mack put his hand over Aidan's to stop him.

"They won't answer, boy. They can't."

Aidan stared hard at Mack. A magpie flew across his mind, raucous call echoing in his ears. The wall behind Mack seemed to tilt to the right. Aidan's breath and heart both stopped, then kicked in again. He pulled his hand and phone away and entered Jack's number.

Jack answered on the first ring, "Aidan?"

"Jack, what the hell's going on?"

Aidan's voice sounded as panicked and unbelieving as Jack knew it would. He nodded to Rita to confirm who he had on the phone, and prayed that God would give him the right words now. "What did Mack tell you?"

"Something about an accident, but it can't be right." Aidan caught the panic rising in his voice and fought to control it, as he fought to control the rising fear that gripped his heart and threatened to choke his breathing.

Jack's heart broke for the boy. Of all the hard tasks he'd been called to perform today, this had to be the worst. Tears rose in his eyes as he confirmed, "It's true, Aidan. I'm sorry."

It was wrong. The news was wrong. Aidan was sure of that. Someone had given Jack the wrong information. Mistaken identity at the hospital, perhaps; or wrong diagnoses. His father was hurt, maybe, unconscious, unable to speak for himself. Maybe all three had been knocked out and were unable to give their names. Maybe the unthinkable had happened, one of them could have been killed, his grandmother, perhaps, or his sister. Certainly not all three, and not his father. There had to be a mistake. "Jack, go to the hospital. Don't call them, they'll tell you anything. They can't all be gone. Maybe one, but not all three. Please, go there and find out."

Jack's voice cracked a bit as he answered, "I've just been to identify the bodies."

"Oh my God." Mack and the band watched as Aidan's eyes grew large, as the color drained from his face and he sank back as far as the chair would allow. "Tell me what happened."

"They were on the A2 outside Ballymena. A lorry came up, going too fast, the driver lost control and hit your father's car." Jack paused, debating over the next piece of information, unsure whether it would help or hurt. "They were killed outright."

The walls around him tilted harder to the right and the floor below him blurred as Aidan took Jack's words in. He was silent so long Jack finally asked, "Aidan?"

32

"Sorry. I'm here. Oh my God, Jack, it can't be true. It just can't." He begged the guardian angels he had always been taught protected him, and the saints he'd been taught he always could talk to, he even begged God himself, please, please don't let this be true. He felt himself shake from head to toe, saw his free hand trembling, lost the battle to keep his tears from spilling over. "Oh God."

Mack took the phone from Aidan, who offered no resistance. "Jack? It's Mack. I'm going to do whatever I can to get Aidan home as soon as possible. Is there anyone he needs to call right now, anything we need to take care of before we get back?"

"No, there will be plenty to do once Aidan gets home, but I can't think of anything that needs tending to right now." Jack heard faint voices in the background. "Is Aidan okay?"

"He's alright." Mack watched the boy who sat stone-faced before him. "He'll be okay. Why don't I call you back in a bit, as soon as I have our flights worked out?"

"Sure. Call anytime."

Jack hung up and turned to Rita. "May I never live to see another day like this."

Rita wiped fresh tears from her eyes. "The poor boy, he'll be gutted by this."

"Gutted? Aye, that's just the tip of it. I don't see how he'll go on without them. You should have heard him on the phone, he was that desperate, begging that I was wrong."

"He's in shock." Rita placed a comforting hand on Jack's arm. "We all are. I don't know how you've been this far through it all and stayed so strong, only a few tears you've shed and all."

"I have to be strong, now don't I?" Jack recalled his own shock at the phone call he'd received, his own disbelief, how he was sure his heart would give out when he viewed his neighbors' bodies. Rita, love, he thought, I'm not strong at all. I've no clue how I'll cope, let alone get that wee boy through the days ahead. Still, it would do no good to admit his weakness and fear. The task of helping them all through this nightmare had fallen to him, and he'd not let anyone down. "It's good they found my number in Daniel's wallet, with his phone being shattered like it was. I can't imagine how they would have tracked Aidan down otherwise."

Rita pulled fresh tissues from a box on the side table. "I'm only glad it was you and Mack that broke the news to him. Imagine if some stranger had called, the Gardai or someone from hospital. It's hard enough hearing news like that from friends; from strangers, I can't even think what Aidan would do."

"Either way it's hell, isn't it?" Jack watched Rita, his wife of thirty-eight years, as she pulled her cardigan closer around her and dabbed again at her eyes. They needed a break, he thought, someplace bright to lighten her mood. "Here, I'm taking you out for tea."

"I've got sliced ham and some potato soup all set for tonight," Rita protested.

"We can have that tomorrow. We'll be busy enough the next few days, you should have a break tonight. Where was that tearoom you liked? We'll go there."

Rita noticed, as Jack retrieved their coats from the front hall, how slow his steps were, deflated, void of their usual sprightly spirit. She knew this day had been so much harder on him; he'd borne the brunt of everything painful so far. As he slipped her coat on her, she smiled and told him, "We'll go to your steakhouse instead."

Aidan turned to the faces around him. "It's true. They're all gone. Jack's identified the bodies." He closed his eyes, as if in doing so he could stop his world from breaking apart. "Mack, I need to get home."

"I'll sort everything out." Mack glanced at his watch. "Why don't you all gather your things while I make some calls. Meet me back here by eleven-thirty."

Michael and Niall entered the room they'd shared next door to Mack's. "I can't believe it." Michael sat on the edge of his bed, saw the stunned look in Niall's eyes and knew it reflected his own shocked expression. "His whole family. Just like that. Gone."

Niall tried to picture Aidan without his family. "He'll be lost without them. Michael, he won't know what to do. Seriously. I've never seen a family so connected to each other, have you?"

"No," Michael agreed and thought, certainly not mine. He pictured his own parents, his father tall, strong, overpowering, a bull in a toy store not caring how many kids he knocked down; his mother petite, demure, elegant, pearls always against her neck, the child in a toy store who would always let the bull run over her. Connected? They could barely stand to be in the same room together. "You and your folks, you're just as close."

"I am close with my dad and mam, but they're pretty independent. I think it comes from farming; you have to be self-sufficient. They carry on without me, same as if I was there." Niall wondered, if they were gone, would I carry on? As soon as he thought it, he blocked the question. He couldn't think on it now.

"I better call my folks." Niall checked his watch, calculated the time difference, and guessed his mother would be in the kitchen, preparing dinner. "We're coming home early." He told her when she answered his call. "Aidan's family was in an accident."

Anna Donoghue nodded to her husband, Will, and turned off the radio they'd been listening to. "We were just going to call you. The news reported an O'Connell family in an accident outside Belfast. Was that Aidan's family?"

"Yes, mam, it was."

She nodded to Will again. "Niall, the people in that accident were all killed."

Niall felt sick inside. "Yes mam."

Anna pictured the young man who had come home with her son twice in the past year. They'd all laughed at how he'd call home at least twice each day to share a joke, check how they were, or share some new farm adventure with them. "Oh dear," she said, "Aidan must be heartbroken."

"He is. When we get home I'd like to go on to Derry with him, unless you and Dad need me on the farm."

"No, you go ahead. Give Aidan our love, and call when you can."

"Thanks, mam." Suddenly aware that time was short and anything could happen, Niall added, "I love you both."

Michael texted Susannah, "Spain off. I'll explain later. Will call soon." He knew she would not be happy. She'd just have to deal with it. He thought of calling his parents. His mother almost always answered the phone; with his luck this one time his father would instead. He wondered how he'd feel if it had been his father killed instead of Aidan's. Relieved, he knew, and hated himself for the thought.

Patrick held the door open to the room across from Mack's that he'd shared with Aidan. As they stepped in, he noticed the Niagara Falls brochure on the floor by Aidan's bed. It must have fallen out of his coat pocket, Patrick thought. Their conversation from the night before came back to him. If it would change things now, he'd go on any ride Aidan wanted, ignore all his fears and laugh the day away if it would erase the phone call from Jack and the heartbreak Aidan now suffered.

Patrick motioned to Aidan's suitcase. "Here, let's get your gear together first, then I'll gather up mine."

Aidan retrieved his shaving gear from the bathroom and dropped it into his suitcase. "That's everything."

"What about your other shoes?" Patrick pointed under Aidan's bed, where the heels of two black shoes stuck out. "And here, isn't this your shirt?"

Aidan collected the shoes and shirt and piled them in his suitcase, his movements robotic, detached.

Patrick checked the bedside table and found Aidan's travel alarm clock, the one his father had given him before they'd left for their tour. "Here." He handed the clock over.

Aidan held its light weight in his hands and ran his fingers over its smooth exterior and round face.

"Look, you can see our time and yours, wherever you are in the world," his father had demonstrated with great excitement.

"Da, I'm only going to America."

"Now, yes." Daniel's enthusiasm could not be dampened. "Who knows where you'll go from there? The whole world could be yours."

Aidan leaned against the hotel room wall and clutched the clock tight. "Oh God, Pat. This can't be real. It's a nightmare, right? Tell me it's all a bad dream, I'll wake up and everything will be fine."

Patrick shook his head, eyes filling with tears. "No. This is real. I wish to God it wasn't."

"They can't be gone." Aidan felt panic flood through him like a lough crashing through a retaining wall. He pressed a hand tight over his mouth to keep from screaming out. "Oh my God, Pat! I can't live without them! I don't know what to do!"

Patrick thought back three years, to his own father's passing. Even though they'd had time to prepare during his father's three year battle with stomach cancer, when death came the huge, dark hole his father left behind nearly swallowed Patrick. In time, Moira and the twins filled his father's empty space, but the first several months, while he got used to his father's absence, was like a headlong fall into a bottomless abyss.

Now Aidan stood before him, on the edge of that same black hole, terror filling his wide blue eyes, blanching the color from his face. "You got through your mother's passing, right?" Patrick asked. "How old were you when she died?"

"Seven." Aidan pictured his mother not from memory, which had long ago faded, but by recalling the photo his father still kept on his dresser, taken when she was in her twenties, two years before she'd died. She was nearly Jeannie's twin, Aidan had always thought and thought again now. "I had my dad and my gran, though. I wasn't alone."

"True, but you're not alone now. You've got all of us, and your neighbors. We'll help you through."

Aidan looked again at the clock in his hand. He was sure there was not help enough in all the world to get him through what lie ahead.

Patrick scanned the room for any stray clothes and other items he might have forgotten to collect, closed his suitcase, and suggested, "Let's go back to Mack's room, then I'll give Moira a call."

"Why don't you call her from here? Mack's busy with phone calls himself." To answer Patrick's apprehensive look, Aidan added, "I can step out of the room if you're afraid of saying anything in front of me."

Patrick shook his head, "Not afraid at all," which he was, to be sure, but he'd not add that to the list of issues the boy had to deal with. "You're right, best to call her from here."

Moira answered, "Hello, sexy," laughed, and continued, "Oh, sorry, Pat, it's you!"

"Damn, woman, your teasing will land you in trouble someday." Patrick laughed in spite of the situation. "If I didn't know you had caller ID, I'd be hanging up on you right now."

Moira laughed again, "Hate to tell ye, the caller ID's not working."

"Then I should hang up so you can call your other lover."

"Now, ye know I've only the one, and he's due back in eleven more days. Not that I'm counting or anything!"

Patrick sobered and returned to the reason for his call. "We've had a change, Moira, we're coming home early. We just learned Aidan's family were all killed in an accident."

"Oh my God, Pat." Moira was suddenly flooded with guilt for her teasing at such a hard time and for Aidan's loss. "What happened?"

"Apparently their car was hit by a lorry, not too far outside Belfast." Patrick glanced at Aidan, who sat on the edge of his bed, eyes closed, and prayed the boy was so distracted he didn't hear the conversation.

"Aidan must be shattered." When Patrick gave a one-word yes answer, Moira guessed, "Is he there with you now?"

Again, Patrick gave a yes answer. "I don't have flight times yet; I'll let you know as soon as I find out. I was thinking I'd like to go on to Derry with him when we land. I know you've got your hands full with the twins and all, what do you think?"

"Pat, of course you should go with him. We'll be fine. Aidan will need you more."

"Thanks. Where are the twins?"

Moira peered through a window and saw them still racing each other around their yard, as they had been for the past half hour or so. "Out playing," she answered. "Would you like me to call them in?"

"No, let them have fun. I'll talk to them later."

"Alright." Moira felt again the pang of sorrow each phone call caused, as they both coped with the separation Patrick's job sometimes forced on them, made so much more sharp this time by Patrick's news. "Please give Aidan our love, and tell him we'll be praying."

"I will." Patrick pictured Moira starting dinner in their kitchen, as she would be now, and their twins running outside, screaming, laughing, filling their world with so much joy. If he could, he'd close his eyes, make a wish, and be with them all right now. "I love you."

"Love you too."

Aidan heard their conversation despite his efforts to close his eyes, shut down everything inside, and fade into the background. He wanted to tell Pat the trip to Derry wasn't necessary; he should just go home and be with Moira and the kids. He'd missed them so much, it wasn't fair he should be delayed now. He knew Patrick would have none of his protests, and would follow him home regardless. This nightmare would impact them all, adding one more layer of complication in all their lives.

Mack arranged flights, canceled the five remaining shows, and released a press statement announcing shows canceled due to family emergency with further details to be posted on the Macready's Bridge website. His head throbbed harder with each task done. He thought again of the night before and Aidan's phone call home, and the many times he'd seen first hand the bond of love that held Aidan's life together. How he would ever see that boy through his whole world collapsing Mack didn't know. He wished he, himself, had someone to turn to, that he wasn't carrying this gigantic burden alone.

Kate.

The name caught him off guard. Not that he didn't still think of her ten times in a day; she was never far from mind. But call her? That was entirely different. After all this time, he had no right to intrude in her world.

Still, she knew him better than anyone, she'd always had a large, compassionate heart, and he could think of no one else to turn to. As he dialed Kate's number, he whispered a quick prayer that he was right.

Her phone rang once, twice, three and four times. He was just about to hang up when he heard "Hello?"

"Kate, it's me."

"Mack. How are you?" She motioned for Deirdre, her sales clerk, to take over behind the counter and stepped away. "I'm at work, I can't talk long."

Mack could picture her smoothing the sides of her swept back auburn hair, straightening her skirt, running her manicured fingers along the outline of her mouth.

"I know. I'm sorry. I just wanted—" he stopped. How did he say what he wanted?

Kate heard the strain in his voice. "Mack, are you okay?"

"I am. I just, well, I'll be in Derry a few days and I thought we could meet up for coffee, or dinner, or something." Twenty years married, eight years divorced, and Mack still found himself tongue-tied by Kate.

Years ago, Kate would have dropped everything and come running the minute Mack called. She had fought so hard to rebuild her life after their divorce. She wasn't sure what Mack was up to, but she'd come too far to slide backwards now. "I don't know, Mack. We've both moved on."

"Please," Mack begged. "I know you have a new life. I don't want to start things up again, I just want to talk." He paused. "It's going to be a hard week."

"What's hard? What's going on?"

"One of the boys in the band I'm managing just lost his family in an accident."

"Which boy?" Kate asked, then admitted, "I've followed your work with Macready's Bridge."

"You have?" Any other time, Mack would have pursued her statement, sure there would be a spark of interest behind it. Now he had more urgent matters on his mind. He answered, "Aidan, our guitarist."

"Oh Mack, how terrible."

Mack suddenly wondered why he had bothered Kate. What had he been thinking? She had moved on. She didn't need his problems. "Kate, I'm sorry. I shouldn't have called."

Kate pictured Mack's weathered face, and imagined the worry lines that would now fill it. He had always involved himself in his clients' lives, taking their problems to heart, helping them work out the many issues that came along. Something in that face had always stirred her heart; it did so now. "No, Mack, it's fine. Of course we can meet up."

"I'm not sure what the week will look like."

"Call when you can and we'll find a time."

She was an answer to prayer, Mack thought. No, more than that. An angel. A beautiful, wise angel he'd once caught and then had been foolish enough to let slip out of his hands. Grateful she'd seen beyond the hurt he had caused and was still willing to open her heart this one, wee crack, he said, "Thank you, Kate. I appreciate it."

"Take care of yourself, Mack. Call anytime." Before she returned to her dress shop customers, Kate ran her fingers around her naked ring finger. So, she had lied to herself after all, told herself she was over Mack, yet one phone call from him and old feelings were stirring, the good ones as well as the bad. She'd have to be careful seeing him.

3

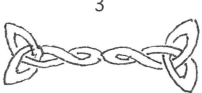

Aidan alone stayed awake on the nighttime flight from New York to Belfast. One by one Michael, Niall, Patrick, and even Mack drifted off. He would have loved to join them in that other state where the concerns of the day were set aside and one's heart and mind could rest. So many details clogged his mind though, so many fears and memories crowded in, he had no hope of sleep. With Mack's help he'd started a list of people he needed to call, the priest, Jeannie's school, his father's solicitor, a few friends. He had started a separate list as well of tasks that needed doing, closing his father's garage for a while, collecting any belongings Jeannie had left at school, and all of the arrangements funerals entailed.

"Making out lists helps get all of these worries onto paper and out of your mind," Mack had said; but he'd been wrong. New details and questions bombarded his mind as soon as old ones were added to the lists.

He pulled his phone from his pocket to look up a name; the screen picture hit him like a fresh fist in his gut. Dad, Gran, Jeannie and himself at Dunluce Castle, the last Sunday of February. Dunluce had always been one of his favorite sites, grey and brown stone ruins rising out of the soil, perched precariously on the edge of cliffs. He always tried to visualize what the castle would have looked like in the 1500s and 1600s, before part of it fell away into the sea, before warring parties had blown parts of it away and wind and time eroded what was left. The ruins had been quiet that day, not many visitors braving the cold winter winds to explore the vast grounds. He and Jeannie had hid among the ancient ruins, chasing each other when found and laughing when caught. They'd all listened to his grandmother recite the history of Dunluce, from the McQuillans to the MacDonnell family and beyond. Later, while his gran and Jeannie rested, he and his father had walked the long line of stairs down to the hole beneath the castle's foundation where the sea flowed in and out.

"Would this gap have been here back in the day?" Aidan had asked. "Or has it just worn through with time?"

"I'm guessing time," his father had answered as he studied the rocks, "but it would have made for a great hidden entrance, wouldn't it?"

They had stood several minutes there, watching the cold blue sea waters race to shore, deposit their gifts of sand and stone, and rush back out for another load.

"Tuesday you head to America," his father had spoken at last. "Are you ready?"

"Gran's made sure all my packing's sorted," Aidan had replied, but his father shook his head and placed a hand over his own heart. "I meant here. This is quite an undertaking for you and the boys. You're going to face many new things while you're there. Do you think you're up for it all?"

It had been funny at the time, because Aidan and all of Macready's Bridge had had the same discussion just two nights prior and were sure they were ready; suddenly, standing next to his father, with the enormity of the cliffs, the enormity of the sea, and the enormity of what lie ahead staring him in the face, Aidan had felt very small and unsure. He'd leaned in closer to his father and said, "No, not sure at all, but I'll do my best."

His father had smiled and put a strong arm around his son's shoulder. "You're a good lad. You'll be fine."

Aidan stared again at the picture, recalling his struggle to set the camera on just the right angle and height to capture them all, with the half-disintegrated castle walls behind them. Jeannie's pure, silvery laughter rang in his mind now, and his granny's rose bath powder scent, the wet wool smell of his father's grey jacket and the calm voice that matched his father's steady, patient manner, the constant that held all their lives together. Aidan stared at the picture before him until his eyes filled and the picture blurred.

Stop it, he ordered himself. You can't fall apart. Not here. Not now.

Aidan thought of the trick they'd all learned, shutting everything inside down when performing. Close your eyes. Clear your mind of everything except that one, immediate thing you had to do. Concentrate on that one thing and lock everything else away. It had worked when Patrick had the flu the month before, when Niall's favorite aunt had a heart attack last fall, and two weeks ago when Michael had a bitter disagreement with his father. They'd all had to learn how to perform when their heart wasn't in it, to mask their feelings and just keep going. Aidan went into performance mode now as the plane flew over the ocean, a dark void underneath, as they crossed time zones below, as the whole plane full of passengers slept and he alone sat awake, staring out the window at nothingness. He held everything together as they landed at Belfast, gathered luggage and instruments, and filed through immigration clearance.

Aidan scanned the faces of people waiting to meet travelers until he spotted Jack and Rita. Funny, he thought when he reached them, I didn't remember them looking so old. He realized the haggard looks they both wore would be from the accident and the burdens suddenly thrust on them.

Rita hugged Aidan. "I'm so sorry, love."

He hugged her back, hugged Jack, then stepped aside, fighting to hold his composure. "You remember Mack and the guys, don't you?"

Jack shook Mack's hand. "I've booked the van you wanted, over by the next counter; you just have to sign for it. I've also called for hotel rooms, but to be honest, between our house and Aidan's you might not need the hotel."

"Thank you Jack. I think we'll stay with the hotel, although I'm sure one or two of us will stay at Aidan's overnight." Mack guessed there would be times each of the boys, devoted to Aidan though they were, and even himself, would be grateful to escape to the hotel for a break.

After Mack and the boys had loaded suitcases and instruments into the rented van, Jack suggested, "Mack, you can follow me, we'll be home in no time. Our Rita's got a lovely meal all prepared for you."

"You must be tired." Rita saw they could each use a shave, and their faces were drawn. "Before we eat you can take showers at our place if you'd like."

Before anyone could answer, Aidan fixed his eyes on Jack and asked, "Where are they?"

Jack had known the question would come. He'd dreaded it and where he knew it would lead.

"The morgue." He spoke softly, as if the word was one never to be spoken out loud.

"I need to go there."

"You don't have to. They can send the forms you need to your father's solicitor, or right to you. Why don't we just go home."

Aidan shook his head. "I need to see them."

Rita placed a hand on Aidan's arm. "You don't want to do that." She spoke as a mother trying to gently turn a child's course of action. "Don't let how they are now be your last memory of them."

Aidan knew Jack and Rita were trying to shield him from something even he knew would be horrible. The ice running through his blood moved to persuade him to follow their advice. His mind, though, was set on its course.

"I have to do this. You don't have to go, though."

Jack saw the resolve in Aidan's eyes and knew he would not be put off. He would not abandon the boy. "I'll go with you."

"I'll go too," Niall added, just as Aidan knew he would.

Aidan turned to Mack. "Why don't you, Michael and Pat go with Rita. I'm sure they don't need me dragging a whole entourage behind me. You can store the suitcases and all in my house. We won't be long."

"I should go with you," Mack started, thinking of his duty as Aidan's manager, but the boy made sense. Jack knew the way to the morgue, he didn't, and Niall, as Aidan's best friend, would go no matter who said otherwise. "You're right though. You don't need all of us. We'll meet you back at your house."

They parted. Soon Jack's car pulled into the parking lot of the low stone building that served as the coroner's office and mortuary. The woman who greeted them recognized Jack, who introduced, "This is Aidan O'Connell, Daniel's son."

"Alice Gerrity," the woman introduced herself. As she led them to her corner desk, she thought, how young the boy looks. How sad.

Alice led Aidan through a series of forms, pointing out, "Read this part, sign here, you'll need to take this one with you." While no day was easy on her job, some were harder than others. Aidan followed each instruction, wrote down names and notes on the paper she provided him, and did so with such composure she half wondered if he fully understood what was going on. When he put his pen down, closed his eyes and rested his head in his hands a moment, she knew his composure was just a front.

"Do you have any other relatives?" she asked Aidan as she placed his signed forms in a folder.

When Aidan shook his head no, her heart broke for him. This was the worst case she'd seen in several years; she knew Aidan's image would haunt her for days.

Alice gathered the last of her papers and asked, "Do you have any questions?"

"I do." One question. He'd thought of it earlier, but was only now ready to ask. "The other driver. What happened to him?"

Alice reviewed a report on her desk before answering, "He was checked out at the hospital and released."

"No injuries?" She shook her head. Aidan felt anger rise inside him and struggled to check it. "What was the cause of the accident, again?"

Alice handed Aidan the police report. "Lorry driver using excessive speed," he read under cause of accident. Underneath that, Aidan spotted the words "citation for use of mobile phone while driving."

Aidan let the words sink in. "If he hadn't been on his phone, the accident could have been avoided?"

"I can't say how much that contributed to it," Alice told him, agreeing with him in her heart yet prohibited by her professional role from taking sides. "I'm sorry."

Aidan noted the driver's name, Malachy Achill, residing in Belfast. Treated and released. They had to be kidding. He'd find Malachy Achill if he had to search the whole city over. He'd send him back to the hospital, really give him something to be treated for.

Aidan let his anger play itself out in his mind for a minute. Then he handed the report back to Alice, and asked, "Can I see them now?"

Alice nodded and pushed a button to summon Harry, the assistant who would take over with Aidan while she helped the next set of people who had come in. Before she greeted them, Alice excused herself, stepped into the ladies room, and allowed herself a few tears for the young man who'd just stepped away.

Harry led them deep into the bowels of the building, their footsteps echoing down cold, silent halls that smelled of gallons of antiseptic. The air was heavy with fear and death, or did Aidan only imagine that? It seemed the walk took forever, and felt like they walked through quicksand. He had to pull hard to lift each foot off the floor, and the door seemed miles away no matter how many steps he took. At last they were there, Harry ready to admit them to hell.

Before they stepped in, Jack tried one more time. "Aidan, are you sure you want to do this? Better to remember them the way you do now, instead of seeing them this way."

He wasn't sure. In fact, he didn't want to do this at all. He wanted to run as fast and far as he could from this room, from the horrors it held. He wanted to run all the way back to Niagara Falls, to the fun they'd been denied. To Chicago, where the skyscrapers were as exciting as the nightlife. To Memphis, home of the blues, or Nashville and the Opry, to Cleveland, where they'd toured the Rock and Roll Hall of Fame. To Los Angeles, where three weeks ago four starry-eyed Irish musicians strolled the streets of Hollywood amazed and amused. He wanted to run clear to Antarctica. But there was no running away from what lie ahead.

"I'm going in," he told Jack. "You and Niall, though, you can wait out here."

Niall had his own job to do, looking after his friend. "I'll go with you."

Niall and Jack waited inside by the door, while Aidan followed Harry to a spot two thirds of the way along the left wall.

"My sister first," Aidan whispered, not sure why he was whispering. Who did he think he'd disturb?

Harry checked his notes, pulled a handle, and there before Aidan was his beautiful sister, golden hair neat and straight, eyes closed, arms at her side like she was asleep, or pretending to be, the way they did when they were kids, only this time there was no life behind the sleepy disguise. Aidan reached out, touched her fine, soft hair, closed his eyes, and after a moment nodded for Harry to continue.

"My grandmother next."

This woman bore little resemblance to Cathleen O'Connell, whose eyes always shone with life, smile rarely gone from her face, so full of energy any room she entered needed no electricity. "Spitfire" had been his dad's nickname for her. Now, she didn't look asleep, like Jeannie; she looked empty. Gone.

Aidan nodded again, but found he couldn't speak. There was no need to. Harry only had one place left to go.

Aidan looked past the injuries his father had suffered, to the man who had been the center of his life, the steady hand, the teacher, the singer whose voice he'd inherited, the source of music, the key to everything good in Aidan's life.

He shouldn't be this silent or still, Aidan thought. He wanted to scream, to shake his father awake. He wanted to wake the three of them. Get up, damn it, he wanted to yell. Don't do this to me!

Everything inside Aidan screamed, this can't be real! It was real, though. He could feel his whole body shake and his heart give a violent jump.

I will not pass out, he ordered himself. I will not lose control. I will make my father proud.

Aidan reached out, touched his father's hand, hated the cold lack of response. He whispered some kind of thanks to Harry, nodded to Jack and Niall, and strode through the cold, sterile halls and out into fresh air.

Once outside, in a refuse bin by a bench, Aidan threw up all the horrible stench of that room, all the stillness, all the ice in his stomach and panic rising through his body. He rid himself of it all while Jack and Niall stood by, silent witnesses to his agony.

Then he sank onto the bench. "I'm sorry."

Niall shook his head. "No sorries needed. You just did the hardest thing in the world."

"Here, have these." Jack handed Aidan a roll of mints to help erase the taste he knew Aidan would have.

Aidan leaned back against the hard wood boards and squeezed his eyes tight shut so the tears he felt coming wouldn't fall. "I can't believe this is happening."

"I know." Niall sat back as well, stunned himself at the turn of events they'd been handed.

Jack let Aidan relax on the bench a few minutes, settle his mind, collect himself, and then said quietly, "Let's go home."

Aidan stood at the door of his house, key in hand, unmoving. When he opened the door, the world he entered would be different. Everything familiar would be outweighed by the shadow of those who would no longer inhabit its spaces. There was nothing to do but enter, yet he stood a moment longer, and prayed that they would send him the strength to bear the vacuum the doors held back.

Inside, Aidan found his father's tea mug left on the coffee table, half full, and his sister's makeup bag and coral and royal blue sweaters on the steps to go back upstairs when they returned. Couldn't make your mind up on color, could you, he thought. To Niall, who'd entered with him while Jack had gone next door, Aidan said, "They must have left in a hurry." He could just hear his grandmother calling, pleading, threatening Jeannie to hurry or she'd be left behind, which would only have ended when his father took the keys, went outside, and started the car. That always brought the tardy Jeannie running.

Niall almost said, "I'm glad I don't have a sister to deal with," his standard answer whenever Aidan told him Jeannie's latest antics and mishaps. They would be the worst words possible now. He clenched his teeth to keep the words locked inside.

The blue and white kitchen, Aidan's grandmother's domain, had been left in its usual order, dishes washed and left to dry in their rack, towels neatly folded over the oven door handle, canisters lined up like sentries along the counter wall. "Hurry or not, she'd never leave this room untidy."

"Neither would my mam." Niall replied. "Must be some gene they're born with! The clean kitchen gene."

"Must be." Cathleen's kitchen was too full of her voice, her image. Aidan retreated to the front room, but found no escape. Daniel and Jeannie loomed large in the air.

"What would you like first, love?" Rita entered, bearing a large tray with sandwiches and steaming hot soup. "Something to eat? Or a nice hot shower? Or maybe you'd like a wee nap?"

"No nap." Aidan shook his head, and looked to Mack who had entered, along with Jack, Michael and Patrick, after Rita. "I should probably start in on some of the calls we listed."

"Eat first," Mack suggested. "You haven't eaten much at all since yesterday."

"None of us have," Aidan pointed out. "You hardly touched your burger and fries, Niall never finished his fish and chips, and Michael and Pat, you both bailed on your roast beef sandwiches."

"Meals first, then." Rita gathered plates and bowls from the kitchen, and set them, with the food, on Aidan's dining room table. "I've made the minestrone soup you like so much, Aidan."

As they ate, Michael took in the many photos of Aidan and his family that hung on walls and stood on tables throughout the house, pictures of Aidan and Jeannie at various ages in school, Aidan and his father playing their guitars and singing together, various combinations of the four of them around town or visiting various locations around the countryside. Jealousy overwhelmed Michael. The only picture he recalled in his house was his parents' wedding picture hanging over the mantle in their large living room. For all the crystal, fieldstone, brass and marble that adorned his family's spacious, elegant home, Michael found Aidan's home rich in what really mattered. The contrast left him aching inside.

"Which would you rather do," Mack asked as Rita cleared their lunch dishes away, "traditional wake, or viewing at a funeral home?"

"Absolutely no funeral home!" Aidan turned to Jack and Rita. "Remember when Mrs. Clancy passed on, and her family used the funeral home? My gran hated that, made my dad promise we'd never do that to her."

"We'll have a lot of setting up to do, then." Jack and Rita began a list of foods they would need and people they could call on to help. Michael and Niall were kept busy with trips to the store, while Patrick helped Jack collect chairs and a good supply of whiskey and stout.

Mack guided Aidan through the list of calls they'd developed and decisions each of the calls brought about. Aidan kept at the list until it was done, brushed off any suggestion for a break, and made decisions, even the most painful ones, by considering options, closing his eyes a moment, choosing, and not second-guessing once a decision was made. Always the member of the band to seek out the most fun, the most adventurous of the group, the maturity Aidan now displayed was a side of him Mack had never seen before, one that made Mack sit back more than once and re-evaluate his impression of Aidan. The boy had more strength and wisdom in him than Mack had realized.

Aidan sat back, closed and rubbed his eyes, then looked at them all. "That's it, done. Everything's set."

"Well done," Mack replied; but Aidan, deep in his heart, felt it was anything but well done. It was just done. For all he knew, he may have made all the wrong choices. He'd done his best, guessed at what his dad, his gran, his sister would have wanted. If his choices were wrong, so be it. He was tired, his head throbbed, his heart felt like an aching stone, as if stones, in all their cold weight, could feel the pain of breaks.

"Whiskey." He looked to Jack. "I'd really like a whiskey." He drank the glass of honey brown liquid Jack set before him, aware that all eyes were on him as his request was not like him, he was so much more an ale man. He only hoped the whiskey would let him sleep. Whether it was the drink or exhaustion that worked, soon he was asleep and, for a short time, at peace.

Patrick took his turn on the sofa that night, while Michael and Niall returned with Mack to the hotel and Jack and Rita went home. While Aidan slept, Patrick listened to the sounds of the house settling and the gentle whisper of tires on pavement outside. Moira rose like a vision before him. Soon, he told the vision, I'll be home soon.

Jeannie's art portfolio stood by the recliner in the corner of the room. Aidan had talked so much of his sister's art. Patrick opened the portfolio now and sifted through her work, drawings of her grandmother's gardens, her father's guitar, buildings around town and, towards the back, portraits of Aidan, Cathleen and Daniel, each done in charcoal, in delicate colors, with clean, confident strokes. She was talented, alright, Patrick thought as he returned the portfolio to its spot by the chair.

A sudden urge to talk to his brother, Donald, seized him. Ever since Donnie had moved to Australia two years ago, they'd had a harder and harder time connecting. Patrick calculated the time difference between Derry and Sydney, realized Donnie would be at work and not able to talk now, and made a mental note to call his brother the next day. He fell asleep recalling the fun, and the fights, they'd had growing up in the outskirts of Sligo, walking the beach at Strandhill with their father, the younger Donnie always his big brother's shadow.

4

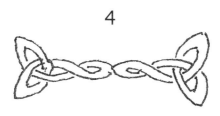

What are the colors of grief we wear? We wear black, the color of darkness, the absence of light, a solid black cloak that envelops our heart. Does it serve as an insulating shield protecting us from further pain, as if we haven't already been plunged into a world that could not possibly be any more painful? Or does the black cloak hold things in, all the memories, all the nearness of the one we've lost, like a winter coat holds in the warmth of our bodies?

We wear blue, midnight blue, a blue so thick it is almost black, the blue of deep loneliness, a penetrating blue, the hottest part of the heart's flame. The color of expectation unfulfilled, as the thing we've always seen in a particular place is no longer there, and its absence so clear it shouts out, and no presence echoes back to fill that space.

And we wear grey, the color of the mist that descends upon our world and clouds our way, so we can see only a few steps of the road before us, and no further. It's a thick, heavy mist that bears down on us, at times lightening up enough we can walk those few steps, at times so heavy we are forced to stop and rest although no rest comes. We pray for the mist to lift, for our path to be clear; we take tiny steps and pray we won't fall.

Aidan stared out the front window at the rain cascading down, sounding a steady beat against the roof and bricks of the house he had always called home. Funny, he thought, it didn't feel like home now. Every inch of it felt foreign, not as strange as the multiple hotels he and the rest of Macready's Bridge had slept in during their tour, but light years from the warm, familiar place that had always smelled of his grandmother's cooking and baking, whose walls had always echoed his sister's constant chatter or his father's evening guitar strumming and singing. Even his own bedroom felt less a haven and more a temporary shelter to be endured until he could get back to that safe harbor that home had always been.

Aidan turned and gazed into the family room of his house, eyes fixed on the three bodies central to the room, loving them but hating the sight of them now. In a few minutes the doorbell would ring, friends and neighbors would start to file through the room, to console him, although he doubted any of them had the ability to do that, and to reminisce. In a few minutes chairs that had been set in place here and throughout the house would be filled, sandwiches, tea and ale passed around, conversation filling the air that now hung heavy and silent, save for the clatter of dishes and opening and closing of cupboards as Rita continued her endless preparations in the kitchen. He had this one quiet minute with his family, but no words came to mind. All he could do was stare, still full of shock and disbelief at the sudden turn his life had taken.

Then the doorbell echoed through the house, Jack entered the room and asked, "Aidan, are you ready?" and the private moment was gone.

Father Nelligan was the first to stop by, offering a prayer for Cathleen, Daniel and Jeannie, and for Aidan himself and the days ahead.

"The whole parish is feeling your loss," he told Aidan. "Sundays won't be the same without your father greeting people at the door, and serving as usher or anything else we needed. The ladies will miss your grandmother and all of her baking and knitting; and the youth group, they're just shattered over your sister."

"It won't be the same going to Mass without them." Aidan tried hard to not think just how different it would be.

Father Nelligan studied the young man he'd watched grow up over the nine years he'd been assigned to this parish. "How are you holding up? Is there anything you need?"

Aidan shook his head. "I think we've covered everything." Then he forced a smile. "I guess when things fall apart tomorrow we'll find out what I missed. I'm sure my gran will give me a proper earful as well."

Father Nelligan assured him, "Everything will fall into place and your grandmother will be proud of you."

Proud. Aidan heard the word over and over that day.

"Remember you reading at Mass with the Youth Group? Your granny sure was proud of you that day."

Aidan reminded Mrs. Patterson, the leader when he had been in youth group, "She wasn't so proud later that day when Brendan and I were caught smoking out behind the church."

Mrs. Patterson laughed along with him, "No, she wasn't smiling then. But she never stopped loving you."

When Mr. Bennigan, the corner shop owner said, "Jeannie was so proud of where your music has taken you, every day she stopped in and gave us updates," Aidan pointed out, "How many times did she stop in to your store on the way to school full of tales of how I'd been picking on her; and you know she was only saying that for the sweets you'd give her."

Terry Reilly, an auto repairman like Aidan's father, told him, "Every week your daddy would call and update me on your travels. He sure was proud of you and your music." Upon hearing that, Aidan recalled the very painful conversation he'd had with his father when he'd revealed following in his father's footsteps wasn't what he wanted, even if his dream of music fell through. There was no pride in his father's eyes that day, only sadness which he'd tried to cover up. Aidan wouldn't tell Terry Reilly that, though. Instead, he answered, "I'm glad there were times I made him proud."

A steady stream of friends, neighbors, and church family flowed through the house bringing food, offering condolences, exchanging memories.

"Do ye remember when Danny fixed our leaky drainpipe? We had water flowing all over that kitchen!"

"He admitted later it was his first plumbing job."

"Aye. He did dry it all up though, and never took a bit of pay for the job."

"Remember him coming out last January in the ice storm to tow me in when I couldn't get my car up the hill? Wouldn't take pay for that either."

"Remember us fishing out on Lough Swilly, and him tipping over the boat?"

"Remember Jeannie singing Ave Maria at Christmas Mass?"

"And those cinnamon rolls of Cathleen's?"

"And Cathleen taking on Mrs. Pritchard and her rose awards, and Cathleen winning with her red and white one, what was it called?"

"Rosie's Fancy."

"That's right. Whatever became of that rose?"

"Didn't young Aidan ride his bike over the rosebush and kill it?"

Even Aidan laughed at the story of the bike and the rosebush. "It's true," he admitted to Patrick and Niall standing next to him. "I thought she'd kill me when it happened, but she didn't."

"What did she do?" Niall wanted to know.

Aidan could still see it as if he'd just run the rosebush over the day before. "She stared at me and my bike and the rosebush for a minute; then she pulled out her trimmers, clipped off the broken parts and threw them away, and went in to make supper. She hardly said a word all night. The next morning everything was back to normal, her smiling and all, but I never forgot the hurt look in her eyes that night. I'd rather have her hit me a thousand times over than ever face that look again."

Tim Dougherty entered with his parents close behind; Aidan recalled the last talk he'd had with Jeannie about her infatuation with this classmate of hers.

"I don't like him," he'd said. "I know that look in his eyes."

"Is that so? Funny, it's the same look you have when you and your friends are out sizing up girls."

"That's different."

"That's dumb!"

Jeannie was right, he knew, so Aidan tried a different approach. "I just don't want to see you hurt. See him if you want, but see other boys too. Don't let your heart get stuck on Tim."

Now Tim stood before Jeannie's casket ashen-faced, red-eyed. "I can't believe she's gone," he whispered.

"I can't either." Aidan thought the boy before him would keel right over. "Here, have a seat."

"We were going to a dance next month. A formal."

"I know. I saw pictures of her dress." Aidan recalled Jeannie's excitement as they talked over the phone about the royal blue dress she'd bought. He closed his mind to the thought of how beautiful she would have looked in it. He told Tim, "She really liked you."

"I can't believe she's gone," Tim repeated. His parents stepped in and suggested it was time they leave.

Oh Jeannie, if I'd known your life would be cut so short I'd have let you do anything you wanted with Tim, Aidan thought as he watched them leave.

"We've got to get him to take a break." Mack nodded in Aidan's direction.

Michael watched Aidan rise, shake hands with another neighbor, and sit back down with a sigh. He collected a fresh cup of tea from Rita, took it over to Aidan and suggested, "Time for a break."

Aidan set the cup and saucer on the same table where he'd let three others grow cold. "Thanks."

"You should step away for a bit." Michael glanced outside. "It's stopped raining; go get yourself some fresh air."

"I can't leave them."

Aidan spoke in such a quiet tone Michael was lucky to catch the words at all. "Sure you can." He sat in the folded chair opposite Aidan. "Here, I'll stay right here with them."

"Nothing will happen while you're gone," Patrick, coming up behind Aidan, confirmed. "Your gran would push you outside herself if she were here."

"You're right." Aidan rose, stretched, and was almost out the back door when a voice boomed out, "Aidan O'Connell, where are ye boy?" The next thing he knew, he was wrapped in a tight hug.

Stepping back from the hug and the man hugging him, Aidan exclaimed, "Oh my God! Charlie! I haven't seen you in forever."

"It does seem that long, doesn't it?" The tall salt-and-pepper-haired man eyed Aidan more closely. "Last I saw you ye were only waist high and look at ye now! Why, you're as tall as the crosses of Clonmacnoise."

Aidan hugged the two men standing behind Charlie. "Tommy! Sean! How are you all?"

"Doing well," the second stranger, a short, stocky man with cap in hand, replied.

"Wish we weren't meeting this way," commented the third, a reddish-haired man.

"I know." Once again, Aidan's attention was drawn back to the three dark wood boxes that stood out in sharp contrast to the cream colored walls and sage carpet of the room that held them.

Charlie shook his head. "'Tis a dark day in all of Derry, with the likes of your daddy gone, and your gran and wee sister besides."

"Saddest day ever," the second man, Sean, said softly.

Tommy noticed Aidan's pale look and still stunned eyes and tried to change the subject.

Glancing past Aidan he asked, "Would these be your bandmates?"

"Yes. This is Patrick, Michael, Niall, and our manager, Mack, coming over with the tray of pints."

"Good manager, there!" Charlie lifted a glass from Mack's tray.

Aidan observed the man who had guided their music so well the past year, and so smoothly brought them through the past couple of days. "He's okay, think we'll keep him another few weeks."

Mack gave a mock hurt look. "The trials I suffer with you lot!"

To his friends, Aidan introduced, "Charlie, Sean and Tommy. These were my daddy's old bandmates."

"Former," Charlie corrected, grimacing. "The word 'old' is a bit too scary anymore."

"Oh, right. Sorry." Aidan grinned.

Tommy nodded to the boys beside Aidan. "Your daddy told us you had your own band now, and a fair bit of success from what we hear."

"If we're successful it's down to Mack, not through any fault of our own!" Aidan watched, grateful all over again for their help, as Jack and Rita passed plates of sandwiches and cakes around the room. Then he told Charlie, Sean and Tommy, "My dad was so excited you were all getting together again. He really missed you guys."

"Too bad it took so long," Tommy sighed. "Oh, the music and time we've wasted."

Aidan told him, "You got together in the end. That's what counts."

Sean said, "That was your daddy's doing. He called us one day, said it was far too long since Annie had seen us all, and would we put her out of her misery."

Aidan stared at Annie, his father's favorite guitar, now standing silent in the corner by the fireplace. All his memories of Annie in his father's embrace flooded back, the smile Annie always brought to his face, the gentle way he fingered her strings, the harmony they always filled the house with. When she started to blur in his eyes, he turned back to Charlie, Sean and Tommy.

"What do you remember most about my daddy? Aside from the music, I mean?"

Tommy's eyes, like his mind, traveled back across years. "It's always the music," he started, "aside from that, though, when I think of Danny I always think of his positive spirit. Nothing ever got him down. Your mam's passing, that's the only time. He was sad a good long while after that; but otherwise, he always believed he could take on any challenge, he could fix anything that needed fixing, and no matter what the world threw at him he'd come out on top. I always wished I could be more like your daddy that way."

Sean nodded agreement at Tommy's recollection, then added his own. "Your daddy always made people feel better about themselves. There wasn't a time we were out that I didn't hear him hand a compliment to someone, or take the time to listen to their troubles. If they weren't smiling before Danny came by, they all smiled after. He was a healer, a light on any dark day."

How many times had he seen that himself, Aidan thought, his father in action, passing out compliments like roses, listening while customers waiting for car repairs poured out their troubles, sending them off with fixed cars and hearts. His father cast a wide net of smiles, alright. He closed his mind to the question of how many people in and around town would miss his father's ready praise and open ear.

Charlie waited for them all to clear their minds and hearts, then fixed his eyes on Daniel and Roisin's son. "I remember your daddy won your mam away from us all."

Tommy and Sean closed their eyes, holding memories in. Mack and the Macready's Band boys looked on, curious, having never heard the story. Aidan smiled, proud that his father had won, even while his heart ached for his mother and now the man she had married.

"Go ahead, tell the story," he invited.

"Your mammy's beauty was stunning," Charlie began, watching Aidan. "All gold, she was, hair and skin, and her eyes when they lit with a smile. Her voice was like glass, smooth, delicate. She was like an angel come to earth, a breath of heaven come to bless us all with a glimpse of paradise.

"We each competed to coax her to turn her heart our way," he continued, eyes no longer set on Aidan, but turned back in time to a day when he and his bandmates were young and free. "Tommy here thought his pipes would cast their spell like the piper of Hamlin setting the mice in a trance. Seanie, you thought your fiddle would steal her away, or the flowers you brought her every week. I was sure my charm would blind her to the rest of you lot!"

Charlie joined the rest of the room in laughter at the thought that his charm could entice anyone, let alone the fair Roisin. He finished his story then, "Rosie loved us all in her way, but her eyes and heart were stuck on your daddy. His guitar strings entranced her, his handsome face, and I have to admit, he was a wee bit better looking than me, just by a hair mind you, his handsome face captured her heart. Truth be told, the rest of us never stood a chance."

"Rosie's Ring." The name of his father's band slid off Aidan's tongue as if it was magic, an incantation that, when whispered with the right mixture of reverence and belief, would shower down fortune and countless blessings on the speaker's life. "My daddy always said she was his touchstone, that his whole life turned around when she married him."

"Aye, she would turn anyone's world right again," Tommy agreed.

Charlie sighed and brought himself back to the present. "We were wondering, would you like a bit of music tomorrow? Was it Shannon's you were going to after Mass?"

"Yes, Shannon's, and if you'd like to play there, that would be fine."

"Right. Well, we best be off and leave you to try and catch some sleep, unless we can do anything else for you."

"Thanks, Sean. No, the music's enough. I'm so glad you stopped by."

As he left Sean said, "Your daddy was very proud of you."

Tommy told Aidan, "Just keep following your daddy's footsteps, boy. You'll do fine."

Charlie gave Aidan another bear hug and whispered, "If you aren't the image of your mother."

Patrick thought over Charlie's story. "Your mom must have been quite a woman for all four of them to fall in love with her."

Aidan pictured his mother, golden, like Charlie said, delicate, gentle. "From what I remember, she was."

"Did the band break up after your mom and dad married?" Michael thought of the conflict he and his bandmates would struggle through if they all fell for the same girl. "That must have made for some hard feelings among them."

"No, they kept at it till I was about eleven."

"What made them stop?"

Aidan thought back. "Daddy was busy raising two kids, Charlie's wife went through cancer, Tommy got changed to the night shift where he works, and Sean just got left behind, I guess."

"I wonder how long we'll stay together." They all stared at Patrick as if he'd asked if the world would end that night. "Not that I think we're going separate ways anytime soon," he added before they all could protest.

"You'll be stuck with us till you're an old man," Aidan teased Patrick, and added, "Oh wait, you're already there!"

They all laughed, but later that night Aidan tried to picture what life without Macready's Bridge would be like. He couldn't picture it; but then, he couldn't picture life without his family yet he was facing it anyway. The house was quiet. Jack and Rita were home, probably sleeping, even though they'd offered to stay. Mack was asleep on the sofa despite Aidan's protest that he'd sleep better at the hotel. At the moment, all Aidan could picture was this room, and the three long wooden boxes it held, and he thought he would be crushed between the walls closing in around him.

He grabbed his coat and stepped out into the back garden. Cool, clean air filled his lungs. Voices from the street rose up around him. He wasn't alone, yet privacy wrapped around him like a wool afghan, safe and warm. High above the city lights, he studied the stars that spread out across the clearing sky.

"Daddy, how many stars are there?"

The child's voice caught him off guard. Suddenly he saw them, father and son, standing in the same spot he now stood.

"Oh, millions," the father had answered.

"How many is that?"

"You know all the peppermints in Mr. Bennigan's store?"

"The *whole* store?"

"Yes."

"That's a lot!" Even in the dark, the seven-year old's wide-eyed amazement was clear.

"Well, there's about ten hundred times that many stars in the sky."

The boy edged closer, felt the strength and safety of his father's arm around his shoulders. "Is my mom one of them?"

The father was silent a long minute. "I think she is."

"Which one?"

"You see the brightest one, right there, over our house?"

The boy studied the sky, then nodded. "That's her," the father said, and they both felt comforted by the thought that she watched over them while they slept.

Aidan shook his head to clear the memory away, but still studied the stars and wondered, which one was his father? His sister? His grandmother? He noticed four stars shining brightly together, forming a square; while part of him knew people didn't transform into stars when they died, the larger part of him hoped they'd joined with his mother and that all four were watching over him now.

In his dream that night Aidan saw his family's picture again, the one on his phone, only this time the image was at a terrible angle, like they were sliding off the world, like the last half of the Titanic sticking up grotesquely pointed towards the sky, and then being swallowed by eternity. Aidan woke with a start. He felt the same way he imagined the Titanic's survivors felt, in their lifeboats, staring hard, unable to comprehend the vast, unbroken horizon before them, no lights, no shadow of ship's hull, only a horrible emptiness where their vessel should have been. His house felt the same, no springs creaking as his father shifted in his sleep, no gentle snoring from his grandmother's room, no playing of the cd's Jeannie always fell asleep to. He thought he would suffocate under the enormity of the silence that filled the house.

Mack rose from the sofa he'd slept on despite Aidan's protests and stretched to loosen aching muscles. Seven a.m. showed on his phone, a half hour before Aidan's alarm was set to go off, yet Mack could hear Aidan's careful footsteps on the floorboards above him.

Probably afraid to wake me up, he thought. He called up, "Aidan, are you alright?"

"Yeah."

Aidan's tone, subdued, told Mack otherwise.

"Did you want to get ready first?" Aidan called down.

"No, you go ahead. Take your time."

While Aidan showered and dressed, Mack laid out the pastries Rita had set aside for the morning, and heated tea water. When he came back down from his own shower, he saw none of the tea or food had been touched.

"Mack, could you help me?" Aidan held out his tie.

"Sure." As he fixed the knot and tightened the black and grey striped tie, he watched the boy's eyes focus on some distant, invisible place and heard his short, uneven breathing.

"You look fine, Aidan. You'll be just fine."

Aidan glanced past Mack to the room where his family rested. "I don't know how to do this." He begged Mack, "How do I let them go?"

Mack rubbed Aidan's shoulder the way he would have if the boy had been his own son. He had no magic words, no advice that would make any of the day ahead easier. All he could offer was, "Just take it one step at a time." His words felt useless, empty.

Rita and Jack arrived from next door, Rita bearing a hot dish of egg and sausage casserole. "This will stick to your ribs better than a bit of cake."

Jack squeezed Aidan's shoulders. "Right sharp looking you are, there. Your gran would be proud."

"I hope so," Aidan whispered, and shook his head at the plate Rita offered.

"You have to eat something, dear."

Aidan wanted to please her. She'd worked so hard, not just this morning but ever since he'd come home. He knew if he tried to swallow anything it would stick in his throat or, if it managed to slide down farther, sit like a rock in his stomach.

"Maybe later," he told her.

Niall and Michael arrived, followed by Patrick and Moira.

"Oh Aidan, I'm so sorry." Moira hugged him. "Conor and Caitlyn made this card for you. It's not much, but they wanted to send you something."

Aidan smiled at the drawing of flowers and a rainbow, and hugged Moira back. "It's a beautiful card. Thanks."

"My mom and dad will be at the church," Niall informed him.

Michael started to say, "My mother sends her condolences," but the words sounded hollow to him and he let the moment slip by.

Impossible to avoid the sight of the three caskets in front of him at church, Aidan stared at each one separately while memories flooded his mind and tore at what was left of his heart. He saw his father as he saw him every morning, dressed, pacing himself through tea and breakfast, never hurried, always structured with his timing, then heading out for work. He saw Jeannie, the exact opposite of his father, rushing upstairs to find a lost book or homework assignment, stuffing her breakfast toast down her throat, washing it down with a hurried cup of tea, dashing back upstairs to finish hair and makeup before flying out the door to catch a ride to school with their father. He saw his grandmother running the morning as a director of a play, hurrying the actors to their stages, supplying what they needed to carry out their roles, everything under control, everything as it should be and, unlike the director, always with a smile glowing in her bright green eyes and cheery face. Even while he'd been away, the image of their morning routine had started his mornings, set the tone for his days, anchored him like a compass marking a position on a map, setting a course for wanderers in a forest. Now the compass was broken, and he wondered how he would ever find his way.

Other images filled his mind as well, pictures of relatives long since gone, an aunt and uncle on his father's side, his mother's sister, grandparents, great grandparents, and beyond, where images were nonexistent but stories fixed them in place and time. He could feel them all with him throughout the Funeral Mass, all of the O'Connell and Fitzsimmons ancestors through the ages, joining together to receive back their own. If he closed his eyes, he could almost hear their ancient voices. Months later he would ask Father Nelligan, "Why did they not call me as well?" Now, though, he tried to close his mind to thoughts and feelings, tried to fall back again into performance mode, although he found it much harder to come by. He tried to absorb Father Nelligan's words, reassuring the packed church that God had Cathleen, Daniel and Jeannie safely with Him, and that His love would see them all through the days ahead; but the words flew out of his mind as fast as they entered, and vanished in the air.

The weight of his father's coffin on his shoulder seemed a ton, yet Aidan found, when it was time, he did not want to set it down. He wanted to hold it forever, never let it go, knowing once he let it go his father was gone forever, they all were gone forever, there would be nothing left of them to hold onto.

Michael watched Aidan as he stood by the graves while others filed out of the cemetery, services concluded. Would he ever miss anyone that much, he wondered. His mother? Possibly. His father? Never. Maybe that was the wrong outlook, though. Maybe there was a way to penetrate his father's stone exterior. What could he and his father share the way Aidan and his dad shared fishing and music? Nothing was the only answer that came to mind. A sense of loss filled him that rivaled his friend's.

Anna Donoghue hugged Aidan while her husband, Will, looked on. "That was a lovely Mass."

Will said, "Niall's told us what a fine job you've done of handling things."

"I couldn't have got through this without Niall and the boys. Are you going to join us at Shannon's? Niall can ride with you and show you the way."

Will shook his head. "We need to get back to the farm. Always work to be done there, you know."

"Niall always says how busy you are out there. I'm sending him back home with you."

"No, Aidan, I know he'd feel better staying with you a bit longer. He'll be home soon enough." Anna kissed Aidan's cheek. Her soft touch and scent reminded him all over again of his grandmother.

Mack caught sight of Kate turning towards her car and caught up with her. "I didn't know you'd be here. I would have sat with you."

"I didn't know if I'd be able to leave the shop until last minute." Kate observed the tired lines on Mack's face. "You look done in. Are you sure you're up to dinner tomorrow?"

"Yes, I'm sure. I'll pick you up at half six."

"I'll meet you at Patterson's at seven."

"Fair enough. Thank you."

Patrick nodded towards Aidan and told Moira, "I'll be right back."

Aidan stood transfixed, staring at the three fresh graves.

"This is the hardest part."

He turned to face Patrick. "I can't do it. I can't just leave them here alone."

Patrick remembered his own father's funeral, and his mother's six months after. "I know. Stepping away is the hardest thing in the world."

"How do I do it, Pat?"

"You just put one foot in front of the other and walk away."

"And leave them behind."

Patrick nodded. "Not their spirits, though. Their hearts and spirits will follow you."

Aidan wanted to believe Patrick, just like he'd wanted to believe the same words from his father when his mother was gone. It was partly true, he knew, but over the years he felt his mother less and less; now it would happen again with the rest of his family.

Still, it was time. He nodded to Patrick, took one last hard look at the gravesite, and stepped away.

The gathering at Shannon's parted when Aidan entered, allowing him space to walk to the bar where a freshly poured shot of whiskey stood waiting. He held the smooth glass, hoping no one would notice how his hand shook, studied the amber liquid a moment, then raised the glass for all to see.

"For my family."

"For Daniel, Cathleen and Jeannie," friends echoed, raising their glasses.

Then another round of stories began. On and on the memories went till Aidan's head spun like a thousand laser lights flying at him too fast to take them all in. He followed the shot of whiskey with a pint of stout, accepted a ham and cheese sandwich of which he ate half, and shook off the second pint offered him.

Sean, Charlie and Tommy played in the background, sometimes slow airs, sometimes jigs, sometimes traditional songs accompanied by the packed pub singing along. Then they stopped, and Charlie called Aidan over.

"The next song's yours, boy." He held out Daniel O'Connell's guitar.

Annie shone honey gold in the light. Her darker fingerboard showed scratches and other signs of wear. Love marks, his father called them. Aidan stared at her as if she was charged with electricity and he'd be stung by touching her.

"I don't think I can," he apologized to Charlie.

The eyes of the crowd were on him, though, and his father's bandmates expecting him to join them. He took the chair Tommy had moved into place for him, took Annie from Charlie, surprised that she didn't bite, nestled her under his arms feeling the same warmth and firmness he was sure his father felt in her, and something else, his father's presence, as if in holding Annie he was holding his father. Aidan prayed for strength to get through just one song without breaking down.

"You know the song, boy," Sean whispered. "Rosie's Ring. For your dad and mam."

Aidan started the song and the others joined in the stirring ballad about the ring of life drawn around one, Rosie, and how light from that ring shone on everyone around her. The last line Aidan found hardest to sing.

> "and the light from Rosie's ring
> still shines in the dark
> and guides my way home."

Aidan stepped away from the stage then, faced the friends who had gathered and said, "Thank you all for being here, for being such a large part of my family's lives. I'll be going home now, but please, stay on, enjoy yourselves."

Back home, Aidan restored Annie to her stand in the corner next to his father's chair. He sank down into the recliner, thought right away he should sit somewhere else, and realized it no longer mattered, the chair's owner was gone. He loosened and pulled off his tie. "That was a long day."

Jack opened a bottle of brandy he'd brought from home, poured several glasses, and passed them around. "One last toast," he announced, "to Daniel, Cathleen and Jeannie."

Aidan swallowed half, then raised his glass again. "To friends. I could never have made it through these last few days without you all."

"What did we all agree on when we started working as a group?" Patrick looked at each of his bandmates and Mack to see if they remembered. "We're all in this together."

"All the way," Michael agreed.

"We never expected we'd go through anything this hard," Aidan pointed out.

Niall nodded. "True, but times like those we stick that much closer to each other."

Rita entered the room, wiping her hands on a kitchen towel. "Aidan, love, your kitchen's all cleared and the food stored away. You're set for the next few days."

Aidan rose and hugged her and Jack. "My daddy and gran would be so grateful for all the help you've given me. You've been the best neighbors ever."

"We'll be by tomorrow to check on you."

Aidan recognized the same tiredness in Jack's eyes that he knew filled his own. "You don't have to. You and Rita could do with a break."

Jack studied the boy before him. The strong front Aidan put up now would break soon enough, Jack knew. He would serve Daniel and Cathleen a while more. "We'll be by just the same."

After Jack and Rita left, Aidan turned to the rest of the room. "It's time you all went home."

"Moira's going home in the morning, but I'll stay on a few more days."

"No, Pat, you'll go home with her." When Patrick started to protest, Aidan insisted, "You've been missing those kiddies of yours every day since we left. You've done everything you can here; you'll go home with Moira."

He turned to Niall, but before he could speak Niall informed him, "I'm staying the night."

Aidan knew better than to try to change Niall's mind when his heels were dug in. Instead, he told Michael and Mack, "I'm going to bed. With any luck I'll sleep for a week. You two should go home and do the same."

"We'll go back to the hotel," Mack replied. "Tomorrow we'll figure out what's next."

5

Jack watched Rita fill a basket with tea packets, biscuits and napkins and asked, "Don't you think the boy's got plenty over there already?"

Rita sank into the kitchen chair across from him. Thoughts of Aidan lay heavy on her heart as they had all night. "I know I'm overdoing it; I just don't know how else to help."

"There's not much we can do." Jack recalled the sight of Aidan at the cemetery, standing firm, not shedding a tear, and the way he held his composure at Shannon's Pub after. "He's got some strength in him. He can take what lies ahead."

"I don't know, Jack." She saw again Aidan's bright blue eyes, always laughing before, but now deep with pain. "Now they've been laid to rest, he'll have nothing to turn his mind to. He'll be lost."

Already, to Jack, the house next door bore a gaping hole, as he missed the sounds of Cathleen calling family in for dinner, or Daniel's car leaving for work in the morning and arriving home at night. He was sure Rita missed the familiar patterns as well. He'd felt her tossing and turning throughout the night. He studied the woman across from him. A sight heavier than when they'd married, hair gone as white as his own, with a few more lines on her face, he wondered what it would be like if she were gone. When she were gone. No! He wouldn't let his mind go there. Without her, he'd be just as lost as Aidan next door was now.

As he watched, her large brown eyes filled with tears. "Oh Jack, I don't know how he'll get through this."

Jack covered her hands with his own. "I don't either, but that wee basket you're filling's a good start."

Rita kissed Jack's cheek as she returned to her work. "Maybe while you're in town today you could pick up some of those crisps he likes."

Niall moved quietly through the family room, picking up newspapers and setting them in a stack by the corner chair, gathering pieces of mail, cards and notes, and placing them on the coffee table, folding the blanket he'd covered himself with the night before and stacking it on top of the pillow.

He heard footsteps coming up the walk and hurried to the door before anyone could ring the bell.

"Rita," he whispered, "come in."

She glanced around the room. "Is Aidan not up?" she whispered back.

Niall shook his head. "He was a long time falling asleep last night. I could hear him turning over and over, getting up and walking from room to room. It was going on three when he finally settled down. I've turned the phone down so it doesn't wake him; I don't think a few missed calls will hurt anything."

Rita noted Niall's tousled hair and unshaven face and the circles under his eyes. She nodded towards the sofa, "I don't imagine you slept well yourself. Would you like help with anything this morning?"

"No thanks. I'm just going to read for a bit until Aidan wakes up."

"Set this off to the side, then, and come next door if you do have a need." She hugged Niall. "You're a wonderful friend to Aidan."

"You and Jack are as well." Niall watched Rita walk back to her house, then set the basket in the kitchen and returned to the sofa. Rita had been right; between listening to make sure Aidan was okay, and sorting through the myriad emotions they'd all been through since the phone call in New York, sleep had eluded him the better part of the night.

While they all were close, with the tight bonds that come from working long hours together and sharing a common interest and goal, he and Aidan, closest to each other in age, both still living at home and neither in a serious relationship, had formed the deepest friendship. When their turns came to share a hotel room in the rotation schedule Mack had set up, they would talk long into the night about music, about girls, and most of all about their families. Niall remembered one conversation above all.

They were three weeks into the tour, which had gone very well so far, far better than any of them had imagined, with very strong ticket sales, even a few sold out shows, and audiences who were enthusiastic beyond belief. After their Kansas City show, Aidan had been unusually quiet. When asked, he'd just told Mack and the boys he was tired. Back in their room, though, Niall had pressed the issue.

"I'm not buying the tired excuse. What's going on?"

Aidan had shrugged and stretched out on his bed. "I guess it's just the traveling. The distances are farther here than back home, bus rides longer; it's just wearing on me."

"Nope. Not buying that either." Niall had looked straight at Aidan. "I can see it in your eyes; you've got something on your mind."

Aidan had finally relented, fixing his eyes on a spot on the hotel room wall, boring through it to some distant place. "I miss being home."

Once he'd let his secret out, Aidan had sat up, swung his legs over the side of the bed, and confessed, "I must be crazy! Here we are having the time of our lives, everything going perfect, and all I can think about is home. That's nuts, isn't it?"

"Not so crazy," Niall had assured him. "Why now, though? We've been away before; it's never gotten to you the way it is now."

"I know." Aidan thought a bit. "It must be the distance. Before, my da was only a short ways away. I could call him any time, and if I needed anything I could get it in an instant, almost. Now it's so much harder. I can't just ring him up anytime I want, and he can't just fly over."

Niall had suspected they'd all felt the same way; he knew he did, knew his mam and dad were fine on the farm but admitted to himself it felt odd to not be able to contact them at will. Aidan was that much closer to his family. Niall could see the distance would be that much harder for him to adjust to.

"Why don't you give them a call?"

"Now?" Niall nodded. Aidan checked his travel alarm clock. "It's too early, five a.m. there."

"I'm sure your dad wouldn't mind. I'll bet he misses you as much as you miss him."

Aidan had called, and spent twenty minutes filling his father in on the tour, pressing for updates on Jeannie and his grandmother, teasing and laughing with his father. Niall had lain down on his bed, on his side with his back to Aidan to give him some semblance of privacy, but had heard most of Aidan's side of the conversation anyway, and had been amazed once again at the depth of the bond between Aidan and his father.

Now, sitting on Aidan's sofa, Niall wondered, if three weeks' distance was hard for Aidan to adjust to, how would he ever cope with this much more drastic separation?

Moira placed her hand on Patrick's as he turned their car onto the narrow road that led to their house. "You've done nothing but worry all the way home."

Patrick pulled his eyes off the road for a second to look at her. "I know. Poor company I've been. I'm sorry."

"No apologies needed. We'll be home soon, though; Conor and Caitlyn will want a smile from you."

"I'll be smiling for them. It's just hard to get Aidan off my mind."

"I know." Moira found it just as hard to clear her mind of visions of Aidan seated alone at church, despite the friends gathered around him, bearing the weight of his father's coffin as he carried it out of the church.

"Do you know, in all the time I've known Aidan I don't think there's a day I didn't see or hear him on the phone with his family."

"I remember when we saw them at Christmas, how Jeannie hardly took her eyes off him." Moira smiled at the memory. "He was her hero, wasn't he?"

"Remember the pearl ring he gave her for Christmas? He must have gone to a dozen stores looking for just the right one. We thought he'd have to design one himself the way he was going."

"And didn't she show everyone that ring twenty times over!"

Sorrow clouded Patrick's face again. "He's going to be so lost without them."

Moira gave his arm a light squeeze. "Maybe in a week or two we can have him over to spend a few days. But now, look, there's your own house, and Conor and Caitlyn waiting for you."

Patrick admired the scene, single level cottage painted cream yellow with marine blue shutters and door, rising up from the green grassy field that surrounded it, with Sligo Bay's gentle blue waves in the background. He remembered the day he and Moira had found it, a few days after they'd found out she was pregnant with twins. She had been so excited at the news, he'd had to hide his fear that two wee infants would be too much to handle. They were driving to his parents' house to break the news when they'd passed by this cottage. Back then the cottage had been in need of paint and repair, thatched roof redone and new glass for broken windows; but the vision of what it could be had hit them both at the same moment and they took the homeowner's plunge. Now the house gleamed fresh and clean in the sun, exuding an air of hospitality and contentment. Two red-haired children chased each other around the side yard, stopping at intervals to watch the road, shouting and running to the road when the car they'd searched for was spotted. As Patrick and Moira drew closer, he could hear their calls, "Daddy! Daddy! You're home!" He pulled the car to its spot by the house, climbed out, found his seven-year old twins so tightly attached to his legs he couldn't take a step, and allowed himself to be dragged to the ground and tickled until they were all laughing, everything else forgotten.

Aidan woke to mid-afternoon sun casting shadows over his pale green bedroom walls. The house was still. In the half-world between sleep and fully awake, Aidan thought, Jeannie's at school, Dad's at work, Gran must be next door. Then he spotted his black suit draped over his chair and remembered why the house would be silent. Thinking he was alone in the house, he stayed in bed, listening to the silence, feeling the weight of it, the strangeness of it, how much he hated it. The clock by his bed read three-forty; he thought he should get up, and he thought he was far from ready to face the whole-house silence. Only when he heard a knock on the front door, the door opened and voices engaged in conversation did he remember Niall had spent the night and would still be there now. He rose, quickly pulled on clean jeans and his favorite ocean blue sweater, ran a comb through his hair, swallowed a shot of mouthwash in exchange for brushing his teeth, and hurried downstairs.

"I can't believe I slept so long. I'm sorry. You should have woke me up."

"You needed the sleep." Niall observed the dark shadows under Aidan's eyes. "You could do with more."

"You've been stuck here all day. I hope you at least got yourself something to eat. God knows there's a whole kitchen full of food." He turned to Mack, realizing he must have been the knock and voice at the door. "Why do people do that, bring so much food? I'll never be able to eat everything that's left. You should each take some home. I should have sent some back with Patrick and Moira."

Mack and Niall could both see Aidan's emotions close to the surface in his stormy blue eyes. "I had a sandwich a bit ago," Niall said. "Let's get you some food and tea."

Aidan shook his head. "I'll get something later. You need to head home."

"I'll be staying tonight," Mack informed them. "I've got dinner plans first, then I'll come back."

"Neither of you are staying." Niall started to protest, but Aidan held up a hand to stop him. "You're tired. We're all tired after the tour and the last few days. You know you can't wait to get back to those sheep of yours. Mack, you don't need to stay either. I'll be sending Michael home too. I've got Jack and Rita next door; trust me, they'll be checking in every few hours."

"They've already stopped by twice," Niall told him.

"See? I'll be fine. You've all been a tremendous help, but it's time for you to go home."

Michael stepped into his empty Dublin apartment, and was struck by how his footsteps echoed as he walked through the rooms and turned lights on against the evening darkness. All during the bus ride home from Derry, his mind had been occupied by thoughts of the overwhelming loneliness Aidan would now have to struggle through. Now, inside his own home, Aidan faded to the background; and Michael was forced to face his own life.

"It's always like this," he reminded himself. "Every time you come home from being out on the road you have to adjust to the quiet, to not having the others around." He tried to convince himself this was like every other time. Deep in his heart, though, he knew this time was different, and not just because of Aidan's crisis.

Michael studied Susannah's photo on his phone, the one he'd taken at a flower stand on Grafton Street the previous autumn as she'd inhaled the aroma from a bouquet of bright orange lilies, eyes closed, enraptured. God, she was gorgeous. And trying, and right now, not happy with him. He dialed her number.

"Leave a message. I'll call back."

Michael cringed, as he always did, at her curt message. Did she never realize how off-putting she sounded? "Suze, it's me. Sorry I haven't called. It's been difficult. I'll explain later. Please call back soon."

Susannah Tierney saw Michael's call come in. She waited until his voicemail message was complete, and a full ten minutes after that, before calling back.

"I'd just about given up on you."

"Suze, I'm sorry."

"I got your texts. I know what's going on." She glared at his picture on her desk since she couldn't glare at him face to face.

"Then you know why I haven't called."

"No. That's the part I don't know."

Michael's muscles tensed the way they did whenever he sensed an argument coming on. "We've all been helping Aidan out."

"I know that," Susannah's voice broke in. "What I don't know is how *you're* feeling, what's going on with *you*." When Michael didn't respond, Susannah continued, "The truth is, I never know what's going on with you. We argue about hot topics when we push each other too far, we have fantastic sex, but you never let me beyond the wall you've built around who you are inside."

She was right, Michael knew. The wall was real, very few people were allowed access to the inner world he guarded as if the Book of Kells itself were stored inside. Even his best friends and bandmates only penetrated to the point he allowed and no further.

"What would you like me to say?" he asked at last.

Susannah slammed her coffee cup down. "Nothing you think you have to to please me. Tell me something I don't know, something from your heart."

Michael sorted through all the thoughts and feelings he'd carried deep inside since that Starbucks morning, his anguish over Aidan's loss, his sadness and anger that he, himself, enjoyed none of the family riches Aidan's life had been so full of, then said, "Aidan's lost everything, he's completely crushed right now; and I'm afraid I'll never have in my life all that he had, all that he's lost."

Susannah was so stunned she couldn't speak at first. After his words had settled in her heart she asked, "Even with me?"

"Even with anyone." Michael hated himself for the way his words felt and how he knew they sounded to Susannah. If she wanted truth, though, there it was, hard and cold.

Susannah's voice finally came across the stillness over the phone, "I guess Barcelona's out, then."

"Barcelona?" Michael exploded. "I've just told you about Aidan, and about what I feel. Who gives a crap about Barcelona? Why do you do that? Why does everything come back to you and what you want?"

"What I want?" Susannah shot back. "Tell me one time since February anything's been about what I want? It's all been about you! You and the band! You on the road! You've barely had time for phone calls, and you missed the biggest event in my family's life last month."

"Here we go again!" Michael was too tired, too at odds with himself, to care if he stepped over any lines now. "Your father's birthday party. Haven't we argued that one to death yet? Are you going to throw that back at me the rest of our lives?"

Susannah's long silence confirmed he'd cut deep, maybe too deep. Remorse flooded in, he hated himself with fresh loathing for hurting her, shoved aside the internal reminder that, in the end, it was always he who gave in and apologized. "Suze, I'm sorry. I shouldn't have said any of that. Ignore me, I'm tired and have too much on my mind."

"I should ignore you." Michael had a feeling Susannah meant another, more total idea than he'd intended. "I agree, though, you've had a lot on your plate. Take some time, get yourself sorted," she advised, and added, "Michael, I love you, but I won't wait forever."

Michael stared at her picture long after their conversation ended. Get himself sorted? Where would he even begin?

Susannah thought back to the night eighteen months earlier, when she'd attended an art exhibit opening party with her best friend, Diane. There amid the paintings and sculpture, the food stations and wine bar, he stood discussing the details of a painting before him with Gavin, the artist, pointing out light and dark and the symbolism of the heron tucked in the shadow. Susannah had caught her breath, struck by Michael's clean profile, the cut of his claret colored shirt against his throat, the smile in his eyes. When she ran into him, almost literally, at the cheese and vegetable table he'd laughed, and his clear, strong laugh drew her further in.

"So sorry. My fault. I see cheddar and lose all sense and sight for anything else! Would have been tragic for my red wine to splash all over your lovely cream sweater."

"Oh no, my fault," she'd countered, matching his wit. "I see celery and am instantly oblivious!"

"Maybe we should head to the biscuit station instead. Or does shortbread render you unconscious?"

"Comatose! But let's risk it."

As they'd moved around the room, revisiting pieces they'd each already seen, he'd sounded so knowledgeable about artwork she had finally asked, "Are you an artist yourself? Art professor? Art critic?"

He'd laughed again. "No. I'm a hotel front deskman by day, and singer at night. You should come hear me sometime."

"I'd love to. Where?" She imagined some intimate nightclub or concert hall. When he answered, "Tomorrow night, Boyle's Pub," she'd been shocked and disappointed.

"A pub? You? Seriously?" Diane was horrified when Susannah filled her in on Michael later that night. "You can kiss that relationship goodbye before it even starts."

Still, intrigued, Susannah had ventured out to Boyle's and came home head over heels in love. She'd followed Michael to Kelley's Pub the week after, and The Golden Harp the week after that. From then on, Michael saved her a seat near the front of any place he appeared.

"You're my lucky charm," he told her one night.

She'd moved in close and breathed into his ear, "Is that all I am?"

The memory of that night in particular stood out as Susannah stared at Michael's photo now. She wouldn't wait forever; but, despite their cat and dog fights, despite the career that now took him farther away for longer periods of time, despite what Diane and their other friends said about how Michael was beneath her, how she could do so much better, she would wait a while longer.

Niall pulled his suitcases and instruments out of the rental van and asked Mack, "Would you like to stop in for tea?"

Mack glanced at the van's clock. "Another time I'd love to. Right now I have to drop this van off, get home and get changed."

"That's right," Niall grinned, "the fair Kate will be waiting. Good luck tonight."

Mack brushed Niall's words off, "It's just dinner and a chance to talk, nothing more."

"Sure," Niall replied. He'd seen the wistful look in Mack's eyes whenever he'd spoken of Kate; as Mack backed out of the driveway and headed down the road, Niall prayed some spark would be rekindled for Mack and the woman he'd never stopped loving.

"We didn't expect to see you for several more days," Will Donoghue called out from the barn entrance as he watched his son glance around the farm in search of his father.

Niall set his gear down outside the barn and hugged his father. "Aidan sent us all home."

"I thought he'd at least keep you on a bit longer."

"I think he needs a little time alone to wrap his head around all that's happened."

"He's got a lot to adjust to," Will agreed. He eyed his son top to bottom. In the two months Macready's Bridge had been gone, Niall had grown taller, or was that just his imagination? He had put a few pounds on, Will guessed from the inactivity long bus rides would produce. He needed a haircut, tired lines framed his dark brown eyes, even his skin seemed pale and dull. A few days of fresh air and farm work should cure that, Will thought.

"It's good to have you home, son." Will whistled for their family dog, Farley. When the collie-sheepdog mixed breed dashed from the yard to the barn, Will smiled at Niall, "There ye go, the two of you can bring our sheep home."

After months rehearsing and touring, and the heaviness of the past few days, Niall felt the walk to the field where his family's sheep grazed was heaven. He soaked up how clean the air smelled, how quiet the hills and fields around him were, how bright the waning sun lit up the waters of the lough at the back of their farm. He was sure the sheep all smiled at seeing him, and ran a little faster following him home.

"I'm sorry you've come home to such a simple meal," Mrs. Donoghue apologized as they sat down for their dinner. "If I'd known you'd be home, I would have made a proper roast for you."

Niall scanned the dishes of stew, salad and homemade bread his mother had set on their kitchen table. "Mam, honest, this looks a thousand times better than the meals I've had on the road. You wouldn't need to add a single thing."

Mrs. Donoghue's blue eyes twinkled with the same laughter that so often lit her son's eyes. "So, you're not interested in the berry pie I have for later?"

"Well, now, I didn't say that!"

As she served their meal, Niall's mother asked, "Do you think Aidan will be alright on his own?"

"I don't know, mam. He looked so alone when I left." Niall could still see Aidan standing in the door, watching Mack and himself leave, empty brick house looming large behind him. "I know his neighbors will help, and truth be told he'll probably sleep the better part of the next few days, but he's got a rough road ahead. I don't know how he'll get by."

"If I know you and your bandmates, you'll be right alongside Aidan's neighbors helping out." Mr. Donoghue passed the butter dish to Niall.

The conversation then turned from Aidan to the latest news from town. Niall listened more than he spoke, relishing the easy, natural conversation that flowed between his parents, one of the by-products of their twenty-seven years of marriage. Niall thought again how blessed he was to have the parents he had, the country life he'd been born into, the decades-old house he'd grown up in. As his mother cleared their dinner dishes off the table and returned with her berry pie, as his father turned the topic of conversation from town news to questions over what they'd grow in their garden this year, Niall tried to imagine this kitchen, this farm without his parents, realized the hole they would leave was too painful to even consider, and focused instead on the discussion of squash versus peas in the garden, which varieties of tomatoes would be planted, and a better way to stake up the beans this year.

Mack stared into the closet of his Portrush home. "What should I wear for ye, Kate?" he asked the empty room. "A suit's too formal. Slacks and shirt too plain. I won't get through the night without a shirt and tie will I?" His eyes fell on the dove grey shirt and black diamond tie the boys had given him for Christmas. Perfect! That, plus black trousers, and his black leather jacket, the one styled like a suitcoat without feeling so formal or stuffy, that would impress Kate without overdoing.

Why did he still feel the need to impress her, he wondered as he sat across from her at their table at Patterson's an hour later. Hell, she knew him inside and out, every fault, every wrinkle, every line, like he knew all of hers. Why, then, could he not relax around her?

"We'll start with bruschetta. Kate, what then for you?"

"The fillet medallions with garlic potatoes, and I'd like a glass of Pinot Noir."

"I'll have the salmon, and some of the Marlborough Sauvignon Blanc." Mack handed both menus to the waitress. When she was gone he said, "Kate, thank you again for being at the funeral yesterday."

"How is Aidan today?" she asked.

"He's sent us all home. I'm not sure we're ready to see him off on his own, but I think he feels guilty about holding us up."

Kate recognized the worried frown that spread across Mack's face now as the same one she'd seen so many times throughout their married years. Beyond the frown, she had to admit he still looked handsome, and still carried himself with style, his black casual suit had been just the right touch. Kate was surprised to find her thoughts scattered, her composure just the slightest bit unnerved. She'd have to work to maintain her focus tonight. "He hasn't sent you all away forever. I'm sure he's just tired and needs a day or two to clear his head."

"Yeah, you're right."

"Life comes at us a million ways, Mack. We all have our turn at a crisis; we all find our way through. Aidan will be okay."

Mack took in how the soft light played in the colors of Kate's hair, held back tonight by a pearl clip that matched her pearl earrings and necklace, how her graceful hands with blush colored nails, never red, she never went in for garish nail polish, lingered on her wine glass, how confidence oozed out of every pore in her, reflected in each of her movements. "You certainly have," he remarked. "Found your way, I mean. You've done very well."

"It wasn't easy, Mack. All the years we were married, I felt I did so many things wrong. I couldn't make you happy."

"You couldn't make yourself happy," he corrected, then added, "we should have adopted kids."

Kate gave a slight shake of her head. "It wouldn't have mattered. I wanted my own children. Someone else's wouldn't have satisfied that desire in me."

"I wasn't much help, had my head stuck in work, always pushing to make a name for myself; I had no patience with you. I was wrong."

Kate laughed. "Listen to us. So many years we spent blaming each other, now we're going to fight each other to take the blame ourselves?"

Mack shared the laugh. "Let's not do that! It's been a hard week. Let's talk about something fun. Tell me how the shop's going."

They talked as they ate, about Kate's shop, about the Macready's Bridge tour, about the economic challenges of both in today's world, about places they wanted to go, and for a while Mack relaxed with Kate and Aidan slipped from his mind.

"I'll give you a ride home," Mack offered at the end of their evening. He caught her hesitation. "No strings attached, no funny business, just a ride."

"No thank you. Thank you for dinner, though. I enjoyed it."

"So did I." He helped Kate slip her coat on. His hand brushed hers, and Kate covered it with her own.

"Take care of yourself, Mack. Get some sleep and try not to worry about Aidan. If you want, you can call me next week."

"Thank you. I will."

Aidan listened to the answering machine messages left while Niall had turned the phone down, mostly messages of condolence, two calls asking when O'Connell's Garage would reopen, one call from Ben, his best friend in school, now living in London, he'd just heard the news, how terrible, he hoped to be home soon and would call in. All of the calls could wait, Aidan thought. He sifted through mail and set the most urgent pieces on top. As he cleared through the stack of newspapers in the family room corner, his eyes fell upon a picture of mangled metal on pavement. At first, the picture didn't register in his mind. Even the headline, "Local Family Killed In Accident," didn't connect with him until the name "O'Connell" caught his eye as he started to set the paper aside.

He stared hard at the photo. God. What a horrendous mess. He could barely pick out the car's doors and top amid the twisted frame and broken pieces lying where they'd been thrown on impact. He convinced himself the dark stains on the pavement were the car's oil and fluids, not blood. The truck itself, off to the left, showed front end damage but little else. The article held few new details. Driver unhurt. Mobile phone. Killed on impact. The words were no longer hollow; their enormity sank in, lead weights pinning his heart to the ground. When he could no longer stand the visual image, he gathered that paper with the rest, and carried them out to the recycle bin.

There in the garden, perched on top of the trellis where honeysuckle grew, was a magpie, black and white feathers as bold and cheeky as the bird itself. Aidan remembered his father's statement in their last chat, "Jeannie saw a magpie." The warning is true, Aidan thought, one for sorrow. He scanned the yard and the neighboring structures for signs of the magpie's companion. There must be another one! Two for joy! Damn it, where is that second bird? None appeared; suddenly Aidan hated that bird, and all the heartache it had brought. Anger rose within him stronger than anything he'd ever felt. He'd show that bird. He'd kill the damn thing! He picked up a rock from the ground and flung it at the magpie with all the energy he possessed. The rock missed the bird, bouncing hard off the fence that surrounded the yard. The magpie flew away, startled. Aidan slammed the door behind him as he stormed back into the house.

His phone rang the minute he stepped inside. As soon as he answered Rita asked, "Aidan dear, are you okay? We just heard a terrible noise from your yard."

"I'm sorry. I dropped something outside," he lied. "I'm fine. Everything's fine."

"I stopped over earlier, but you were asleep. Jack and I are having chicken for dinner soon, would you like to join us? Or shall I bring some over to you?"

"Neither, thanks. I'm going to have some of what's left here, and then go back to bed."

"Alright, dear. Call if you need anything, otherwise we'll see you tomorrow."

Aidan heated water for tea and glanced through the food that filled his kitchen, meat and cheeses in the refrigerator, bread and baked goods on the counter. Nothing appealed to him. He set the hot water aside. Even tea wouldn't fill what he needed. He returned to the family room and sat in his father's recliner. Evening fell, the house grew dark, and still Aidan sat, the silence of the house growing heavier and heavier, the enormity of truth bearing down on him. They were gone. Completely. Forever.

When he was little, and hurt or afraid, he'd climb into his father's lap, feel strong arms wrap around him, hear his father's heartbeat and know he was safe. If the pain or fear was severe, he'd snuggle into his father as tight as he could, demanding more comfort, more reassurance. Now Aidan pushed into the recliner as tight and hard as possible, but no comfort came. He pushed tighter still, but the chair gave nothing back. Finally the wall of reserve that had held him together for days collapsed, and he cried the tears of a child whose most prized possession was irretrievably broken. When he was all cried out, he fell asleep in the chair.

6

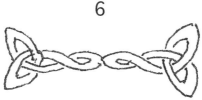

"These are the last two forms to sign for now."

"For now," Aidan repeated and smiled at James Maloney, his father's solicitor. "I'm beginning to understand that means you'll have more for me next week."

"It's an endless process, to be sure." Jim Maloney slid the signed forms into a folder and reviewed the papers before him. "Did you know the house was in your grandmother's name, and all paid for?"

"Yes, we had a party last year to celebrate the event."

"That's an accomplishment worth having a party for," Jim agreed, then returned to his papers. "The garage is in your father's name, he owes some money on the building, and there are monthly bills for the business."

Jim set his papers aside and slid his eyes over the son of his former classmate. The boy had his mother's golden hair, oval face, high cheekbones and shining blue eyes. Jim wondered if Aidan carried his father's strength. He'd displayed plenty enough at the funeral service, sitting tall and straight in his black suit in the church's front pew, hardly showing emotion throughout the Mass, stoic as he helped carry his father's casket, composed as he greeted people afterwards. He'd shown plenty of strength then, but would he have enough for the long days ahead? Jim pictured Daniel again, young as they went to school and as they played after, older as Daniel started performing music and Jim and their mates would follow wherever he played, beaming with pride the day he and Rosie married, and again when Aidan and later Jeannie were born, heartbroken the day he buried Rosie. Aidan seemed so much like Daniel now, Jim thought, perhaps not in physical features, but in his demeanor, straightforward, asking and answering questions with little hesitation or emotion, unlike others Jim had seen who were so distraught at the loss of a loved one they could barely navigate the paperwork end of things. Jim watched for Aidan's reaction now as he asked, "Have you thought what you'll do with the garage?"

Aidan shook his head. "I'm hardly the one to fix cars. My dad knew years ago he had a better shot at Jeannie following in his footsteps."

Aidan's answer was straightforward, just as Jim expected it would be. "Well, you have a few options; you could sell up, or you could keep it and hire someone to run it for you."

"Do I have to decide now?"

Jim smiled again. "No. Not at all. I'm just pointing out where things stand and what you'll need to think on over the next few months."

"Terry Reilly, he's a friend of my dad's, he's taken most of my dad's customers on since... since the accident." Aidan hated that he still tripped over the words. "He works for another garage, but I've heard him a couple of times tell my dad he'd love to own his own place someday. I'm pretty sure he'd be willing to take the garage over, at least until I decide what I want to do."

"That sounds like a good plan. If you want to go that route, we should draw up an agreement between you both."

"I'll call him this week." Then Aidan admitted, "I know there are books to keep for the garage. I don't know how to do any of that."

"I could recommend an accountant to help you if you'd like."

"That would be great."

"What about the bills at home? Are you able to handle them?"

"So far, yes."

"Fine." Jim gathered the papers before him, placed them in the same folder as the signed forms, and sat back. "You look tired, and you've lost some weight. I'm a little worried about you."

Aidan smiled to reassure the man who had been his father's friend and solicitor for as long as he could remember. "I'm fine. I'll eat and sleep better now that I'm getting some of these details worked out."

"Right. Well, call me any time you have questions or need anything. I'll call you in a day or two on the accountant and we can meet again soon."

"That's fine." Aidan rose and shook Mr. Maloney's hand. "Thanks again."

Aidan stepped out to find the rain clouds that had hovered over the city all day had broken, and for the first time in days sun filled the space around him. The fresh, clean air felt almost medicinal, healing after his appointment with Mr. Maloney, each signed form signaling one more layer of detachment between himself and his family. When had the trees gone from bud to full leaf, he wondered, as he walked the city sidewalks. He watched children run through the pavement fountain in front of the Guildhall, laughed as the fountain's intermittent spray caught one of the young boys off guard, soaking him, then caught himself laughing and felt a fountain of guilt wash over him. He stood a while in front of the Guildhall, struck by the light and shadow the sun cast on its terracotta stones, and the multi-colored reflections of its windows. How many times had he stood here with Jeannie as she drew this, her favorite building, working with charcoal or colored pencil until she was satisfied she'd captured its colors to perfection. He turned to the city's ancient walls, and Shipquay Gate behind him; his grandmother's voice rose in his mind, reciting historical and more current events. He wished he'd thought to record her stories so he would have them forever. Eventually, he knew, they would dim and the walls would become lifeless black and grey stones he would pass with little notice.

Aidan checked his watch and found he still had an hour before he was to meet Ben at Flaherty's, their usual gathering place. With time on his hands, and Mr. Maloney's words still filling his mind, Aidan headed for his father's garage.

The sign "Closed Due To Family Emergency" still showed where he had taped it to the door's small window. I should replace that, he thought as he slipped the key in the deadbolt lock, turned it until it clicked, and entered his father's domain.

The air smelled of grease and dust. The spot where cars in need of repair usually stood seemed ten times larger in its emptiness. Across Aidan's mind flashed every time he'd observed his father work his magic repairing cars, listening, diagnosing, then operating like a fine surgeon, screwdriver and wrench the scalpels he used, intense in his work, his mastery always amazing to behold.

Aidan surveyed the garage once more. His father's overalls hung on their nail hook on the side wall, gloves in their familiar spot on the tool chest, tools, as always, stored away in their proper beds. Aidan ran his hands over the tool chest, fingering spots where red paint had worn away from years of use.

"Always keep your tools in their proper places, then you'll always have them when they're needed."

His father's voice sounded so clear, so real, Aidan spun around, expecting to see his father behind him, ready to tackle another job. Of course, his father wasn't there. He never would be. Aidan felt foolish for even thinking otherwise. He hurried to the stairway in the back and climbed to his father's office, a corner of his father's life he had never entered before.

Like the workspace below, Daniel O'Connell kept his office neat and organized. Waterless hand cleanser and paper towels stood on top of the filing cabinet. Pencils and notepad sat by the phone. His father's careful handwriting listed appointments, names and phone numbers on the desk-sized calendar. Taped to the wall in front of the desk, Aidan found pictures: himself, Jeannie, his father with his grandmother, and his mother, this last photo faded, worn at the edges as if his father removed it and ran his fingers over it from time to time. Aidan studied the picture, her gentle smile, the sun reflecting off her golden hair.

Footsteps and a loud "Hello" broke into his thoughts. "Who's up there?"

Startled, Aidan glanced through the rectangular window in front of the desk and found Terry Reilly standing below. Relieved, he called back, "Terry, it's only me, Aidan."

As he scurried down the stairs, he heard Terry answer, "Thank God. I was afraid someone had broken in."

"I'm sorry. I was just collecting some of the books and papers I need."

"I saw the side door open, and thought I'd best check. I keep an eye on the place you know."

"I do know, and I'm grateful." Thinking again on Mr. Maloney's words, Aidan guessed now was as good a time as any for the next step he had to take. "Terry, I was wondering, I know you've been helping with some of my dad's customers, do you think you'd be interested in taking the garage over for a bit? Just until I decide what I'm going to do with it long term?"

Terry flashed a broad smile, "Aye, I'd be glad to take over." Then his expression sobered. "Mind, I wish it wasn't necessary. I'd much rather see Daniel himself back here where he belongs."

"So would I." Aidan glanced at his watch, not so much as he feared he'd be late, more as a way to stop Terry from reminiscing. He couldn't handle that, not in this shop, not when he'd have to then face his friends. "If you're sure, Terry, I can have my dad's solicitor draw up some papers for us."

"Aye," Terry repeated. "I'm sure."

Aidan glanced at his watch again so Terry could see he was pressed for time. "If you don't mind, I need to finish collecting the books, then run off to meet a couple of people."

"Of course. I'll see myself out."

"I'll call you in a day or two about the garage. And Terry, thanks again for all your help. I know how much my dad would appreciate it."

Thankful to have that task done, Aidan hurried back upstairs, as his watch had shown the time to be later than he thought. He located his father's books in the desk's top drawer, folded the desk calendar so it partially fit in the books, pulled the photos carefully from the wall and tucked them, in a clean envelope he found, into the books. He took one last slow look around his father's home away from home, and left, pulling the "closed" sign down and locking the door shut behind him.

Aidan found two surprises upon entering Flaherty's: Ben was not there yet, and Rosie's Ring was.

"Young Aidan, come over here!" Charlie called out, waving for him to join them as they unpacked guitars and fiddle in the far corner of the pub.

"Where have you been hiding yourself?" Tommy asked.

Sean thought Aidan's jacket hung looser than it had at the funeral three weeks earlier. "How are you?"

"I'm fine." Aidan was sure Sean could see through his lie. "So, you three are carrying on?"

"We are." Charlie paused, an empty gap in his words that matched the hole Daniel had left in their music. "And yourself?"

And myself? Aidan wondered, sorting through several responses. I'm hungry, but nothing tastes good. Bone tired, but can't sleep a wink. I've a world of weight on my shoulders, and wish to God my father was here to help me sort it all out. He chose to say none of these, replying instead, "I'm just taking things one day at a time."

"That's all any of us can do." Tommy nodded toward an empty stool in their corner. "Why don't you join us up here?"

"No, thanks. I'm meeting friends." Aidan pointed to Ben, grateful he'd shown up just then.

"Go on with ye," Charlie waved him off. "Mind, we might call you up for a song or two anyway."

Aidan slid into a vacant booth as far as he could get from where Rosie's Ring had set up. Ben joined him with two pints in hand, set one in front of Aidan, and informed him, "Kieran and Brendan are on their way."

Aidan's smile dissolved.

"You don't want to see them?" Ben asked as he slid in across from Aidan.

"I do. It's just—" Aidan paused. He couldn't even explain it to himself, let alone Ben. Today was the first time since the funerals that he'd ventured away from the house for more than an hour. As he'd left the garage and headed towards Flaherty's he'd already begun to feel the house pulling him back like a powerful magnet, the need to stay close by where they'd been, to feel connected to them in that one central spot they had always eventually come back to. No, they wouldn't come back now, he knew; still, there was comfort in sharing the air, the walls, the fabrics they had all touched. The irony, he knew, was after an hour home alone he'd be just as desperate to escape that air, those walls and fabrics.

Ben looked on, puzzled. Instead of trying to explain, Aidan lied, "It's just my neighbors are expecting me back for dinner. I didn't think we'd be out that long."

"See how things go when Kieran and Brendan get here," Ben advised. "You could always call and have your neighbors start dinner without you. I'm guessing they'd be happy to know you were out having fun."

"You're right." Aidan changed the subject, "How's everything going in London?" He eyed Ben's three-piece suit. "Successful by the looks of it, I'd say."

"Top of the world!" Ben beamed and stuck his thumbs under his lapels, as if to announce to the rest of the growing crowd at Flaherty's, "Look at me!"

Aidan lifted his pint. "Here's to you; you've worked hard for all your success."

Ben set his pint down, untouched. "I'm no success. The bank's downsizing; I may be out of a job in a month or two. I had an interview here in town this afternoon, and I've got another one in Belfast on Monday. Or did ye think I got this dressed up for you?"

Aidan faked disappointment. "I was hoping!"

"Sorry to disappoint. I don't know what's going to happen, I might have to move beyond London, maybe Canada or America if these interviews don't work out."

"Funny how life works, isn't it?" Aidan shook his head. "You think you're all set, everything's turning your way, and in the turn of a head it's all thrown upside down."

"It is." Ben gave Aidan a closer look. "I'm so sorry I couldn't be here for your family's wake. How are you getting on?"

"Okay." When Ben raised his eyebrows, unbelieving, Aidan shrugged, "Alright, I'm doing lousy. Life is hell right now."

"It must be. God, you and your family were all so close, I don't think any of you breathed without the others."

"We didn't, which means I pretty much don't breathe now."

"You should come back to London with me for a bit."

"Hmmm, London," Aidan smiled, remembering, "we talked about that so many times, you and me hitting the streets of London, blowing them all away with our musical abilities."

"Never too late," Ben encouraged. "You could stay at my place if you don't mind the sofa."

"And we'll busk around the city and dazzle them all?"

"Sure."

Aidan shook his head. "That was a dream. Now you're stuck in office land, I'll bet you haven't touched a guitar in years; and me, well, now just isn't the time."

Before Ben could respond, Kieran strode in and took the seat next to him. "Look what the wind blew in!" Aidan couldn't tell, from watching Kieran's eyes pass over Ben and himself, which of the two the comment was meant for. As he eyed Kieran, trying to decide, Brendan joined them, carrying four fresh pints.

"You do have room for these, don't you?" he asked both Ben and Aidan.

"If you're buying, I've got the room." Ben pulled one of the glasses in front of him.

Brendan set the other glass in front of Aidan. "Haven't seen you here since—" he paused, "well, in a bit. Glad you've come out of hiding."

Aidan let the comment pass. "How's the loading dock going?"

"Same as ever." Brendan nodded to Kieran, who worked alongside him, "Wouldn't you say?"

"Too right. Nothing ever changes there."

"Are you two still thinking of opening an arcade?"

"Yeah, someday," Brendan answered Ben. "Hard saving up for it though."

"This economy's not helping," Kieran added.

"Have you ever figured out a business plan like I suggested?"

Brendan and Kieran exchanged glances that gave their answer away. "Not yet," Kieran admitted with a sheepish grin.

"You two will never change!" Ben's tone was teasing; inside, though, he thought them both fools, and would have written them both off as bad business risks if they hadn't been friends. "Okay, here's what I want you to do. Make a list of what you would need to start your business up, nothing fancy, just the very basics. How many people would it take to run your business, what hours and days would you be open, what licenses or permits do you need? Scout around for locations, something with good traffic, again, nothing fancy."

As Ben walked Kieran and Brendan through the initial steps they'd need to take, as they analyzed the economy, and how to plan for their business goals, Aidan realized the difference between them all. Ben had studied hard to receive his business degree, was willing to move to London when the bank he worked for requested, and had pushed hard for the promotions he'd received. Aidan himself had practiced long hours to hone his musical skills, would take whatever gigs he could to gain experience and exposure, and had at last seen his hard work begin to pay off with Macready's Bridge.

Brendan and Kieran, though, would drag their feet on the work needed to reach their goals. They'd always have minds full of visions that never quite came true.

Aidan could see Ben ten years from now in Armani suits and Ferragamo shoes, driving a Porsche on visits home from London or even New York. He could see Kieran and Brendan still meeting at the same pub, still pulling shifts at the loading dock, or possibly on the dole with wives nagging at them and children running wild.

And himself? Hell, he couldn't see into next week or next month, let alone years down the line.

Kieran waved his hand in front of Aidan's face, "Hello, Planet Earth to Aidan."

"Huh? Oh, I'm sorry. I guess I got sidetracked."

"You were off someplace else, alright," Kieran agreed.

"I was telling the boys here you're coming to London with me," Ben informed him.

"We're coming along," Brendan added.

Aidan felt trapped. "Wait, I never agreed I'd go."

"It would do you good to get away," Kieran advised.

Before Aidan could answer, Charlie called out, "Aidan O'Connell, come up and give us a wee tune!"

Aidan froze. In talking with his friends, he'd forgotten Charlie's vow to call him up. Now, there was no way out. As Aidan stared at Charlie, as all of Flaherty's patrons stared at him, the same thing happened that happened at home each time he thought of picking up his guitar. Where he'd long heard his own voice running through songs in his head, now he heard his father's. Instead of seeing his own hands hold his guitar and dance over its strings, now he saw his father's work worn hands. The sight and sound overwhelmed him to the point where he could not sing or play. It was hard enough falling apart over music at home; in public, it would be a disaster.

"I'm sorry," he apologized to Ben, Kieran and Brendan. He glanced at his watch in the pretense of checking the time. "I didn't realize it was so late. Jack and Rita are holding dinner for me."

Aidan turned to Charlie. "I'm sorry. I have to leave." He glanced at his watch again to lend his lie credence.

"Call me about London," Ben called out to him as Aidan hurried towards the door.

"I will," he promised, and rushed out before anyone else could stop him.

"You're doing it again."

Moira's voice broke through Patrick's thoughts. "What? What's that?"

"Watching the kiddies while your mind's a million kilometers away," she flashed a quick, understanding smile, "or at least a few hundred kilometers."

Patrick exhaled a deep breath. "I'm sorry. I just can't get him out of my mind."

"Neither can I," Moira admitted. "He looked so small standing in that empty house when we left."

"Aidan's always been confident, almost cocky, when we've worked together, like he could take on the world and win; but that was when he had his family behind him. Now, I don't know. I'm worried he'll fall apart without them."

Moira slid her arm around Patrick's waist and kissed his cheek. "Sure, he's got a hard road ahead, but he's also got you and the boys to stand by him.

Right now, though, you've got your own kiddies to tend to."

Patrick hugged Moira back. "You're right. I'm sorry."

"Don't tell me, tell them." She pointed to Conor and Caitlyn who were fighting by the driveway.

"I won!"

"Did not!"

"Did too!"

Conor pushed Caitlyn just hard enough that she lost her balance and landed on the ground.

"Hey! There'll be none of that," Patrick ordered.

"Daddy, I won, didn't I?" Caitlyn rose, rubbing her backside extra hard for effect.

"I'm sorry, I didn't see."

"You promised you'd watch!"

"It's Uncle Aidan, isn't it?" The way Conor watched Patrick, blue eyes wide as Sligo Bay behind them, face full of understanding, melted Patrick's heart. He drew both children close to him.

"It is," he answered Conor.

Caitlyn forgot about her hurt pride. "He's still sad, isn't he Daddy?"

"Yes. I think so. Do you think if he came out here to visit us you could get him to smile a bit?"

"Yeah!" Both kids beamed and chimed in unison.

Patrick glanced at Moira, who nodded consent. "I don't know when I can get him out here, but let's call him. First, though, you've got a race to run again, and this time I promise I'll watch the whole thing."

The twins lined up at the stone wall to the left of the house and waited for Patrick to count off one, two, three, go! They dashed from the wall to the boulder that rose from the ground in the middle of the yard, slapped the boulder as hard as they could, and raced to the edge of the driveway, Conor just two steps ahead of his sister.

"I won!" Conor cried out, then looked to his father for confirmation.

"You did indeed." Patrick had a sense, from Caitlyn's crestfallen look, that she had won the earlier race. "You both ran well, though. Now, I'll bet Mam can make us some toast with jam while I call Uncle Aidan."

Aidan's phone rang several times and then went to voicemail. "Just checking in with you," Patrick said. "I hope you're finding your way through things there. Moira and the kids and I would like you to come out for a visit. Call me as soon as you can."

Chores around the house called then. Patrick weeded the vegetable garden, staked up tomatoes and beans, and repaired the wire fence that kept rabbits from helping themselves to free salad. Moira hung and later folded three loads of laundry, and weeded her flower garden. Even though the kids had a day off from school, Moira insisted they spend an hour studying, and after lunch an hour reading.

By suppertime Aidan still had not called back. Patrick waited till they had all eaten their fill of Moira's roast and Conor and Caitlyn were outside playing tag. As he sat in the yard watching them, balancing a plate of Moira's gingerbread on one knee and holding a mug of strong, hot tea, he asked, "Do you think I should call Aidan again?"

Moira read the worry that clouded Patrick's eyes and multiplied the lines across his ruddy face. "You know he'll be okay," she pointed out. "We all pray for him every night."

"I know, but I'll feel better once I talk to him."

Moira stepped back into the house, picked Patrick's phone up from where he'd left it on their coffee table, and handed it to him. "Maybe he'll be home by now."

When Aidan still didn't answer, Patrick's worry increased. He dialed another number; Moira listened in, curious as to who he was calling now.

Mack saw Patrick's number come up and caught the voicemail message while Patrick was still on the phone. "Hi Pat, how are you?" He turned down the flame under the chicken and peppers he was grilling.

"I'm fine. I was just wondering, have you talked to Aidan this week?"

"No. I saw him last week though." He thought back to his stop by Aidan's house the Thursday before. "I was in town, and we went out for lunch."

"I've tried calling him and haven't got through. I was just worried."

Mack had to laugh. "Patrick, tell me a day when you don't worry over something! He seemed okay. A bit tired, still a lot to sort through, but nothing to worry over, I don't think."

"It's just not like him to not return my calls. You're right, though; probably just me being silly. I'm sure he's just busy. He'll call back when he can."

Patrick hung up, finished his tea and gingerbread, and called out, "Who's ready for music time?" As Caitlyn and Conor ran in, cheering and picking out their instruments, flute for Caitlyn and guitar for Conor, Patrick gave Moira a tight hug.

"Thanks for putting up with me."

"Ah, ye daft man, go build the fire before your kids try to do that themselves!" The feel of his arms around her, though, stayed with Moira as she washed the last of their dishes and settled in for their Friday night tradition. She laughed over missed notes and Patrick's animated face whenever it was he who played a note wrong. She gathered in her heart how the firelight shone off Patrick's fiddle and reflected in the eyes of their children as they played with and learned from their father. When the twins had gone to bed, she and Patrick curled up on the sofa and watched the last of the fire's embers burn out.

"I must be the luckiest woman in the world."

Patrick turned his head from the fire to her. "Are ye daft? You've got nothing but a wee cottage and just enough furniture to fill it, no more than two pairs of shoes to your name, and I'm not quite showering you with diamonds and pearls now am I?"

"Shoes are overrated," Moira answered, "I've got your ring on my hand, that's jewels enough for me. And the cottage, it's filled with our children and all the love it can hold."

Before the dying embers and Moira's rhythmic breathing lulled him to sleep, Patrick whispered a special prayer of thanks for the wife God had blessed him with.

Mack hung up from Patrick's call and returned to the grill, but now Patrick's worries gave rise to his own. Aidan had been okay, hadn't he? He'd just finished a shower when Mack had stopped by, evidenced by his wet hair.

"Sorry, I slept in a bit," he'd apologized. Hell, the boy was allowed any day he wanted to sleep in, for all he was dealing with.

For the blankets and pillow on the sofa, Aidan had explained, "I fell asleep watching a movie last night."

True, the boy looked tired, but the depth of pain in his eyes and circles underneath them were understandable. He looked a little thinner as well, but he ate a good lunch, lasagna, his favorite, and seemed to be fine. Mack had dismissed all these until now.

Patrick's call left him wondering, though. Aidan, for all the times he could be casual, even careless, never left phone calls unreturned. Aidan stayed on Mack's mind all while he ate his dinner, and while he walked his Irish setters, Kellan and Seamus, around the grounds of his home. As he settled down for a night of wine and old movies, he thought to call Niall, who'd always seemed to have the closest connection with Aidan.

"Hey, boss, how are ya?"

Niall's upbeat tone relieved Mack. If anything had been wrong, he was sure Niall would have known. "I'm fine, and you?"

"You know me; life on the farm is just grand!"

Mack pictured the old stone house and steel buildings that made up the Donoghue's farm. "That's your answer for everything, now isn't it?"

"It's the one that works for me. But you're not calling about that. What's up? Is it Aidan?"

"Well, yes."

"Oh my God," Niall breathed before Mack could explain. "What's wrong now?"

"Probably nothing. I just wondered when you talked with him last."

"Let's see. Today's Friday. I talked with him Tuesday. No, Wednesday. Why?"

"How did he seem? Was he okay?"

"Sure." Alarm rose in Niall. "Mack, what's wrong?"

"Patrick called him this morning, left a message, and Aidan hasn't called back. Patrick's a little worried."

Niall had to laugh. "For a man of faith, Patrick sure worries a lot."

"He does. On the other hand, Aidan always returns his calls."

Niall nodded. "He does, but he said something about a friend coming into town. I'm sure he's just out with his friend."

"That'll be it," Mack agreed. "Thanks. I'll let Patrick know. Aidan did seem okay though, didn't he?"

"Sure, for all he's going through. He's getting by okay."

"Thanks Niall. Tell your folks I said hi."

Mack talked with Patrick and reassured him Aidan was most likely out with friends and would call back soon.

Then he thought, since he'd already talked with the other two, he should check in with Michael as well. When his call went in to voicemail, he said, "Just calling to see how you are. Hope everything's okay. Call anytime."

After the phone calls, Mack turned The Maltese Falcon on the television, and settled on the sofa with burning turf in the fireplace casting warm light around the room and Kellan and Seamus asleep at his feet, and let everything else drift from his mind.

Niall set his phone down and turned back to the fire he and his parents sat in front of. He had to laugh to himself, they always chose a cozy fire over the television he'd bought them for Christmas the year before. Someday he'd figure them out.

"That was Mack," he informed them, even though he knew they'd heard his end of the conversation.

Mrs. Donoghue set her crocheting aside. "Is Aidan okay?"

"I think so. Patrick was worried that Aidan hadn't returned his call, he checked with Mack, Mack called me."

Mr. Donoghue looked up from his newspaper. "Do you think there's reason for concern?"

"I don't think so. Patrick's always worrying about things." Still, Niall thought back over his phone conversations with Aidan over the past week, searching for any clues he might have missed.

"Aidan would tell you if he was having any problems, wouldn't he?"

Niall turned to his mother. "Probably not. People never do, do they? They always say they're fine unless it's clear that they're not."

Mr. Donoghue stirred the fire and added fresh fuel. "Why don't you call him when his company's gone back home and invite him out here. He might welcome a bit of a break, and then you can see how he's doing."

"I will, thanks."

Aidan stared at the plate of lasagna Rita had brought over, now grown cold just like the tea that filled the mug next to it. Piping hot, the lasagna had held no interest for him; now it didn't stand a chance. He wrapped it in foil, tossed it in the trash bin and washed Rita's plate off. Above the television he'd fallen into the habit of turning on he could hear his grandmother's voice calling them to meals, then asking his father about neighbors or customers at the garage. He could hear his father discussing school work with Jeannie, and Jeannie chatting away with friends, or telling their grandmother the latest drama at school. He turned the television up louder to drown out their voices.

Annie called him from her stand in the living room corner. His own guitar called from her case by the stairs where he'd left her when he'd first come home. The incident with Rosie's Ring that day gnawed at him. Maybe he'd given up too quickly; maybe he should fight more to push past the barrier that held him back. He pulled his guitar from her case, checked her tuning, and arranged his left hand fingers in the G chord position along her neck. After weeks away from her, the guitar now felt awkward and unfamiliar in his hands. He strummed her strings a few times, played at picking out a few tunes, but his heart wasn't in his attempt. After a few minutes he packed his guitar away in her case and stood the case in the corner opposite Annie.

The house around him felt as hollow as he did. Everything he saw spoke their names, the sage colored curtains his grandmother had made, the cream walls his father had painted, the shadow box filled with porcelain animals his sister collected. They were everywhere he looked and in every sound he heard; yet the house still seemed too empty and too large.

"Maybe Ben's right," he admitted to the air around him. "Maybe I should get away for a bit. But where to?"

Patrick, Niall, Michael, Mack, Aidan knew they'd each offer their homes to him for as long as he wanted. There was always London with Ben. None of them suited though. How could he explain to them he needed space from people's sad expressions and careful conversations as much as he needed to escape the house full of memories?

"I could just tell them I'm going fishing."

As soon as the idea struck, it felt right. He'd avoid Lough Swilly, where he fished with his father the most, and head in the opposite direction. He wouldn't set a time to return, just tell Jack and Rita he'd be back in a few days. The more he turned the idea over in his mind, the more it seemed the right thing to do.

7

Rain slashed against Michael's windows as he peered at the Dublin streets below. Businessmen, students and tourists all hurried into shops and pubs to escape the rain. He should be hurrying too, he knew, or he'd arrive late for dinner at his parents' house. Still, he stared out the window, coffee growing cold in the mug he'd held the last twenty minutes or so.

He glanced around the apartment he'd chosen and decorated with great care, the mocha and cappuccino walls, burgundy rugs and curtains, chocolate brown leather sofa and chair. He admired the shine of the hardwood floors as his floor lamp shone down, and the wrought iron Celtic knot wall piece he'd found in Kilkenny last fall. The apartment showed the same ambiance it had held since he'd decorated it, but today it felt different, unsatisfying. Van Morrison's voice spilling out from the corner stereo didn't brighten the rooms, nor did the espresso aroma left over from brewing a half hour earlier. He might as well be out walking the wet Dublin streets, he thought.

He spotted them turning the corner, strolling down the street under his window, laughing over some private joke. They neither ran to outpace the rain nor sought a pub or storefront's shelter. Even from his vantage point above them he could see the light in their eyes, the smiles that never left their faces; they were clearly in love. Watching them,

Michael knew what was lacking, why his apartment felt so empty and cold. He grabbed his phone and dialed a number before he could change his mind.

Susannah's "Hello" on the other end didn't sound as perky as Michael had hoped. On the other hand, she didn't ignore the call or hang up; a good sign, he thought.

"How was Spain?"

"I didn't go."

Something in her flat tone made Michael guess he was the reason her trip fell apart. Guilt flooded him as he asked, "You didn't? Why not?"

"Let's just say the timing was wrong. What can I do for you?"

"I'd like to take you out to dinner tomorrow night."

Michael could see Susannah studying the space in front of her, weighing the mental pros and cons, before answering, "Yes, okay. What time?"

"I'll pick you up at seven."

"I'll meet you at eight. What restaurant?"

"Fitzroys." Michael spoke before he could call the words back. Would she remember?

She must have. Her tone softened, "Alright. Fitzroys, eight tomorrow night."

The fact that she hung up right after, didn't ask Michael how he was, didn't extend the conversation in any way didn't trouble Michael at all. She'd agreed to see him. That's all that mattered. Michael left for his parents' house not caring anymore that he'd be late and would face his father's wrath for that and for so much more.

"Are you mad?" Diane set her coffee cup down hard on Susannah's table. "I thought you were through with him."

"I was." Susannah fingered the gold bracelet he'd given her for her birthday, turning its delicate chain in slow circles around her wrist. Funny, she thought, if she was through with him, why did she still wear the bracelet? "I don't know, Diane, there's something about him, something that pulls me back to him every time I think I should break our relationship off."

Diane rolled her eyes. "Please tell me you're not in love with him."

"Would that be so bad?"

"Let's see. You were in love with Bryce the banker, Liam the solicitor, Diarmid the investor, oh, and Brian, who manages all of his father's properties. Only, you really weren't in love with them, you just thought you were at the time. Didn't each one of those 'loves' end in disaster?"

"They were different." Susannah ignored Diane's cynical stare. "Michael's different. They never made me weak in the knees the way he does."

"Weak in the knees is a physical condition, not a good gauge of love."

"Then what is a good gauge?" Susannah watched Diane shift in her chair, unable to come up with a good answer. When she couldn't Susannah spoke out, "Ever since I first met Michael you haven't liked him. You've tolerated him, but nothing more. Why is that?"

"He's not one of us. He doesn't fit in our world."

Susannah stared at Diane as if her words had been a physical slap. "I can't believe you're saying that!" She shut her laptop down in one swift, angry motion. "I think we're done planning for the day."

"He's a musician, for God's sake." Diane tried one more attempt to help her friend see reason.

"What will you do when he's flat broke and can't get a proper job?"

Susannah gathered her notes on the upcoming fashion show she and Diane were planning to raise funds for the abused women's shelter they both supported, and slid them into her carry bag with her laptop.

"I'm sorry," Diane apologized. "I just don't want to see you hurt."

Susannah sat back down at her dining room table. "Diane, I know you mean well. We've been friends for so long, I don't want to have a falling out with you. You don't know Michael like I do. Oh, I'm in love alright. If he was flat broke and couldn't get a job, I'd love him just as much as I do right now." She thought back over the others Diane had mentioned. "The others, they were fun but they were never meant to last. Michael feels like the real thing."

"Would you marry him if he asked?" Diane held her breath, afraid of Susannah's answer.

Susannah considered Michael's wall of reserve, and their many conflicts. Could she live with all the problems their marriage was sure to face? Could she handle the loss of friends she was sure to lose, like Diane, if she married Michael? Then she thought of what her life would be like without him. Could she handle the pain of letting him go? She shook her head, and answered Diane, "I don't know."

"I'll only be gone a couple of days." Aidan finished stowing his fishing pole and tackle box in the car's back seat, and turned back to Jack and Rita. "Are you sure you don't mind watching the place?"

"Not at all, boy." Jack answered. "Do you know where you're going?"

Aidan nodded towards the bridge that crossed the river nearby. "I thought I'd head out along the Foyle and see where it takes me."

"Take this with you." Rita handed over a box with a thermos and foil wrapped package.

Tea and scones, Aidan thought, smiling inside that he'd guessed correctly, Rita wouldn't let him go without providing some kind of care package. He tucked the box on the front passenger seat and then hugged Rita. "Thanks for looking after me."

"Go on with ye," Rita brushed him aside. Inside, though, her heart burned with the same warmth she'd known when her own children, Lizzie and Jerry, hugged her in response for something she'd done. Her heart ached, watching Aidan slide into his car, as she realized how much she missed her children. Dublin and Galway weren't so far away, but Lizzie and Jerry were so busy with their own lives now they made it home with less and less frequency.

"Mind you drive careful now," Rita heard Jack say as Aidan started his car. "Take care of yourself."

Aidan waved and was off.

"Do you think he'll be okay?"

Jack squeezed Rita's shoulders. "Aye. He needs to get away a few days. Too many ghosties in that house."

"He looks done in," Rita acknowledged.

"Too much on his plate." Jack turned Rita towards their house. "Time away will clear his mind and set him back on track. Now, did you save a few wee scones for your husband?"

Aidan followed the A-5 along the River Foyle, crossed over at Strabane where the Foyle met the Finn, and continued to Ballybofey, where his father had sometimes stopped. From there, the elder

O'Connell had scanned the river and the skies, smelled the air, drank tea while pondering which path to take, and then struck out, pole and gear in hand.

"What are you testing for?" Aidan had asked a few years back, always keen to gain his father's wisdom. "What's in the air, or the water, you choose from?"

Daniel O'Connell had glanced over the rim of his mug to his son, then winked and grinned. "It's the fairies, boy. I'm waiting for them to tell me where to fish."

Aidan half believed his father. It could be true; fairies had been known to do all sorts of things, and if a fairy had taken a liking to his dad and wanted to help him, who could blame them? His dad was a likable guy.

Or, his father could just be teasing. "The fairies, is it? And where are they telling you to fish today?"

Daniel studied the river again and pointed to a shaded spot along the right bank. "Over there." As they cast their lines, he proceeded to teach his son what he really did look for, the flow of the water, where the sun hit and where the shade would disguise them from the fish. He spoke quietly, in part to not alarm the fish and in part to preserve the peacefulness of the river and the day.

Aidan could still hear his father's words as he stepped out now, poured tea from Rita's thermos, unwrapped a scone and sank his teeth into it, scanned the overcast skies, thankful it had not yet started to rain, and studied the Finn's waters.

"Alright Da, where are your fairies telling me to fish today?"

He didn't expect an answer, and wasn't surprised that none came. That's the way it would be now, he realized. Every decision to be made he'd have to make on his own. Choosing which waters to fish was just the start. Aidan finished his snack, stared at the river again, and drove west, following the Finn's course.

Aidan recognized the spot outside Cloghan where he and his father had once caught salmon and decided he'd start out there. The empty house walls that had closed in on him fell away as he stood on the riverbank and cast his line. Open space filled his eyes with soft green hills and soft grey skies. The television's constant background voice was replaced by the river's conversation and the chatter of birds in the surrounding trees. As he inhaled the rich fragrance of soil and water and clean, fresh air, Aidan could feel his muscles start to relax, letting go of tensions he hadn't realized they'd been locked on. He felt as free as the waters flowing by him and wondered for a bit where his spirit would take him if he let it travel at will.

When he caught a grilse, he cheered, held it up, and admired its silver belly and spotted scales. Then he turned and it hit him, there was no one to share the joy with. Hit him so hard, he slunk down on the ground as if fists had brought him down. He strained to hear a "well done" from his father. When the air around him echoed silence, he realized the next awful truth: fishing, the sport he loved almost as much as he loved music, would never be the same. Aidan watched the grilse's eyes blink, blink again, puzzled as to what new, strange world it had suddenly found itself in. He felt as sorry for the fish as he did for himself, released it from its hook prison and set it back in its river home, and wished he had as easy an answer to free himself from his own incarceration.

Aidan packed his gear up and headed back to the car. Once behind the wheel, he knew he wasn't ready to return home. He gazed at the Finn's waters flowing by, mesmerized by their steady course past trees and rocks, and the liquid music they made. Where did they lead next, he wondered. He decided to follow them to find out.

Outside the Dublin city limits, Michael found the countryside relaxing, as he always did. Open fields and flocks of grazing sheep and cattle always had a way of calming him no matter how much stress he carried, as he did now. Facing his father always felt like facing a lion. If it weren't for his mother, he wouldn't go home at all.

As Michael pulled into the lane that led to his parents' home, he was struck, as always, by the coldness of the stone house that stood at the end of the lane. No sheep grazed nearby, no barking dogs animated the grounds, no cats sunned themselves in windowsills. No children's laughter or sounds of play graced the air. No flowers or ivy softened the granite exterior, no colored curtains brightened the windows, only straight, bland, white sheers. Over all the years he'd grown up here, he'd felt the cold silence; now, as he parked his car, careful to stay within the pre-worn grooves in the gravel, his spine and arms shivered involuntarily.

As Michael entered his parents' home, the vibes of his father's usual sullen mood rose in the air along with the aroma of the roast beef his mother had prepared for their dinner. Faint sounds from the kitchen confirmed his mother was still, as always, tiptoeing around his father, trying to keep peace. He inhaled, held his breath a moment, then called, "Hello."

Heels echoed on the stone hallway floor. Michael could picture his mother in her customary heels, silk dress and pearls before she turned the corner. "We'd almost given up on you."

"I'm sorry." He dropped a quick kiss on her cheek. "I had to deal with a last minute phone call before I left."

"Your father's ready to eat." Marie Sullivan took her son's raincoat and hung it in the hall closet. "You best go in and sit down now."

Michael drew another, deeper breath, steeling himself as he entered the dining room.

Edward Sullivan held a level gaze as Michael entered the mahogany paneled, claret-draped dining room and sat in his customary side chair. A full minute passed before Edward said, "You've got no respect for your mother, late for dinner like this."

"She said dinner at half-six. It's half-six now. Technically I'm on time."

"You're meant to be here earlier. You know that."

"I had business to tend to. You know what that's like."

Michael had never taken pleasure in confronting his father, but tonight, for some reason, he found it rewarding, the little digs here and there almost intoxicating. He knew he'd hit his target each time his father's neck muscles tightened.

"You know nothing of business, traipsing off to the far corners of the earth with that rag tag bunch you call a band."

Michael's mother entered bearing a platter of roast beef smothered in onions, surrounded by mushrooms, potatoes and carrots, which she set in front of Edward. "Start slicing, please, while I bring more wine."

More? Michael thought, amused. We've not had any yet. He held his tongue though. He might enjoy baiting his father, but he would never hurt his mother if he could help it.

Marie Sullivan prayed over the meal while Edward looked on, impatient to start eating. After passing full plates around, Marie turned to Michael. "Tell us about your adventure in America, Michael."

Michael winced. Her choice of words made the tour and, by association, his whole Macready's Bridge experience, sound like a lark, a passing hobby while he searched for the career that would transport him to adulthood. If his father had said those words, Michael would have challenged him. Instead, he answered, "We had a grand time, Mom. I've told you some of it along the way. New York, well, you've been there, you know that's amazing. L.A., Hollywood, you can almost touch the magic that fills every particle of air there."

"And your shows, they all went well?"

"They were wonderful. The crowds every night were crazy for us. Best time of our lives." Then Michael thought of Aidan. "It's just too bad it ended the way it did."

Michael's mother set her wine glass down. "How is Aidan doing?"

Michael thought a minute. "It's hard to tell over the phone. We all thought we'd visit him next week, maybe take him to dinner, and get a better sense of things."

Edward set his knife down hard on his plate. "What are you all doing while this friend of yours is taking time off? Are you all just lazing around, not working? Nothing?"

"We can't very well work without our guitarist."

"Hire a replacement."

Michael glared at his father. "For the love of God, the boy's just lost his family. Let's give him some time."

Edward glared back. "And what about your business degree? Do you ever plan to use that? Or was Trinity College just another waste of time and money, like everything else in your life?"

"Edward, please," Marie pleaded.

"Shut up! Stop defending the boy. It's all your softness that's brought our son to this state. He knows nothing about the hard things of life, fighting for jobs, fighting for food and housing."

For a moment, no one spoke. Marie held her hands clasped in her lap, eyes fixed on the roast left on her plate. Michael stared at the wine glass frozen in his hand. Edward stared at his wife, then his son.

Finally Michael found the words he wanted. "She hasn't made me soft. She's taught me the love you've never shown me." He pushed his chair back. "Dinner was wonderful, Mom. Thanks."

"Don't go," Marie begged, "I've made your favorite apple crumb cake for after." She followed Michael out to the hall.

"Don't come back until you've found a proper job!" Edward shouted after him.

"He doesn't mean what he says."

Michael slipped his coat on. "Yes he does, Mom. He hates everything about me anymore. I can deal with that, but I hate that you're stuck in this house with him. You could come back to my place if you want."

Marie glanced behind her. "I'll be fine. You just have to learn how to handle your father."

"I'll learn that when he learns to respect me."

"Alright, Finn, let's see what you've got to show me."

Aidan turned his car not in the direction the River Finn flowed, but opposite, curious to see where she came from. He wished he'd thought to bring his camera as he passed new farms and fields and drove through small towns he'd never visited before. Twice he pulled into empty spaces and sat, admiring the way fresh sunlight played off a field or the mystery of what used to be a stone cottage, now left to ruin. Disintegrating rain clouds chased each other across the sky as he drove along, following the Finn's course as she wound her way below him past farms and fields, lost at times behind trees and hedges gone wild, reappearing as a slender ribbon reflecting silver in the sun. His car rose up hills, higher and deeper into the countryside. Aidan lost track of time; when he finally reached Lough Finn, the river's source, and spotted the picnic area, he realized how hungry he was and pulled in. He gathered the last of Rita's tea and scones and the cheese sandwich he'd packed for himself, and settled in at a picnic table for a late lunch.

Aside from the lough's waves gently lapping against the shore and the odd gull or two wheeling overhead, spying Aidan's sandwich and protesting in retreat when they realized his food would not be shared, the only other sound Aidan heard was silence. Not the same oppressive silence that haunted his house, this silence calmed, and stirred the imagination. Aidan studied the sweep of the large hills lowering down to the lough, and occasional farmhouses scattered on the hillsides.

"Now that's a hard life," he remarked to his car as he imagined farming on the steep hillsides that surrounded the lough. "It would be tough enough on a fair weather day, but in the wind, or a hard rain? Not for us at all!"

As Aidan sat and listened, he was sure he could hear farmers of old calling their dogs and herding their flocks, and farther back to the days of monks and earls, and even clear back to St. Patrick himself spreading the word of God. He imagined he could hear the Celts, and Vikings, and Normans in ancient battles. He remembered the legend of the lough and swore he could even hear back to Feargamhain's calls for help, and the great splashes of water as Finngeal ran to her brother's rescue, drowning in the process.

Another voice called out, one older and greater than all of these. It whispered across Lough Finn's rippled surface, its calling card scent filling the air. Aidan recognized it as the same voice that had called to him the last few days of the Macready's Bridge tour, the call that had been pushed aside with the sudden shift his family's passing had caused. Now he collected the remainders of his lunch, returned to his car, and drove toward the ocean to answer her call.

He reached Gweebarra Bay and left his car in a car park while he walked out on the beach. The bay stretched out before him, filled with the Atlantic's own waters, endless waves rolling in, kissing the shore, and rolling out to rejoin the larger body. Occasional boats bobbed on the water, gulls wheeled overhead, water lapped at his feet; Aidan stood by the shore until his eyes and ears, heart and soul had had their fill of the sights, sounds and smells of the ocean.

Aidan so lost himself in the ocean's mesmerizing pull that he was surprised to see the sun had started to slip towards the horizon. He hadn't figured where he would stay the night, and first he thought he should return to his car and drive home. Compared to the openness of the ocean, though, his house seemed more suffocating than ever.

To the right, Aidan spotted rows of caravans dotting the hillside and thought, if they have any vacancies, I'll stay the night and unwind a bit more.

"Aye, we've got a camper available." Fingal O'Brien, the owner of the caravan rentals, peered beyond Aidan to the empty car outside. "Is it just yourself then?"

"Just me," Aidan confirmed.

"And you'll just be wanting it the one night then?"

"One, maybe two if it's available."

"You can have it the week if you'd like. Mind, it's booked the week after, and every week through the summer, but this week it's yours for the taking."

"I'll take the two nights, and then decide on more if that's alright." Aidan signed the register and paid up. "Is there a store nearby? I didn't think to pack food."

"Nearest store's back in Dungloe, a ways away. It will be closed for the night though. There's a coffee shop around the corner for light fare." He eyed the young man, took in his thinness, and something sad about his eyes. "If it's dinner you're wanting, our Sheila's made more chowder than we could eat in a week." He handed the keys to one of the caravans over to Aidan. "Last camper on the end, front row. Sorry it's a bit of a hike for you. You get yourself settled. I'll send our Sheila around with chowder and a good hot cuppa for you."

"Oh, don't bother," Aidan started to protest, but Mr. O'Brien waved him off.

"Go on with ye. You can leave your car where it is. Sheila will be down in five minutes' time, soon as fresh water's heated."

The camper would be small for a family, but Aidan found the size perfect for his needs, a double bed in the bedroom, with a quilt showing the blues, greens and tans of sea and sand, the living room holding a sofa and two chairs in similar colors and a sea green rug. The kitchen fit a table and four chairs, an icebox under the sand-colored counter, and a small stove. Windows in the living room and bedroom opened to the ocean, now showing the sun slipping closer to the horizon, covering the waves with a lavender-rose blanket.

Three short knocks echoed on the door, then Sheila O'Brien stepped in. "Aidan? I've got some dinner here for ye." She set a tray on the table. "Chowder, tea, and some bread from the morning. I'll be making fresh tomorrow, so don't worry that you're taking the last of our supply."

She opened a cupboard and pulled a mug out for Aidan. "Dishes are here, silverware in the drawer by the sink." She pulled a package out of her coat pocket. "Thought you might enjoy a few oatmeal biscuits as well. I'll be heading in to market tomorrow; if you give me a list, I'll pick a few things up for you."

"I couldn't ask you to do that. Thank you for this though. This should suit fine until lunch time anyway."

"Alright, you eat that now while it's hot, and let us know if you need anything else tonight. I'll check in with you tomorrow."

Susannah arrived at Fitzroys fifteen minutes late, just long enough for Michael to worry she wasn't coming. He heard her rich, smooth voice, turned, and watched her make her way to where he sat at the bar, aware that at least a half dozen other guys also watched her move. Her signature Chanel perfume reached him just before she did, not overpowering or flowery, but tantalizing, drawing him in the same way her green eyes did, and the soft shine of her golden hair in the restaurant's low lights.

"Nice choice of restaurants." She watched as he ordered a Sauvignon for her and a refill of his own Pinot Noir.

Michael had wondered if Susannah would remember the first time they'd been here. She unbuttoned her raincoat, Michael helped her slip it off and found she'd worn the same black slacks and black, green and purple blouse she'd worn here on their first date. So, she did remember.

He winked. "I hear they have the best steak in town."

She smiled back. "I heard the same thing."

"That's still my favorite outfit of yours."

"You remember?"

"Remember our first real date, the first time you agreed to go somewhere with me when I wasn't singing?" Michael drew her to him and set a light kiss on her lips. "I'd die before I'd forget that perfect night."

Susannah turned her head away. So, he hadn't been forgiven yet.

They sat at the same table they'd first had, ordered the same crab salad starter and the same Caesar salad. Susannah varied her dinner choice; instead of steak, this time she chose lamb.

"I see a new Monet exhibit is coming to town next month." Michael prayed Susannah's passion for the French artist would be piqued. "I can get us tickets if you'd like."

"I'll let you know."

So, she wasn't hooked yet. "Fair enough."

"Diane's having a dinner party next weekend." Susannah was instantly mad at herself for letting this out; she'd meant to hold it in a few days longer.

"I'd like to take you," Michael offered. "If I'm invited, that is."

Susannah set her wine glass down. "Michael, I just don't know. This last argument, the past few weeks, it's all been so painful." She saw the same troubled look in Michael's eyes she knew was in her own. "We just can't go on this way."

Michael nodded, "You're right."

Susannah sat back, stunned. "Then you agree? We shouldn't see each other any more?"

"Not see each other? No, I didn't mean that at all! I agree we can't go on like we have been though."

Michael had rehearsed all day what he would say, how he would say it. He'd tried to anticipate every reaction and objection Susannah might have. Now the moment was here and he had to choose: Should he carry his thoughts inside him a little longer, or say what was most on his heart? He'd always hated these relationship crossroads; so many times he'd made the wrong turn, and ended up traveling alone once again. If he spoke his heart now, if his timing was wrong, Susannah might never give him another chance. If he didn't speak up, could he stand one more day building his hopes up and worrying they might be destined to fall? Michael's heart vibrated in his chest with such force he was sure it would burst through the skin and bones that housed it, and all the words he'd planned scattered in every direction like sparrows fleeing a hawk. Still, he knew he had to push through the one opening he had before it was gone.

"Suze, I've had a lot of time to think lately. You're right, we need to make some changes. I know this isn't the direction you were expecting from me, but I know I don't want to lose you. You're the best thing that's ever come into my life."

Michael reached into his jacket pocket and pulled a small box out. "Susannah, will you marry me?"

Even as he started to speak, Susannah begged in her heart that he wasn't about to say the words she was so not ready to hear. As he reached into his pocket, she begged he would not draw out the box that appeared. Susannah's eyes grew as large as the dinner plates on their table as she stared at Michael, then at the red velvet box, then back at him. The sounds of dishes, conversations and music from the restaurant around her faded away as her own pulse beat hard in her ears. "Michael, we've never talked about this before."

"I know. I'm sure I'm not what you've dreamed of. I keep too much inside me, and life as a musician's wife would not be easy. You could do so much better than me. But no one else would ever love you more than I do."

"Michael, I don't know if we're right—"

Susannah caught herself and stopped mid-sentence. She'd almost said it. Before she did, she'd better be sure the choice she made was for the right reason. True, they had serious differences and so many issues to work through. Was she basing her decision on that, though, or on what Diane had said the day before? Susannah thought of Diane, and of the circle of friends they had practically grown up with, some of whom had stopped calling Susannah over the past few months as her relationship with Michael had intensified. Was she about to turn Michael down because he interfered with her social status? Or was he really wrong for her, and time for them both to face that fact? If she turned him down, how would she feel if he accepted her words and walked out of her life for good?

Michael watched as Susannah thought, eyes closed to him and everything else around them. She was going to reject him, he knew. She was going to say no, they would finish their dinner in polite silence, or with small, meaningless chitchat, then they would part and he'd never see her again. Maybe he could salvage this before they reached that end.

"Susannah, my timing is terrible. You need more time for me to prove myself to you. Let's just forget I asked the question. Let's eat and talk about other things or, if you want, we can just call it a night now." He picked the box up and started to return it to his pocket.

"No." Susannah's hand on his arm stopped him.

His heart sank to his shoes. "No, you won't marry me?"

She smiled and raised a hand to wipe away the tears that had filled her eyes. "No. I mean, no, don't put my ring away. Oh, Michael, I don't care what you are, musician, fish merchant, you could even be the man who picks up other people's refuse. I know our marriage won't always be easy. I love you, though. I don't want to live my life without you. Yes, I'll marry you!"

Michael could barely keep his hands from trembling as he slipped the square cut diamond ring out of its box and onto Susannah's slender finger. She held it up, admired its delicate braided gold band and the small rubies, her birthstone that sat one on each side of the diamond. "Michael, that's the most beautiful thing in the world."

He smiled and kissed her hand. "No, you are."

Later that night, with the soft music of Norah Jones filling his apartment's empty spaces, with candles casting soft shadows on his bedroom walls and floor, Michael watched Susannah as she slept beside him. For the first time since he'd met her he felt calm. All the worries he'd carried about whether she was "the one," or whether he'd end up the way his parents had, had vanished. He brushed a strand of hair away from her face, carefully so as not to wake her. For once he could almost reach out and touch the happy life he'd dreamed of, the same life Patrick had found, the same one Aidan and his family had known. For once he believed he could make his dream come true.

8

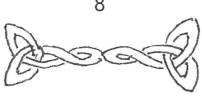

Aidan rose early the next morning, stirred from sleep by the hum of a boat's motor passing over the water across from his camper, and the smell of the sea the boat crossed. Outside his window a light rain fell, but the clouds overhead were light in color, sun appeared to break through on the horizon, and the waves rolling onto the shore called his name. Aidan took a quick shower, threw on jeans and a clean sweater, sliced and ate what was left of Sheila O'Brien's bread and the last oatmeal biscuit, drank a quick cup of fresh tea, and hurried out to greet the day.

The beach curved around to the right of him, and stretched out far to the left, where the town of Portnoo rose up along the hillside. Aidan chose to bear right, saving the longer stretch for the afternoon. As he walked, he drank in the sight of the unbroken horizon, the waves in their endless procession to shore, how the water mirrored the sky overhead. To his right, a grassy hill rose. The sand felt like a soft cushion under his feet as he followed its gentle curve. As he walked, the light rain diminished to a fine mist, then evaporated as the clouds overhead broke into pieces, which shrank in size as he walked. The boat that had woke him disappeared in the distance, other boats took its place; when he turned at the tip of land that separated his beach from its neighboring one, Aidan discovered other people had emerged and dotted the stretch between the caravan park and the water.

I'll check out the cafe for lunch, then drive into town to stock up for the next couple of days, he thought, but found upon returning to his camper that Mrs. O'Brien had left fresh bread and cheese, apples, and cinnamon coffee cake, with a note, "I'll stop by with stew tonight unless you're not going to be home."

"Mam, I'm running into town for some wiring and supplies for Dad, is there anything you need?"

Niall's mother stepped into the hallway, wiping her hands on a kitchen towel. "No dear, thank you. You'll be home in time for dinner, won't you?"

"Sure mam."

Niall found a parking spot two blocks from Boyle's, the hardware store his father had shopped at all of Niall's life. Smaller and far more limited in selection than its more modern counterparts in larger towns nearby, John Boyle, the owner, made up for what it lacked with his innate knowledge of tools, supplies, and just what would work for repair problems his customers brought him. Ten minutes after entering Boyle's, Niall walked back to his car with a bag full of goods and his father's change in his pocket.

As he unlocked his car door, a pair of voices across the street froze his hands and his heart. Keeping his head down, Niall lifted eyes to the couple stepping away from their car to the cafe nearby.

Gary, his best friend all through school, appeared with Mary, his girl, or at least she was until he'd left for the ill-fated Scotland tour. He remembered their last night together, at Rafferty's, their regular pub. Mary wore yellow that night, standing out bright against her dark skin, dark hair and eyes, exotic as her gypsy roots always shone. Gary had been there that night as well, with Jane, the four of them so often together the bartenders at Rafferty's had started setting a table aside for them each night.

That night Gary and Jane had left early, while he and Mary stayed until closing, prolonging their separation as long as possible. When Rafferty's closed Niall drove Mary home. There, in her parents' driveway, she'd promised, "I'll be waiting for you to come home," a vow they'd sealed with a kiss so passionate it would have led to much more if her family's dog hadn't started barking, waking the house up, lights going on upstairs and then down.

Mary had hurried inside the house and, weeks later, out of his life. He could still see the words she'd written in her last letter, "I don't know how to tell you, so I guess straightforward is the best way; Gary and I, we've gone for coffee and dinner a few times and, well, you'll be gone so long, I don't think I can take it. I've started going with Gary".

He still had the letter, tucked in the back of the bottom drawer of the desk in his room. He hadn't been able to bring himself to throw it away.

Now Niall quickly unlocked his car, slid inside and closed the door in one movement and drove away as fast as he could. If Gary or Mary saw him, he never knew.

Aidan scanned the rows of campers, and the small building that served as the caravan park office, hoping to catch sight of Mrs. O'Brien. When he spotted her by the camper next to the office, he walked her way.

"Mrs. O'Brien," he called out.

"Call me Sheila," she offered as he came closer.

"Sheila, okay, thanks. I just wanted to thank you for lunch, it was delicious. About dinner, though, please don't put yourself out. I'm heading out to the store in town, I'll be fine. In fact, is there anything I can get you while I'm there?"

"No, dear, but please, don't feel you're putting me out." Sheila eyed him up and down, his thinness pulling her heart's strings, and his solitude, on holidays alone. "I enjoy cooking. Fingal and I have more food than we need, with just the two of us. You'd really be helping me out, helping us finish what's left before I cook our next meal."

"That's very kind of you, but truly—"

Sheila cut him off, smiling as she did so. "Aidan, our son, our only boy, has moved to Australia for work. Feeding you makes me feel like I'm looking after him. I'd very much like it if you just let me continue, please."

She had the kindest blue eyes, and freckles splattered across her wind worn face, and Aidan hadn't the heart to refuse her. Each morning, while he was out, Sheila would drop off cheese and bread, or sandwiches, along with biscuits or scones and fresh fruit. By dinnertime, he'd find a fresh dish of soup ready to be heated, brown bread and butter, and fresh pie or baked goods. There was always food enough for breakfast, and the cycle would repeat itself.

Mornings, Aidan strolled the beach, smiled at shorebirds playing tag with the waves, studied the clouds sweeping the sky and the odd sets of footprints from the night before all but erased by the tide. He examined the treasures the water gave the sand, an interesting stone worn smooth by its journey along the ocean floor, occasional shells and shell fragments, driftwood, a few scattered pieces of sea glass. The most worthy treasures he gathered, thinking Jack and Rita would like them.

Afternoons he walked the road uphill to Portnoo, where he watched boats slide up to the pier, take on new passengers, and head out for fishing or sea bird watching. A father played catch on the beach with two young boys and a girl while their mother looked on. A young couple teased each other, she grabbing his coat and running with it, he chasing her down, both of them falling to the sand, their laughter rising up to Aidan, tugging at his heart to find what they had found.

Fionna Fallon watched the newcomer return from Portnoo down the same road he'd hiked up earlier, just as he had the day before, and the day before that. From her stand behind her easel along the rocky road that looked out over the beach she could see many things, father and children playing catch, boats leaving and returning to the pier, a young couple chasing each other through the waves, and him. Something about him drew her attention more than anyone else who passed by. His strong profile? His charismatic good looks? Both of these, perhaps, but Fionna felt there was something more, something that churned deep inside him. She studied his stride, steady, not stopping along the way, as if he'd had his fill of scenery and was now headed with purpose to another destination. She knew the destination as well; she'd watched the night before as he walked to the camper at the end of the same caravan park where she and her parents were staying, just as they'd stayed one month out of the year every year since she was five.

This time, as Aidan passed Fionna called to him, "Do you have the time?"

Aidan checked his watch. "Half six."

He turned to continue his walk. Fionna thought fast, "Is it that late? Oh no! You couldn't give us a hand, could you? Only, I'll be late for dinner and my dad and mam will be that mad at me."

Aidan hesitated, not wanting to involve himself with any of the locals or other guests here. Then he heard his granny's voice urging him, "Give the wee lass a hand." As he reached out to help her fold down her easel, he gave her sketching a closer look. "That's really good. You've captured the waves just right."

"Do you think they should be a bit more blue?"

"No." Aidan studied the watercolors more closely. "Actually, I'd think a bit more grey."

Fionna tipped her head to the left and eyed her work. "You're right. I'll have to fix that tomorrow."

Aidan tucked the folded easel under his arm, and picked the paint box up with his free hand. "Where are you and your parents staying?"

"Down there," Fionna pointed to the same caravan park Aidan was at. "Second row back, towards the center."

"I'm at the same park," Aidan commented as they started walking.

"I know." She hadn't meant to let it slip out, and froze inside as soon as it had. Aidan didn't seem to notice though, as he continued walking, shortening his long stride so as to not pull too far ahead of her. Out of the corner of his eye, Aidan noted how her copper hair shimmered in the sun as it fell across her back.

"Are you here with anyone?" Fionna asked, meaning parents, and hating how prying the words sounded once they were out.

"No." Aidan kept his eyes focused on the path ahead of him. Fionna asked no more questions; they finished the walk in silence.

"Fionna! Get inside. Your dinner's getting cold." The grey haired woman who opened the camper's door threw a cold glare at Aidan. "Who are you?"

"Aidan." He set the paint box down and offered his hand, which the woman rejected. "I just helped Fionna carry her things back."

"Fine. She's here now, you can leave."

"Mother, that was rude!" Fionna cried out as Aidan walked away.

"Is that what you do every day? Tell us you're out drawing and painting, and all the while you're out there chasing boys down?"

Fionna was so stunned she had no reply. She placed her art materials in the corner of the great central room, and sat at the table where a plate of ham and potatoes had already been set out.

Mrs. Fallon watched Fionna start in on her dinner. She saw herself at Fionna's age, walking to and from her office job alone, spending all her evenings with her parents in their cottage outside of town. She remembered the man who started accompanying her on the walk home, claiming he had to go the same way; she'd often seen him at the bank across the street from her office, he seemed safe enough. She remembered the evening the walk turned horribly wrong, how she'd snuck home after, hid her torn skirt and blouse until she could burn them while her parents were at Mass, the weeks afterward worrying, her realization she was pregnant, and Jerry, dear sweet Jerry, marrying her, saving her.

She watched Fionna now, eating her meal in silence, and softened. "I'm sorry. I didn't mean to be rude to your friend."

"He's not my friend," Fionna corrected. "He's just someone kind enough to lend a hand."

Mrs. Fallon overlooked the correction. "The point is, you don't really know him. Anything could have happened."

Fionna knew her mother was right, people could seem trustworthy on the surface, and underneath be absolute ogres. This young man, though, seemed okay. Aidan. So that was his name. The rest of the night, while her father read Hamlet out loud to Fionna and her mother, another yearly tradition, while her mother knitted five more rows onto her latest blanket project, Fionna thought of Aidan, how she'd love to sketch the contours of his face, how the wind had tossed his golden hair, how a wall hid so many stories behind his deep blue eyes, and how she wished she could know him better.

Fionna's artwork nagged at Aidan while he heated the chicken pie Sheila had left him, while he ate the pie and the salad and brown bread she had left with it, and the apple cobbler she'd left for after. Her drawing stayed on his mind, or rather, what Jeannie would have done with the same seascape view Fionna had captured with watercolors.

Charcoals, he thought, for this Jeannie would have used charcoals, favoring their quick response to paper, how she could blend and manipulate the shades, catch the colors of sea and sky to suit her artistic mind. He would have enjoyed watching her draw with quick, deliberate movements, so focused on her work she wouldn't even catch that she chewed her lip the same way he did when they were most intensely involved in a thing. He would have stood off to her side, careful not to disturb her, admiring how she could capture a view with such perfection. He would have stayed nearby no matter how long she worked, her admirer, and her defender if any strangers approached.

While she worked, his father would no doubt be casting lines in the water, praying he'd snag something special for their dinner. He'd succeed, too; he always did, he knew just how to throw his line, when to let the bait lie undisturbed or when to move it the slightest bit. He had perfect patience as well, letting the fish come to him, never hurrying the process.

Afterward, they'd return to the camper where his granny would fry their father's catch, they would dine on that plus potatoes and vegetables she would have fried alongside the fish, or maybe they'd build a fire on the beach, and dine with the sound of waves for music, and emerging stars overhead for lights. Then he and his father would pull their guitars out and accompany the waves with the sweetest of songs. His dad would even get his granny to dance a wee jig in the sand, the light in her eyes matching the fire's bright flames. They would roast marshmallows his gran would just happen to have with her, and they'd tell fireside stories till they could no longer keep their eyes open. They would fall asleep under the open sky, on woolen blankets, with their jackets rolled under their heads.

Aidan squeezed his eyes tight to block the vision, but couldn't block the memories it generated or the way they tore at his heart. Fresh air would help, he thought, so he ventured back out to the beach, where the sun had started to slide downward. and clouds building off to the west promised rain by morning. Even the diversion of shell hunting did little to clear his mind. When he found a suitable boulder by the side of the hill that rose on his right, he sat down.

"It's not fair," he told the ocean in front of him. "It's not fair that they're gone and I'm here without them."

Even as he spoke the words, he remembered speaking them before. He was in their back garden, he'd just come home from school, his mother had called him out to sit with her. That in itself was odd, she was always at work when he came home, what was even stranger was her worried look which she tried, but failed, to hide with a forced smile.

"Am I in trouble, Mom?" He couldn't think of anything he'd done wrong, but there had to be something.

His mother shook her head, "No, dear, but I do need to tell you something." She motioned for him to sit next to her, and held his hand in her own. "You know I haven't been feeling well?"

"Yes mom," he'd answered, recalling the meals she'd missed recently, and how his grandmother had moved in with them to help with housecleaning and other chores his mother was too tired to handle.

"Well, today I saw the doctor. I've seen a few of them over the past week, I'm sorry I didn't tell you that earlier, I didn't want to worry you. Anyway, the doctor today gave me a name for what's making me sick, it's a long name, don't try to remember that. The part you need to know…" she paused, Aidan could still see her take a deep breath, still feel the trembling in her hands. "The part you need to know is, I'm going to be going away, but your Da, and your Gran, they'll be here to take care of you and your sister."

"Where are you going?" When his mother didn't answer, he'd grown scared. "Mom? Tell me!"

She had kept her brave face on and said, "I'm going to be with your granddad. You remember him, don't you?"

Aidan remembered he'd passed on a few years earlier, but barely recalled his face. At the time he'd been too young to understand what that meant, only that his granddad had disappeared. Now, a few years older, he knew that meant his mother was going to die.

"Mom! You can't! You can't go! It's not fair!"

Now, sitting in front of the sea, with the vision of Jeannie, his gran, and his dad still fresh on his mind, he heard again the words his mother had spoken, "No, it's not fair. So many things in life are not fair. You're young to be learning that now, but someday you'll be stronger for it. Whenever life isn't fair, we have to be brave and move on."

The words should have helped him now, but they didn't. He still hurt, he still missed them all, he still felt angry that life had taken another cruel twist. "You were wrong, mom. It doesn't make me stronger at all."

Mrs. Donoghue watched Niall sit with his father in front of the fire, cup of tea in his hands, a book lying open in his lap, just as he had every night since returning home. She had yet to see him turn a page in his book tonight.

"Why don't you go out for a bit?"

Niall glanced up at her. "What?"

"Go take yourself out for a bit. You haven't been to the pub since you got home."

Niall thought of Rafferty's, and Gary and Mary, and picked his book up again. "Not tonight, mam, I'm tired."

Mr. Donoghue studied his son then agreed with his wife, "Go on with ye, a night out would do you good. Call your friends up and go for a pint."

Niall drank what was left of his tea and set his book on the table next to his chair. "Guess I can't fight you both! I'll go for one pint and be back before you go to bed."

"Be back before sunrise," his father called after him as Niall lifted his coat from its hook, slipped it on, and headed out to his father's truck.

He had two choices. The Ploughman would be open, filled as usual with his father's friends and conversations ranging from machine parts to the going price for wool and the latest schemes for land management. He could join them, have one pint, and be home in an hour. Or, he could take a chance on Rafferty's.

The first thing Niall did when he entered the low stone building with a black and gold sign reading Rafferty's hanging in front was scan the seats to see which of his friends might be there. Thankful that Gary and Mary were absent, Niall stepped up to the bar. "Tim, a pint please."

The bartender smiled and pulled a fresh pint. "Good to see you back, Niall."

"Good to be back."

"What was America like?"

"You can't imagine how big the place is!" Niall started in describing various cities, and some of the highlights of their tour. As he talked, he watched Tim greet newcomers, pull pints and pour drinks for them, catch up with their news, all the while following Niall's conversation and asking occasional questions. He was fascinated, as always, by Tim's multitasking ability, something he, himself, lacked.

When Tim stopped in the middle of pouring a glass of wine, Niall was curious and turned to see what Tim's eyes were locked on.

Gary and Mary stood behind him.

"Tim, a pint for me, and wine for Mary," Gary ordered, then cocked his head towards Niall and added, "and whatever he's having."

Niall turned a cold look Gary's way. "No thanks, I'm set."

Gary nodded. "Fair enough, but you know, you're home now, we're going to run into each other here and there, I hope we can resolve things and be friends again."

"By things, you mean you stealing my girl while I was gone?" Niall challenged. He looked beyond Gary to where Mary stood. "And you, you're no better than him. The two of you deserve each other."

"Niall, please—" he heard Mary call after him, but Niall strode out the door, down the sidewalk to where he'd parked his father's truck. He slammed the truck's door behind him, revved the engine, and peeled away as fast as the truck would go.

On his third evening walking the beach, Aidan stayed longer than usual, watching the sun lower itself towards its ocean bath and the stars dress the darkening sky, listening as shore birds and gulls called goodnight to each other. The ocean waves in their endless whispers told him stories of ships that had come and gone, fishing crafts with fishermen seeking food for their families, sailors testing their skills in wind and heavy surf, tall ships coming and going, great crafts of beauty, sails unfurled, filled with air power, carrying so many dreamers over the centuries who set out to build better lives. The ocean told her story so clearly Aidan could almost see the ships full of emigrants seeking a new world, their loved ones standing on shore watching them leave.

"How did you stand it?" he asked the spirits he knew crowded the beach and hills around him. "How did you ever survive the pain of letting them go?"

He listened hard that evening and long into the night. The ocean's whispers had become their secret language again. The hills were silent.

The next day Aidan went into the O'Brien's office to renew for one more night.

"Here's extra for the meals." Aidan handed over more money than required. "I'm sure they're not included in the camper rent."

Mr. O'Brien pushed the money back to Aidan. "She enjoys looking after others, our Sheila does. I'll not have you paying for the smiles you've put on her face."

As he was paying, the man whose children Aidan had seen playing on the beach earlier that week entered the office. "The bathtub drain's stopped up in our camper."

"I'll be right with you," Mr. O'Brien answered, then turned back to Aidan. "You're all set, Aidan, here's your receipt."

"Aidan?" the man repeated and studied the boy before him. "You wouldn't be Daniel O'Connell's son would you? You look like him."

"I am," Aidan nodded, guarded, trying to place the man before him.

"He's not here with you is he? I've only seen you by yourself. Leave the rest of the family behind have you?"

"No, they're not with me."

"Mention me to him will you? Bill Patterson. We went to school together. Tell him I'll see him at the reunion next month."

Aidan knew it would be wrong of him to not tell the truth, to let Mr. Patterson find out at the reunion. He held his breath a moment, then announced, "My father's passed on. A few weeks ago, in a car accident."

"Oh dear Jesus." Mr. Patterson breathed. Mr. O'Brien looked on, stunned. "That leaves you head of the family now doesn't it?" Mr. Patterson said it more as a statement of fact than a question.

Aidan wished he'd never stepped into the office, that some fairy could blink him away on the spot, that he didn't have to say the next words. "My grandmother and sister were killed as well. It's just me now."

Aidan hated the looks of pity both men gave him, and sought the fastest escape possible. "Thanks for the extra night," he told Mr. O'Brien, and hurried out of the office.

The camper Aidan retreated to no longer felt like the comfortable haven it had been. The accident filled his mind all over again, the phone call, the newspaper photo, the visit to the morgue. These were all he thought of now, all he saw when he closed his eyes. Caught between the choice of running into Bill Patterson or staying inside with ghosts, though, Aidan chose inside, and turned the camper's television up loud to drown out the memories.

When steady rain set in that afternoon and drove the other guests inside, Aidan ventured out to explore the beach. He focused on searching for shells and other sea gifts to keep memories at bay.

He noticed Fionna standing out on the beach across from her parents' camper. For a while he gave up searching the sand, and watched her instead. She held her gaze on the sea, and looked neither to the left nor right of her. When the wind blew hard she held her stand, only moved her hand to gather her long copper hair to the side and hold it in place. He wondered why she wasn't inside with her parents, then remembered her mother's tirade when he'd walked her home. In her place, he might prefer to stand out in the rain as well.

Fionna watched him stroll by, legs taking long even strides, eyes so focused on the ground before him he never noticed her. She puzzled over what would send him out in the rain when he had a warm, cozy camper behind him. She was half tempted to go after him, keep him company on his long walk, uncover his secrets. He was so much a loner, though, always keeping to himself, never stopping to talk with people on the beach or others at the caravan park, she was afraid to intrude on his private world. Fionna let Aidan pass, and returned to her study of the sea.

How far do you go? She wondered as she stared at the unbroken expanse before her. What kinds of adventures lie on your opposite shores? If I were brave enough, I'd find out. Her mind replayed the argument she'd had with her parents earlier that afternoon.

"You always tell me my paintings are lovely, and that I have talent," she had reminded her mother. "I want the chance to develop that talent."

"You'd be wasting your time, and our money," her mother had countered.

Then her father stepped in, ever the realist, pointing out, "You'll find more jobs in the library field, in libraries, in bookstores, or other literary arenas. In today's economy, you need to play it safe."

Play it safe. To Fionna, it seemed she'd done that all her life. While her friends were at university, or moving to other cities, even other countries, taking apartments, traveling abroad, she was still stuck at home. Instead of following her heart, she was still following the path they'd chosen for her. Desperate to break free, she'd argued for a chance to go to art school, dreaming of New York and London, but willing to settle for Dublin if that would gain their approval.

They had vetoed all her ideas. She wasn't brave or independent enough to oppose them and step out on her own. They had won.

Aidan's beach exploration carried him farther than ever down the shoreline; with the sea and sky the same grey, and the sun in hiding, Aidan didn't notice how late the day had grown. Only when he saw evening lights twinkling like stars come down to earth in the cottages and campers along the shore did he think to head back.

Fionna still stood watch when he passed by; now his curiosity took control.

"Excuse me, are you okay?"

Fionna jumped, surprised. "Yes. Why?"

"Not many of us out here on a rainy day."

"No, I guess there aren't." She returned to watching the waves roll in and out in front of her.

"Won't your parents be worried about you?" Aidan nodded in the direction of the camper a short distance behind her.

Fionna glanced back as well. Yes, they'd be worried, but for once she didn't care.

Aidan didn't know what moved him, a sadness in her eyes he knew mirrored his own, or camaraderie with another being choosing rain-drenched beaches instead of warmth and shelter, but he found himself offering, "Would you like to have tea with me?"

A light went on in her deep blue eyes. "I'd like that."

"Should we tell your parents where you'll be?"

"No."

Back at the camper, Aidan turned the kettle on and sliced some of the fresh bread and cheese Sheila had left while he was out. As they ate he asked, "Is it just you and your parents? Any brothers or sisters?"

"Just me. And you?"

"Just me. Do you work or go to school?"

"School. I'm studying library science."

"You don't sound too thrilled with it." Aidan set the sugar cookies Sheila had brought over on the table.

Fionna felt again the pull of her dreams. "No. I'd rather study art. And you?"

"I'm in between jobs." It was truth enough for the moment. "So, what kept you out in the rain today?"

Fionna tried to find the right words to explain. "I love my parents, but sometimes life with them just feels suffocating. I needed fresh air." She looked closer at Aidan, read the depth of a story behind his eyes. "What about you, what kept you outside?"

Aidan looked out to the dark sky and listened to the waves rushing in and out before responding, "Sometimes a silent room is too noisy. I needed fresh air myself."

The kettle boiled, Aidan poured tea for them both, and sat across from Fionna. "Art is it? What would you do with it if you took that at university?"

Fionna flashed the first genuine smile Aidan had seen from her. "You mean besides paint the Sistine Chapel or the Mona Lisa, something of that stature?"

Aidan had to smile as well. "Yeah, besides that."

"I would teach. I'd love to use art the way doctors use therapy. Art's very healing, you know." She thought of how drawing and painting always helped her through her dark moments. "Half the people on medicine these days could do just as well, maybe better, if they had something positive, something creative to focus on instead of their troubles."

You sound so much like Jeannie, Aidan thought. He fought to block memories from overwhelming him again. Focus on Fionna, he ordered himself. Don't think of anything else.

She was even more beautiful in the soft camper lights than she had been out on the beach. Her eyes were a dozen brilliant shades of blue. Her hair was auburn and copper and ginger all blended together. Her nose turned up just the slightest bit, her cheeks carried the softest blush in them, her lips were full, appealing even without the adornment of lipstick. The more he focused on her, the more enchanting she became.

Maybe it was the sound of rain on the roof and waves in their endless dance with the beach, rhythms blending to form a steady pulse in his brain. It might have been her slight smile, both hopeful and afraid to hope. Or perhaps it was one more distraction from memories he wanted to escape. The reasons were muddled; but Aidan stood, pulled Fionna close to him, kissed her, kissed her again when she didn't resist, and soon found himself drawing her back to the double bed. Her skin, smooth and soft, fed the fire in his mind. Fionna responded with fire of her own, releasing all the pent up passion she'd locked away too long. Aidan lost himself in her hair, her body, her scent of jasmine and spice, letting his passion crowd out everything else he thought and felt.

Aidan woke to the sound of music blaring from the camper next door. For a moment, he watched the girl sleeping next to him and thought how sweet their encounter had been, and he smiled. Then he remembered Fionna's mother, and leapt into action.

"Fionna! Wake up!" Aidan jostled her shoulders until she opened her eyes. "Your mother, she'll be frantic that you haven't come home!"

Fionna glanced out the window and saw how dark the night had grown. "What time is it?" she asked as she scrambled to pull her jeans and sweater on.

"Almost midnight. She'll kill us both!"

Fionna smoothed her hair out with her fingers, and pulled her shoes on. "She'll be upset, that's for sure."

"If she finds out you were here she'll have the Gardai after me in a heartbeat!"

"She won't." Fionna threw her long raincoat on over her sweater. "I'll tell her I walked farther down the road than I'd realized, and lost track of time."

Aidan stopped her as she reached the door. "Fionna, about tonight—"

"I know," Fionna cut him off. "It was a mistake, you're sorry it ever happened."

"No, that's not it at all." Aidan saw the deep hurt in her eyes, and wished he had the power to chase it away. "It was really great, in fact. It's just, I'm not one to use a girl, or hurt her, but I'm not looking for a relationship right now."

So, she'd guessed wrong after all. Underneath that vulnerable look he was the same as so many others, running from any hint of commitment as fast as he could. "It's alright." Fionna drew her arm away from Aidan's light hold. "I'm not looking for anything from you."

Again, that rejected look. Aidan needed to make her understand. He held the door closed one more minute. "No, you don't get it. There's been a family crisis, I'm trying to sort through a lot of things right now. I'd be no good in a relationship until it's all sorted."

Fionna looked closer at Aidan, saw the same storm she'd seen in his eyes before, rising more turbulent now, and gave his arm a soft squeeze. "I'm sorry. I hope you work things out." Before she stepped out into the night, she smiled back at Aidan. "It was wonderful to feel someone else's closeness for a change. I will always remember that."

After she left, Aidan stepped outside, stood close to the camper so no one would see him, and listened for sounds of yelling from Fionna's place.

163

None came. He stood a long time, listened to nighttime insects share long conversations with their neighbors, watched the clouds that had hugged the sky all day start to break, leaving the moon to cast patches of gold across the blue-black sea, and an occasional star to wink down at him. As he stood, he sorted through the flood of voices running through his mind.

"I didn't raise you to treat a girl that way." That from his granny, and he could just see the stern look she'd be saying it with, and the forefinger she'd be pointing at him.

"See? You talk about the boys I go out with, and you're no better." Jeannie's eyes would be mocking him as she spoke.

His father's eyes would show more understanding, after all, he was a man, he knew. Still, his father would say, "You best go sort this with the girl, make sure she understands, make sure she's okay."

A fourth voice hovered on the periphery, barely audible, more of his own imagination's making than anything real. It spoke, "I'd hoped for better from you," and the femaleness of the voice, the gentleness and firmness blended in its tone, made him think it was what his mother would say.

His own voice spoke as well, "I can't believe I just did that. That was awful. I'd tear into any guy who ever treated my sister that way, and here I go doing the same thing. What a bastard you are, O'Connell." At the same time, he'd hear Fionna's parting words, and agree, for just that one short space of time, it felt good to hold someone close, to banish the echoes of voices that surrounded him. He thought of Fionna's tender feel and touch, of her intoxicating fragrance, of the light in her hair and eyes, and knew if he had it to do over, he'd make the same choice.

He also knew if he saw Fionna again she would be irresistible, which would put them both at great risk if her mother ever found out. There was no doubting what his next move should be. When morning broke, Aidan settled his account with the O'Briens, thanked them again for the meals they had provided and kindness they had shown, and drove home.

9

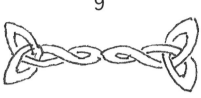

Rita watched from her kitchen as Aidan and Jack sat at their dining room table discussing how to seal a leaky pipe.

He's grown up so fast, she thought. She could still see him riding bikes with Jeannie on the sidewalk in front of their houses, golden hair on both of them shimmering in the sunlight. She could hear their laughter, and occasional arguments, rise out from their backyard. Jeannie should be here now, she thought, they all should be, Aidan and Jeannie filling the house with laughter, Daniel discussing politics and prices with Jack, Cathleen helping her with dinner and, later, tea. Her heart ached at the empty spaces around the table now, and for the young man they'd left behind. He'd grown so quiet, the last few days, so drawn into himself, even showing in his appearance now, clothes in need of washing and pressing, himself in need of a shave. Maybe she could persuade him to let her take care of some of his laundry this week.

Surprised that the kettle had heated to a furious boil while she reminisced, Rita poured fresh tea and returned to the table.

"You look like you haven't slept in several days," she commented as she handed Aidan a cup of tea.

Rita's soft tone was so like his grandmother's Aidan's pulse started racing, something he'd caught it doing too many times lately. He closed his eyes and tried to recapture the performance mode state that had brought him through the first few weeks; he failed, he'd lost the power to shut his emotions down.

"I've been watching too much t.v. at night," he told Rita. "I'll start turning it off earlier."

Then his stomach won the war it had waged all day, and the roast beef and potatoes he'd just eaten turned gigantic somersaults. He rose from the table. "Excuse me."

"He's not fooling me," Rita whispered to Jack when Aidan left the room.

"What? That he's staying up too late? Ye daft woman, he's probably got some of them girlie movies rented, the kind he could never watch with the rest of them around." Jack winked, "Tell ye what, I'll go over there tonight, watch one or two movies with him, then I can tell ye for sure!"

Rita rapped Jack's knuckles hard with her knife. "He's not watching them, and if he was you're a fool if ye think I'd be letting you go watch them as well." She raised a finger to her lips to hush them both, and cocked an ear, listening hard. Jack listened too, and heard the sound of vomiting, and the toilet flushing, and water running hard.

"I told you," Rita whispered, sad to be proven right. "That boy's not keeping any of his food down."

Jack listened and agreed. "Maybe it was the roast, it was a wee bit spicy."

"It wasn't the roast. It's him. He's wound tighter than a spring inside."

"You're right."

"You have to step in. You owe it to Daniel and Cathleen."

Jack watched Aidan's cautious steps as he returned. "Are ye not feeling well, boy?"

Aidan shook his head, embarrassed. "I must have picked some bug up on my fishing trip."

Jack caught the slight shake in Aidan's hand as he spooned sugar into his tea. "How was your trip? You've not said much about it."

"It was fine," Aidan started, then stopped. This was Jack and Rita, who'd been through so many moments of his life they would see through any lie he told now. Instead, he told them, "It wasn't as much fun as I thought it would be."

"Hard going off on your own, was it?"

Aidan nodded to Jack, and closed his eyes again, this time to hold back tears.

Jack placed a hand on Aidan's shoulder. "It's only been a short while, boy. You're bound to miss them still. It won't always be this hard."

"Maybe you shouldn't be in that house alone," Rita suggested. "Why don't you stay here a while? We have the spare room, you could use it as long as you'd like."

Aidan insisted, "I'm fine at home, but I'll remember about the room."

Not long after Aidan returned home Jack heard the television go on, and knew it would be on all night. He picked up the phone, Rita nodding encouragement beside him as he dialed.

"Mack, it's Jack MacLaren, Aidan's neighbor. Rita and me, we're both worried about him."

Mack listened to Jack and Rita's concerns. "You were right to call me," he assured them when they were through. "I've been giving him some space and time to sort things out. I think it's time we stepped in."

Mack then called Patrick, Michael and Niall, and worked out a plan. Finally, he called Aidan.

"It's been a while. I'd like to set a group meeting, a chance to catch up with each other, and start to figure out where we go next."

Aidan shook the blankets out and pulled cushions off the sofa he'd taken to sleeping on ever since the accident, ever since he discovered his family's spirits inhabited their bedrooms, calling out memories so loud sleep upstairs was impossible.

His phone wasn't there.

He shook out the pillowcase, crouched down on his knees and searched under the sofa, then sank back on his heels.

No phone.

He gathered the newspapers piled on the floor in front of the sofa, sifted through them, and tossed them out in the recycle bin. He sorted through bills and papers strewn on top of the dining room table, then gathered them and stuffed them in the top drawer of his grandmother's desk.

His phone was nowhere to be found. All the voicemail messages and pictures of them he'd stored on his phone were lost to him now.

Even though he knew his phone wouldn't be there, Aidan searched Jeannie's room, where prisms hanging in her window cast a dozen rainbows on her soft lilac walls, and the stuffed dog she'd had since she was two sat on the same chair she had always left it on when she made her bed every morning. The phone wasn't in his grandmother's room, whose rose spray curtains and bedspread still carried her powdered scent, where the bride and groom in her wedding photo still smiled out to whoever entered the room. Nor was it in his father's bedroom, where his father's sweaters and slacks still sat folded on his corner chair, Aidan not having the heart to store them away in the closet. Aidan scanned the tan bedspread and rug and the top of his father's bureau, but the phone was in none of these places.

Aidan glanced at his watch. No more time to look now, he realized, they'd be here soon. He rushed through a shower, pulled clean jeans and a sweater on, and had just finished combing his hair when the doorbell rang. As he hurried downstairs, a wave of dizziness hit, forcing him to sit on the stairs until it passed.

"I thought since I called today's meeting I should at least bring lunch." Mack entered and handed Aidan a platter of sandwich meats and cheeses and a bag of rolls. As Aidan set the food on the dining room table, Mack noticed how loose his sweater and jeans hung.

Patrick arrived bearing a box of scones. "Conor and Caitlyn helped make these. They don't look the best, but they taste okay."

Aidan had to laugh at the lopsided scones. "I see they have their father's culinary skills!"

Michael brought a peach pie. "It's safe," he assured them all, "I bought it at the bakery down the road."

"Thank God!" Aidan set the pie on the kitchen counter. "You know, I do have food here, you all didn't need to bring lunch with you."

"My mam said to warm this over medium heat ten or fifteen minutes," Niall instructed as he entered and handed Aidan a container of beef barley soup. "She also said she's feeling abandoned and when are you coming out to see her."

"I'll drive out soon," Aidan promised and motioned to the table where the others sat. "Let's see what Mack wants."

"We should all catch up a bit first," Mack suggested, selecting ham and cheese and a roll, then passing the platter to his left. "Pat, what have you and your family been up to?"

"The kids are growing like weeds. We visited a friend in Connemara last weekend, he raises ponies, now all the twins talk about is when can we have one." He laughed, "Next time we'll have to be more careful where we take those two."

Michael spread some mustard on his turkey sandwich. "Susannah and I are back together, we've worked out the problems we were having." He stopped short of announcing their engagement, then wondered why. Was he afraid of their reactions? No, he realized he enjoyed keeping the news between himself and Susannah a little longer, a secret only the two of them shared.

Niall added a second layer of Swiss cheese and ham to his roll. "I'm home with my sheep. What more could I want?"

When Mack and the others turned his way, Aidan gave a hasty answer, "All the business end of things are sorted for now. Everything's settling down."

Mack eyed them all, Aidan the longest. "Right, it's time we started planning our next album. I don't suppose, with all your ponies and girlfriends and sheep, any of you have found time to write any new songs?"

"I've written a couple."

Patrick and Michael both punched Niall's arms playfully. "Thanks for making us look bad!"

"You don't need my help for that!"

"Alright boys," Mack interrupted, relieved to see their humor kick in as strong as ever. "Niall gets

171

the gold star. You should all start to think about songs you'd like to see on the next album."

"Do you know when we'll be working again?" Patrick's eyes circled the table. "It's just, I need to start bringing some money in soon. Bills are getting a little tight now."

Mack turned his full attention to Aidan, noting now how pale his face looked, eyes flat, their spark of humor extinguished. "What about you? Are you ready to get back to work?"

Four pairs of eyes studied him, waiting on his answer. Ready? Far from it. From the corner of his eye Aidan could see Annie and his own guitar standing in their respective corners. He had no heart to pick them up. He shook his head, "I don't know, I haven't given it much thought. I'm sorry."

Mack watched Aidan set the sandwich platter in the center of the table without taking anything. He'd have to press a little harder, he knew; Aidan would volunteer nothing. "You've had other things on your mind. Maybe now that they're getting sorted, it's time to get back to our work."

Aidan fixed his eyes on the empty plate in front of him. The blue and white floral pattern was his mother's choice, he remembered. He nodded in response to Mack, but didn't trust himself to speak.

Mack turned to Patrick, "Pat, all of you, I can't set dates yet. For now, if any of you want I can help you sort out some solo work to bring a bit of money in."

While Mack and the others discussed the band's future, Aidan stepped into the kitchen, put fresh tea water on, and wondered if he would ever play his guitar again. The knot he'd felt in his stomach all day tied itself tighter. As he reached into the cupboard for plates to go with Michael's pie, a buzzing noise filled his ears. He couldn't figure why, when he turned to the others, the dining room tilted to the left. Then the room went dark.

Mack stood over him calling, "Aidan! Wake up!"

Niall knelt by him, shaking his shoulders.

Patrick and Michael stood close by, fear etched on their faces.

"What happened?" he asked, pushing himself up from the floor, mind still hazy as he rose to his feet.

"Here, sit down." Mack led him to the sofa, then sat in the chair opposite him. "Has this happened before?"

"No." Aidan looked at their fearful faces, and thought humor would help. "I guess I was waiting for an audience."

No one smiled.

"I'll be honest Aidan, I didn't call this meeting so we could plan the band's next steps. Jack and Rita called the other day. They're worried about you. We all are."

"I'll be fine, it's just a bug," Aidan tried to reassure Mack, but Mack didn't believe him any more than Jack and Rita had.

"Jack and Rita feel you're sliding downhill, a little more each week." Mack let that sink in a minute. "I want you to come spend time out with me. Either that, or I'll stay here a while. I don't want to leave you on your own."

"Moira and I would love to have you stay with us," Patrick offered.

Michael added, "I have an empty bedroom, you could stay with me as long as you want."

173

Aidan glanced from Michael to Patrick, to Niall, then to Mack, concern mirrored on each of their faces. He knew they were right; his stomach still churned like a roller coaster, his head still buzzed like a swarm of bees lived in it, he was sure if he stood his legs would buckle. He shouldn't be on his own.

He could stay with Mack, he knew, but he'd feel guilty putting Mack through so much trouble. He could stay at Patrick's, Conor and Caitlyn would love it, but Patrick and Moira had enough on their plate. Michael's apartment, surrounded by city traffic, would not give him the quiet rest he knew he needed. No, if he had to go anywhere, one option stood out far better than the others.

Aidan turned to Niall. "Does your mother really feel neglected?"

Niall nodded, "If I don't bring you home with me now, she'll disown me."

Fionna stood at her easel, gauging the many colors of the evening sun reflected in the clouds above her and the water below her hilltop vantage point. She combined various blues trying to capture the vibrant sky, tried them on her watercolor paper, then gave up, tore the top sheet off, crumpled it and threw it in her paintbox. Maybe the sky was the wrong subject tonight. She turned her easel to the left, where her view took in the beach, the caravan park, and Portnoo in the distance. No, the view was too cluttered, not at all what her mind wanted to paint. Frustrated, she gave up and sank to the grassy ground.

She knew what she most wanted to paint, but he was not there.

The days after Aidan had left were more empty than she'd ever experienced. She was not only once again alone with her parents, now the beach she walked bore a huge hole. No solitary figure strolled along the water's edge to distract her, no mysterious story behind the figure to intrigue her. The beach had once again become just a beach, a stretch of sand and rock and sea to draw as she'd drawn a hundred times over.

Her mind replayed the night at his camper, his solemnity as they talked, the passion and urgency in his hands and body as they made love, his concern for her after. She'd only had one other relationship. The boy had been immature and awkward, with none of the depth and care Aidan had shown. He had been a gift from the gods to break the monotony of her life, a puzzle to solve, and now, a heartbreak to endure.

Fionna thought again of his words, a family crisis to work through. Behind his eyes strength reflected, she thought of that strength now. Maybe that was the greatest gift the gods had given her. If Aidan had strength enough to face whatever challenges faced him, perhaps she did as well. She rose and faced her easel again, set her pencil to paper, and started to draw the beach, the sea, and a lone figure walking the shoreline. As she drew, her heart gained momentum. She would go to art school despite her parents' protests, she would follow her heart and build the life she dreamed of, not the life they chose.

"I'm sure I can line up gigs at the Swagman and the Harp and other places in town, and Mack's promised to help." Patrick slipped an arm around Moira's shoulders to comfort her. "We'll be fine."

Moira hugged Patrick back. "We always pull through. It's Aidan I'm worried about. Are you sure Mack shouldn't have taken him to hospital?"

Patrick shook his head, "I'm sure he'll be okay out at Niall's place. Niall's folks will look after him, if he's worse they'll get him to a doctor."

"You're right." Moira settled back against the sofa they shared in front of their evening fire. "Okay, we'll tighten up on our spending the next month; we can make it."

Patrick kissed Moira's forehead. "Have I told you lately how much I love you?"

"No," Moira teased, "tell me now!"

Rita listened to the silence from the house next door, then turned to Jack. "He will be okay, won't he?"

"Yes, love. He's in good hands. You were right to push me to call Mack, though."

"You would have called on your own if I hadn't pushed."

Jack watched Rita pick up her knitting and start slipping yarn and stitches from one needle to another. "What's that you're making now?"

Rita fingered the rows of pale green and white yarn she'd already constructed. "A baby blanket for Linda, she's new at church, I don't think you know her. Her wee baby's due next month."

Jack had to smile. "You just can't help yourself, can you?"

"What?" Rita gave Jack a puzzled look.

"Mothering others, doing for others." Jack pointed to the blanket. "You've a large heart, love. Don't ever change."

"Go on with ye," Rita waived him off and returned to her knitting. As she worked, she whispered prayers for Aidan, and slipped a few in that God would continue to protect the man she loved.

10

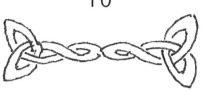

Sunlight glistens across Lough Veagh, whose surface waters are rippled by a soft breeze that cools the summer air. She sits on a bench, he perched beside her, arm around her waist.

Both of them laugh as the boy and girl, so close to adulthood now, chase each other through the field. The boy almost wins, but at the last moment the girl changes direction and escapes. Their laughter rings across the glen, as bright as the sun, as lively as the nearby birch branches swaying in the breeze.

An older woman calls, the boy and girl return. Both women carry out blankets and picnic baskets. They all settle for lunch along the lough's waters, sunlight warming them skin to bone. After lunch he brings out his guitar. The boy and girl sing along while the women pack their lunch leftovers away. Then they set out on foot for the hike to the castle, always their favorite part of Glenveagh Park.

The castle gates are within sight when a sudden storm blows in, wind bending branches, blowing leaves by. Rain starts quick and hard; she knows from the clouds overhead the storm will intensify. They run for cover, she, her husband, her daughter, the grandmother. Only the son remains behind, outpaced by them no matter how frantic he runs.

"Wait," he cries out. "Wait for me!" He screams against the wind and pelting rain.

She looks back once, motions for him to hurry, yet the distance between them increases until they are out of sight. He hears their laughter at being caught in such a storm. Then even their laughter is gone.

Aidan woke with a start. The dream was so real, he felt for several minutes longer the pain of losing them all, even his mother, looking as fresh and pretty as she did in the picture in his father's garage. Even as he took in the room around him, trying to place the soft peach walls, oak dresser, green and rose woolen blanket spread over him, the dream oppressed his spirit.

They were gone. He was left behind.

Voices rose from somewhere below him, then from outside. He listened, unable to make out words, the familiarity of one of the voices catching him, until at last the voice and the room became clear. The voice was Niall's; he was in the guest room at the Donoghue's house. The blankets over him and pillow under his head felt soft, smelled clean, tempting Aidan to relax in bed a few moments longer, till he saw the clock on the nightstand.

"Eleven forty!" Shocked, he threw the covers off, grabbed his jeans and sweater that had been folded and set on the corner chair, dressed and hurried downstairs, where Mrs. Donoghue had just set a laundry basket of clean clothes by the sofa.

"Mrs. Donoghue, I'm so sorry. You should have woke me up."

"You were meant to sleep in." Niall's mother set a fresh cup of tea before Aidan. "In fact, after you have some food you're to go back to bed. Niall and his father are heading out to the field to mend fences. They'll not be disturbing you."

"Oh I couldn't do that."

179

"You can and you will."

The smile she gave Aidan was so like his grandmother's his heart leapt and sank in the same movement. She bustled around the kitchen in the same way as well, slicing bread and buttering it, frying up eggs, even the way she sliced tomatoes and set food on a plate was a mirror of his own granny's actions.

"You get this in ye now," Mrs. Donoghue ordered, "and then you're off for more sleep." She spoke in a stern, no nonsense tone, but the same warm smile lit her eyes.

"Alright, I will." He could no more stand against her than against his granny. "Thank you."

She squeezed his shoulder, smiled again, then turned her attention to the basket of laundry that needed folding.

When Aidan woke again late day shadows played across his walls, and the smell of food rose up from the kitchen. Aidan guessed roast beef and something fruity. Apple? Apple pie? He headed down to investigate and to join the conversation that drifted up with the aromas.

"So, sleeping beauty wakes!"

Mrs. Donoghue rapped her son's shoulder. "Stop that!"

"Oh mam, he knows I'm just teasing."

"I would have been out with you earlier, but your mam, she's pretty tough." Aidan took the empty chair at the kitchen table where dinner was being laid out, and turned to Niall's father. "Thank you for letting me stay here a bit."

"You stay here as long as you'd like, boy." Mr. Donoghue handed him a plate of roast beef, mashed potatoes and gravy. "You're always welcome here."

"Are you feeling any better?" Niall asked with genuine interest now.

"Yeah. At least the world's stopped spinning."

Mrs. Donoghue set a dish of applesauce before Aidan, the source of the fruity aroma. "The rest did you good. Another day of that, then you should be fine."

"I can't be lazy another day," Aidan protested.

"We'll see in the morning." Mrs. Donoghue eyed the plate before him. "Your breakfast stayed down. We'll see how you do with this dinner."

Mr. Donoghue sliced meat and passed around plates for the others, said the blessing, then turned to his son. "You did fine mending that fence today. Tomorrow we'll see if we can get her finished."

"Thanks Dad. We're running a bit low on nails, unless you have another box stashed away somewhere."

"No, that's the end of them. I'll go to town tomorrow and get some more."

"You'll get me my fountain as well."

Mr. Donoghue looked across to his wife. "You've no need of a fountain; you've got a whole pond behind you."

"I still want my fountain."

"They've been on about this for weeks now," Niall told Aidan. "She'll get her way in the end." The last part he said soft enough only Aidan could hear.

"Once the fence is done, we should start in on the sheds, there's a few holes in the roofs that need patching."

"Sure, Dad." Niall handed Aidan butter for his bread. "You can help me with that. From ground level, of course!"

"Don't trust me on a ladder yet, eh?" Aidan passed salt and pepper back to Niall.

"I'm not sure I trust you on solid ground!" Niall retorted.

"We'll find something easy for you, Aidan." Mr. Donoghue turned to his wife, "I hear Peg McGraw's selling some rose bushes. If you ride into town with me, you might pick up a couple."

Mrs. Donoghue winked at Niall and Aidan. "Is that in place of me fountain?"

"Give it a rest on the fountain, will ye? Do you want the roses or not?"

"You know I do."

Their banter went back and forth, a sparring match played out against a background of love that made Aidan smile once he realized it was all in good fun. His own father and grandmother had never matched wits like this, but they had been mother and son, not husband and wife. Aidan wondered if his own mother and father would have bantered back and forth in this way had she lived. When dinner was over, Mrs. Donoghue cleared the table, set dishes to soak, and carried two cups of tea to the living room, where she and her husband sat in opposite chairs and watched the fire he'd built.

Upstairs, Niall knocked and then entered Aidan's room.

"Are you settled in here okay? Anything you need or want?"

"No. Everything's fine here." Aidan laid back against his pillow. "I'm sorry for putting you all through so much."

Niall lowered himself into the corner chair. "It's not your fault."

"Maybe it is."

"In what way?" Niall watched Aidan, curious.

"I could have asked for help earlier." Then, because he had to tell someone and Niall was his best confidant, Aidan revealed, "There's something more. A girl. I met her at the caravan park while I was fishing, and we, well, 'connected'."

"Connected?" Niall repeated, as the full meaning sank in.

"I used her," Aidan admitted, ashamed. "I would never have started a relationship with her, but one night I took what I needed and didn't care."

Niall thought back to all the conversations they'd had since Macready's Bridge had started, about girls and sex, about what turned them on and when relationships felt right or wrong. Aidan always drew the most girls at their shows, but had always held them at a respectable distance, had never given in to the temptation of one night stands. "It's like my granny's always watching over my shoulder," he'd once laughed. "I don't know how I'll ever stand a chance once I'm married!"

"You didn't rape her did you?" Niall asked now, afraid of the answer. He breathed a sigh of relief when Aidan shook his head, shocked.

"Of course not!" A smile flickered across Aidan's face. "In fact, we both enjoyed it."

"Then what's the problem?"

"I told you. I feel like I used her."

Niall studied his friend. "Maybe she wanted that night just as much as you did. In a way, maybe you both used each other."

Aidan thought back to Fionna, so alone and mysterious along the shore, so tied to a solitary life with her parents. That night seemed to be as much an escape for her as it was for himself.

"You could be right."

Niall laughed. "I'm always right! Now, enough of the guilt, okay? I'll see you in the morning."

Back in his own room, Niall listened to the sound of the house falling asleep, silence from the guest room where Aidan slept, the occasional creak of his parents' mattress as they settled in for the night, then peace throughout. He, alone, remained awake, thinking of Aidan's encounter with the girl at the shore, and thinking again of his own encounters with girls, most recently Mary. As angry as he was at her, as deep as the hurt over her betrayal went, tonight he wanted her all over again. He closed his eyes and saw her again, her long, dark hair flowing down to the middle of her back, her large brown eyes shining, as always, with excitement and laughter. He could hear her laughter ring out, clear, musical, captivating. God, he wanted her back, no matter how she'd hurt him.

"Could I win you back, Mary?" he asked the air around him. He ran several plans through his brain; each one ended with him seeing the look on her face when he'd seen them across the street from Boyle's. She was happy, and in love. That had been plain even from a distance. No, he'd leave well enough alone. He laid awake for hours mulling over every other girl in town, wondering when he'd ever have another girl like Mary.

No dreams interrupted Aidan's sleep that night. He woke the next morning to the smell of bacon frying, and joined Niall's family for breakfast.

"You're looking that much better this morning, dear." Mrs. Donoghue set a plate of fried eggs and potatoes before him. "Did you sleep well?"

"I did, thanks. That's a very comfortable room."

"My dad's snoring didn't keep you awake?" Niall laughed at the warning look his father sent him. "Do you feel up to helping me with the fence today?"

Aidan nodded as he spread jam on his toast. "I'd like that."

"You might not like it an hour or two into the job!"

"You'll not be overworking the boy!"

Niall laughed at his mother. "Oh mam, I'm just teasing. I'll be careful with him."

"A bit of work might be just what the lad needs." To Aidan, Mr. Donoghue added, "Mind, don't let our Niall push you too hard. Take a break whenever you need to."

The work was not hard. Aidan helped Niall stretch out wire and held it into place while Niall nailed it to posts that had been set into the ground at regular intervals. Some posts Niall had to reset, Aidan held them steady while Niall poured fresh cement. For a while sun warmed their faces and arms; when misty rain moved in they worked in the barn, cleaning out stalls, raking hay, moving away equipment and supplies that were getting wet from rain falling in through holes in the roof.

Niall's parents returned with five of Peg McGraw's rose bushes. "Set them around there, boys," Mr. Donoghue directed, pointing to the cement pad behind the house that served as their patio. "We'll plant them later."

"No, in the garden," Mrs. Donoghue corrected. "Set them out by my flower garden."

"They'll look best along the patio."

"They'll get trampled on by your dog. They belong in the garden."

"You can't see them as well way back there." Mr. Donoghue set the first one down by the cement, and motioned for the boys to follow suit. "You'll be wanting them where you can see them from that kitchen window of yours."

The next day, they planted the roses by the patio. To protect them, the boys helped Mr. Donoghue surround the patio with low wrought iron railing he'd salvaged from a renovation site he'd come across months earlier.

"If you just hold this last one in place for me, I'll have her set in no time," Mr. Donoghue directed Aidan, then filled dirt and small stones into the holes around the railing's posts.

Aidan liked the cold, solid feel of wrought iron in his hands, the strength and stability it represented, its timeless endurance. He liked, too, working with Niall and Mr. Donoghue. The way the chores were steady, never hurried, and the easy, instinctive way they worked, anticipating each other's needs and next moves after years of working side by side, settled him inside. He was thinking how fortunate Niall was, living in such close harmony with his parents, on such a peaceful, beautiful piece of land, when Mack's car pulled into Niall's driveway.

"Glad to see you earning your keep," Mack teased as he stepped out of his car.

"They're regular slave drivers," Aidan teased back, ducking to avoid the work glove Niall threw at him.

"You look more relaxed." Mack held a small black object out to Aidan. "Here, Rita found this, we thought you might want it."

"My phone! I thought I'd lost it forever!" Aidan clicked on the photo icon. Thank God, the pictures were all there. "Where did she find it?"

"Out back by the refuse bin."

"I don't even remember taking it out there. I was afraid I'd lost all the photos it held."

Mack thought of all the photos of Kate he still had stashed away in a drawer. He rarely pulled them out, but he'd be crushed if he ever lost them. "I'm glad you didn't. You might call Jack and Rita when you have a minute; they've been quite worried about you."

"I will."

"Do you want to stay for lunch?" Niall nodded towards the house. "If you hurry, you can grab a bit of food before Aidan inhales it all!"

Aidan threw the work glove back at Niall, striking the side of his head. Niall chased after Aidan, and trapped him in a mock headlock.

"Hey, you're supposed to be helping me recover, not killing me!"

They all laughed, then Mack opened his car door and slid back in. "I'll have to pass on lunch, Niall. I have other places to get to."

"He looks and sounds so much better," Mack told Kate later that day as they strolled along the Peace Bridge that crossed the River Foyle. "Being out in the country agrees with him."

"Being away from the house agrees with him." Kate sipped the tea Mack had bought her.

"You're right. Niall thought Aidan might stay out there another week or so."

"That would be good for him, for all of you."

Mack watched as she walked, tea in hand, light breeze teasing a wisp of hair from its gold clasp, blowing it in front of her eyes from time to time. A younger woman would have brushed it back and re-secured it; Kate let the breeze play with her hair, unconcerned. "I'm not as worried about him this week, that's true. Do you think I did the right thing, telling the others to sit tight a little longer and wait for Aidan?"

Kate thought before she answered, another trait Mack admired in her. She always thought her words out before speaking, never said what she thought a person wanted to hear. "Yes, you have to give him time, but do you have a deadline in mind?"

Mack shook his head.

Kate stopped along the bridge's railing and watched lights reflect off the Foyle's rippled waters. "You know you have to balance Aidan's needs against the rest of the band's. How long can Patrick hold out, with a family to support?"

"Not much longer. I'm helping him line up some gigs in pubs in and around Sligo over the next few weeks, that will help." Mack's eyes narrowed with worry. "Aidan's just not ready yet."

"If this was any other job, he'd already be back to work," Kate pointed out. "Sometimes the routine and distraction of a job are the best healers."

"That's true," Mack said out loud. To himself, he said "My God, Kate, you look more beautiful than ever, the way your hair shines in the evening light, the way your eyes glow."

"In a few weeks Aidan may have sorted things out and be ready to get back to work. You made the right choice." Kate placed her hand on Mack's, a show of support that sent electric warmth spreading all through him. When she withdrew her hand, the warmth remained.

"Thanks for taking time out for tea with me." Mack resisted the urge to push the stray wisp of hair off her face, or to take her hand back in his own.

Kate smiled. "I'm glad I ran into you at the market. I should have called earlier to see how you all were."

"I wouldn't have expected you to call." Then he decided to risk the next step. "If I called you in a week or two, would you have tea with me again?"

Kate stared into the river so long Mack thought to withdraw the question. He almost did, when Kate spoke at last, "I've never stopped loving you, Mack. You're still the only man who can set my heart racing like it was after all the treasures in the world. My life's far too quiet without you. We had so many bad times, though. I don't ever want to go back to the way it was, and I don't ever want to give you false hope. If I say yes to tea, that doesn't mean we have a future; it just means tea, nothing more."

"Fair enough," Mack told her. He told himself, "There's a chance. Thank God, there's still a chance."

Kate flicked the switch inside the door and entered her living room. "Hello?" she wanted to call out, wanted someone to answer, to come running, glad she was home. Even a cat, she thought, a cat would have been nice. True, she detested the things, always spying, stealing around corners, jumping up on counters and tables and behind her neck on sofas, scaring the heart out of her. They were sneaky and too independent, only coming around when they wanted something. Still, tonight, she would have welcomed the sight of a fat, furry cat strolling into the room, stretching, circling around her legs if only for the dinner she would set out for it. I should have gotten a cat, she thought again.

She crossed the room and looked out through her lace curtains to her view of the Foyle, now sparkling, reflecting Derry's evening lights, and the half moon rising to her left. To her right the Peace Bridge's graceful curves joined the city's two sides; near the center she could spot where she had stood beside Mack a short while earlier.

She had been surprised earlier, at the market, when she'd run into him; not at seeing him there, but at how her pulse had quickened at his sight, how all the details her mind had been sorting, the store's intake for the day, appointments she needed to follow through on, a display she needed to finalize to highlight a new fall clothing line, had evaporated at a turn of her head. She had thought, after all the battles and bitterness of their last years of marriage, after so many years divorced, she would have more control over herself when it came to Mack. True, she'd never completely moved on, spot checking his career as she did, but that had been occasional moments, with as much distance between her checks as there was between their lives. While her mind may have stayed somewhat attached, she had thought her heart and body had let go.

After this evening, their riverside walk and talk, Kate now knew the truth. She turned from the window back to her empty apartment with the realization that Mack moved her to the same depth and fullness as he ever had. Yes, if he called again she would see him. God help her, and her heart, she would see him every time he asked.

Mr. Donoghue surveyed the shed, the roll of sheet metal next to it, his son, and Aidan. "Are you sure you feel up to the job?" he asked his guest.

Aidan studied the ladder and roof. "Sure. I can do it."

"I'll handle the ladder and roof part," Niall assured them both. "Aidan can hand things up to me."

They worked as well together on the roof as they always did with their music, Niall selecting the spots to be repaired, both of them cutting pieces of sheet metal for patching, and drilling screw holes in the corners, then Niall climbing the ladder, securing the patches in place with caulking and steel screws. They both concentrated on their work, exchanging few words. As they worked, Aidan could see Mr. Donoghue fiddling with some repair to the tractor, Farley, the family's dog, lending his master vocal encouragement, Mrs. Donoghue hanging laundry out to dry and pulling weeds out of their vegetable garden, and the Donoghues' sheep grazing in the fields beyond. Aidan recalled all of the times he'd worked by his father's side, repairing various items around their house, the smell of sawdust, the sound of hammer and drill, the feel of different wrenches and screwdrivers in his hands. When memories overwhelmed him, he looked out across the rolling hills beyond the Donoghue farm, the ribbon of blue river in the distance and the few small loughs around them, and filled his mind with green and blue scenery and the sound of songbirds and sheep.

They worked most of the day repairing shed roofs, breaking long enough for sandwiches and tea at lunch, and tea again mid-afternoon. When their job was done, and as Mrs. Donoghue prepared dinner, Aidan and Niall walked with Farley to the pasture to bring their sheep home for the night.

"How many sheep do you have?" Aidan asked, watching Farley, nose to the wind, sniff out whatever scents the light breeze carried their way.

"Twenty-seven. We lost a few over the winter."

Aidan glanced at Niall and grinned, already knowing the answer to his next question. "I'll bet you've given each of them names, haven't you?"

Niall flashed a smile of his own. "Of course! Farms with larger flocks just go by numbers, but to me our sheep are like family, just as Farley is. They've got to have names."

"How can you tell them apart?" Aidan hadn't studied them closely, but they all seemed to look alike.

"I know each of them inside and out." When Aidan cast a doubtful look, Niall added, "I can even tell you which ones are friendly and which one will bite you."

"Sheep don't bite." Then, because he wasn't sure, Aidan asked, "Do they?"

Niall sent a knowing look Aidan's way. Farley's ears raised and twisted, gathering various sounds, front paws bouncing now as they reached the gate of the pasture the sheep had spent the day grazing in. Niall opened the gate and Farley charged ahead to his favorite part of the day, rounding up his charges for the walk back to the barn. Aidan watched, intrigued, as the collie-sheepdog mixed breed ran wide circles that grew ever tighter, gathering the black-faced animals into a huddle, then guiding them toward the gate and home.

"So, what are their names?" Aidan tested as they followed Farley and the sheep.

"Well now, I could tell you any names I wanted and you'd never know if I was telling you the truth. But I'll tell you straight. That's Maggie, and Bridget, and Amber, and Cloud, and there's Ben, and Finn," Niall named each one in turn.

"And which one bites?" Aidan asked, skeptical, when Niall was through.

"Ah, that would be Buttercup."

Aidan cocked an eyebrow, sure now he was being had. "Buttercup bites?"

"She does. You don't believe me, though, do you?" When Aidan raised both eyebrows in response, Niall motioned, "Follow me." He led Aidan to the front of the flock, to a sand colored sheep, one of three without a black face. He nudged her aside until she was separated from the rest of the flock. "Go ahead, put your hand by her mouth."

"You first," Aidan countered.

Niall, knowing the ways of sheep in general and the habits of Buttercup in particular, knew to put his hand just to the side of her mouth, not right in front, an imperceptible move to Aidan. When Buttercup gave no reaction, Aidan, sure he had proved his point, chuckled, "See, she's as gentle as they come."

"You try now."

Aidan stretched his hand full in front of Buttercup, a move to her like waving a red flag in front of a bull. In a flash, she bit at Aidan's hand. He jerked his hand back so fast he almost lost his footing and fell into the sheep behind him. They both laughed hard. It felt good to laugh until Aidan realized what he was doing and stopped.

Niall saw the cloud flash across Aidan's face, gone as fast as it had come, leaving him subdued. It's enough for one day, Niall thought. Out loud, he spoke, "We better get these sheep home. Mam will be waiting dinner on us." They completed their walk in thoughtful silence.

After dinner, Niall brought his pipes out. "Too bad we didn't bring your guitar out here," he told Aidan, "you could accompany me."

Aidan shook his head, stood up and stretched. "I'm worn out, think I'll head for bed."

"Did you see that?" Niall whispered to his parents once he heard Aidan close the door to his room. "He's avoiding music altogether."

"Maybe he's just tired, dear," Mrs. Donoghue suggested. "You both worked hard today."

"The boy's just getting back on his feet," Mr. Donoghue pointed out. "Sure he's tired, and deserving a good night's sleep."

"Could be." Niall had caught the look in Aidan's eyes though, their light gone out as soon as music was mentioned, and knew there was more than tiredness disturbing his friend. "Anyway, I'm off to play our sheep to sleep."

Out in the barn, Niall turned the overhead light on, it's low light casting shadows from the sheep in their pens, the boards that penned them in, and the various ropes, chains and tools that hung from hooks on the walls. The atmosphere, one of Niall's favorites to write songs in, created a magical, mysterious ambiance. As the sheep settled down for the night, and with Farley stretched out near his feet, face pointing to the door lest any intruders invade, Niall tuned his uillean pipes and played notes, experimenting with different tones and combinations until the sound pleased his ear, and a song rose in the night air.

Three songs in, Niall set his pipes down. No matter how sweet the music seemed, tonight he was dissatisfied.

Aidan had never before turned down a chance to join Niall in music. Niall had hoped the weeks that had passed since the accident would have given Aidan time to adjust and start looking to the future. He'd realized at Aidan's house, at the meeting Mack had called, that Aidan was far less ready than he'd hoped. As the flock around him slept, as even Farley dreamed, legs and body twitching like he was chasing a rabbit, Niall struggled to find a way to bring Aidan back to the music that had been his heart and soul.

Aidan lay awake long after the house had grown quiet, its inhabitants and even Farley fast asleep. The only sounds were crickets in their nighttime chorus and the occasional whisper of trees being blown by a breeze. He remembered a similar night many years back, when he was eight or nine and his family had gone to visit friends in the country; he recalled lying in a strange bed in a strange house, hearing unfamiliar noises, goats bleating in the barn, an owl calling nearby. When the tree outside his window knocked against the house in the wind, that was all Aidan could take. He slipped from his bed and tiptoed to the room across the hall where his father slept. Shaking his arm, he woke his father up. His father, without asking the reason, simply offered, "Want to sleep here the night?" and had slid over in bed to make room for his son. Aidan remembered how secure the world felt next to his father.

"Don't think," he ordered himself now, as memories once again tried to rush in. "Let it go." Then, to fill his mind with something else, he tried to remember all the names of the sheep Niall had rattled off earlier. Sleep overtook him around the tenth name, Clover.

Anna Donoghue watched out the kitchen window at Niall and Aidan, hard at work clearing the farm's barn and shed. After studying them a few minutes, she turned to Will.

"Do you think he's okay, working so hard, after being ill?"

Will watched as Aidan held a roll of fence wire steady, and Niall tied it to keep it from unrolling, then pointed to where Aidan should place it back in the shed.

"He'll be fine. Our Niall will know if they need a break."

"He'll know if he needs one himself," Anna agreed, "but he might not see it in Aidan. You know that boy's just putting up a front, wanting us to think he's okay when he's still all broken inside." She could not stop the tears forming in her eyes, and raised her dishtowel to wipe them away.

Will drew her away from the window and led her to a kitchen chair, then sat down across from her. "Do you remember when Maggie Ahearn passed on a couple years back?"

"Could I ever forget? She was my closest friend in all the world."

"She was that," he agreed. "And do you remember the early days, when she'd just gone?"

Anna followed her memory back to that painful time, the first weeks without her best friend. She'd go through the morning, expecting at some point Maggie's ritual phone call in which they'd compare their plans for the day, what meals they were preparing, what vegetables or flowers were growing in summer, or what winter storms were predicted. When lunchtime hit and the call hadn't come, she'd remember there would be no more calls. At market, she would think to check whether Maggie needed vegetables or fruit, and then catch herself. Nighttime was hardest, no tea and biscuits and sharing the day's news, and that tiny bit of gossip that always rendered them both helpless with laughter.

"I remember. Took me weeks to get over her."

"Took you months," Will corrected, taking her hands in his own. "All the while you put on your own front so no one would see your heart was broken."

"You saw, though. You always do."

"Aye. And so will our Niall. He'll keep a close eye on Aidan."

After cleaning the barn and shed, Niall and Aidan helped Niall's father repair a section of the stone wall in front of their house. As they worked, Niall watched Aidan out of the corner of his eye, noting when Aidan looked tired, the times he would shift his gaze to the hills around them and the flash of anguish that would fill his eyes, when his hands would tremble, the telltale signs that his nerves were on edge. At those times, Niall would make up an excuse for a break: "I could do with some bread and butter," or "my arms are killing me, I'm not used to this much hard work," or "did you see that now?" pointing off in one direction or another to follow the flight of a bird overhead, or the way a sudden strong wind bent a tree low, nearly splitting its trunk, or how Marley, the barn cat, chased Farley away from the sunspot on the patio, at which point they'd set aside the work at hand, sit at the patio, and rest until Niall could see, in Aidan's eyes or relaxed body, that he was ready for more work.

After a week of work, an unusually hot, sunny day broke over the Donoghue farm. After breakfast,

Niall and Aidan set out to wash Mr. Donoghue's truck. Niall spotted the golden moment for fun, and turned the hose on Aidan instead of the truck. Stunned at first, Aidan then threw his bucket of soapy water at Niall; soon both boys were drenched and engaged in battle.

Mr. Donoghue came out of the barn to see what all the commotion was about, turned the hose off and announced, "I see I'll get no work out of you two today. Why don't you take yourselves down to the lough, and see if that old boat of ours still holds water."

The lough at the end of the Donoghues' farm was small, but deep and broad enough for rowing and swimming. An old wooden rowboat rested, overturned, on an outcropping of rocks next to the lough, tied to an iron stake that had long ago been driven into the ground. Niall ran his hands and eyes along the bottom of the boat now, found no obvious holes or problems and, with Aidan's help, turned the boat right side up. He then tossed in the bag of sandwiches and fruit his mother had provided and set the boat afloat, climbing in after Aidan. When they reached the center of the lough, they set the oars inside the boat and let it drift at will as the gentle waves directed.

Niall gazed at the hills surrounding them, the pastures where his father's sheep grazed, the farm he'd grown up on, how sun and shadow filled the contours of the green hills surrounding the lough, and the occasional ripple of waves that danced on the lough's clear blue water when a slight breeze stirred.

"Life doesn't get any better than this," he said at last.

"It is a bit of heaven," Aidan agreed, watching swallows play overhead. He loved the chatter between them, and how their metallic blue-green bodies glistened in the sun. He spotted a large old house on the opposite shore. "Whose place is that?"

Niall looked toward where Aidan was pointing. "That's the Gallagher house. Been there a hundred fifty years, I believe."

"It looks empty now."

"It is. The owner passed on a while back, no one's been there since. We'll ask my mam about it tonight, she knows more about the story."

"So this really is your own private lough."

"For now, yes." Niall opened up the lunch sack, fished out ham and cheese sandwiches and packages of crisps for them both, and handed half of them to Aidan. They ate in silence, the only sounds interrupting their quiet reverie were the chattering swallows with their aerial display, Farley's bark in the distance, and the waves occasionally breaking against the boat.

"You've eaten better out here," Niall observed as Aidan finished his sandwich. "You're looking better too."

Aidan considered the contrast from just a week earlier. "When you're at bottom, anything's an improvement!"

"The countryside agrees with you."

Aidan fixed his eyes on the solitary oak in the field across from him.

"You know, our farm's not too far from the studio we record at. You should just stay here until we're done with the next album. We could work on some new songs together." Niall caught the look on Aidan's face. "What's wrong?"

Aidan avoided Niall's look, and focused instead on the wood planks on the boat's bottom, noting the different shades of wood and varying grains and knots. "I don't know if I'm staying with the group."

"What?" Niall demanded so loud it echoed across the pond and the surrounding hills.

Aidan looked back at the oak tree and shrugged, "I don't think I care about music anymore."

The way Aidan said this, detached, distant, scared Niall. "You can't walk away from it. It's in your blood. Aidan, you live and breathe music. Look at all the times you practice while the rest of us are grabbing lunch or dinner, all the new techniques you try, all the different sounds and styles you experiment with. You know music's always been your great passion. You wouldn't be happy doing anything else. You can't leave us either. We need you." The last truth hit Niall to the core. Even if someone else stepped in, the vibrancy and enthusiasm Aidan brought to Macready's Bridge would be missing; their music would feel empty, their job that much less fun.

Now Aidan looked straight at Niall. "I don't know if I can do it any more. My dad—" he drew a deep breath and studied the clear blue waves slapping against the boat. "It was always for him, all the songs, they were the bond between us. I don't think I can play my guitar without him."

There. It was out. The deepest fear, the hardest truth. For weeks now he'd carried it inside, afraid to admit it to himself or anyone else. Now the words were out, yet he didn't feel any better. He only felt empty, and alone even though Niall was there.

"Your father would want you to go on playing."

"Well he's gone and left me, so he doesn't get a vote."

They had grown too serious, Niall realized. He had to do something to lighten the mood. He chose the only sure thing he could think of; he dropped an oar in the water then stood up to retrieve it, letting the boat rock out of control till it capsized and he and Aidan landed in the cold lough. They both laughed, once the shock of cold water passed, then turned the boat right side, shot huge waves at each other, raced each other swimming, then stretched out in the grass and let the hot sun dry them.

As he lay there, half asleep, Niall wondered, what if his family had been killed in an accident instead of Aidan's? Would he find living on the farm intolerable? He doubted it; he drew his strength and peace from the farm, from the quiet solitude and the soft landscape surrounding it. The steady, predictable routine here anchored him and filled his days with purpose. How much would that change if his parents were gone? Would he lose his passion for life? He didn't think so, but he was no longer sure.

Aidan lay on the grass face down, inhaling the clean scent of earth, letting the sun penetrate through clothes and skin down into the very core of his body and soul. Its energy radiated through every cell in his body, filling him with a sense of wholeness he had not experienced in months. He pondered this feeling, and Niall's words, and the truth he had finally exposed. Niall was right, of course. His father would want- no, expect- him to go on with music and with life. The shock of the accident was wearing off now; deep down, where the sun reached the deepest part of his heart, Aidan knew it was time to start stepping back into life. If only he knew how. Lying on the grass, with the sun bleaching everything clean inside him, and the sound of swallows chattering overhead, with thoughts of Mrs. Donoghue's steak pie for dinner that night, and of a peaceful night in a house where others slept, Aidan knew this was the place to start figuring things out.

"Mam, could you tell us about the Gallagher house?" Niall asked over dinner that evening. "Aidan was wondering about it."

Mr. Donoghue sat back and relished the light that spread across his wife's face as her mind traveled decades back.

"The Gallagher house? Oh, that's a grand place! When I was young, I used to walk past it on my way home from school with my friends Sheila and Irene. Oh, the dreams we had of that place, and of young David Gallagher! Several years older than us he was, but that didn't stop us having our dreams." She glanced across the table to her husband, eyes full of love, and continued, handing out seconds of steak pie as she spoke.

"Quite an estate that was back then, horses, sheep, lavish gardens, and oh, the parties they'd throw! I always dreamed of going to one of their parties."

"What happened to the place?" Aidan asked.

"The family fell on hard times. Old Mr. Gallagher, his heart gave out, and Mrs. Gallagher not too far behind. David, well, he was a bit of a playboy, too loose with the money till it all ran out, and then he just disappeared. I heard a couple years back that he died down in London, some kind of industrial accident."

With a start, Mrs. Donoghue pulled herself back to the present. "That's all in the past. The house stands empty now, waiting for a new owner, although for the amount of work she needs there's not a long line of interested parties. Now, who's for some of my berry pie?"

Later that night, after Niall and Aidan had both gone to bed, as they sat in the kitchen with their nighttime tea, Will asked, "Was I a letdown compared to your David?"

Anna stopped stirring her tea and looked into her husband's deep green eyes. "He was only a dream. You're the one I married." She retrieved the last biscuit and jar of quince jam from the counter and set them in front of Will. "And you don't see me looking to change things, now do you?"

He smiled, and drew her down to sit on his lap. "I do love the bones of you."

She laughed softly but didn't move. "Did you see Aidan at dinner tonight? A full plate of seconds he ate. First time he's eaten that much."

"Aye. He's settling down well. Steady hands tonight, too."

"It would be nice if he stayed the summer with us."

"He'll want to be getting home soon enough, but we can keep him a little bit longer."

"We can always keep him and Niall busy with the patio plans."

"Ah, woman, you and your patio plans," Will teased, squeezing her waist and making her laugh more. "Will you never give up?"

"You were right about where you planted the roses," Anna admitted. "Now they're in, don't you think a pretty new table and chairs would look grand?"

"And a fountain," he added. "Don't forget the splash of a fountain!"

"Ah, ye'r that cruel, you are." She rose from his lap and slapped his arm. He laughed, but later that night, after they had folded themselves into bed, she facing him, he watching her soft face, relaxed as she slept, wondering what dreams she still carried inside her large heart, Will determined to set up that patio so it was everything she wanted and more.

The next day he designed a trellis of wood beams that would arch over their patio, recalling a similar trellis Anna had admired the summer before in a garden in town. With Niall and Aidan helping, cutting boards, securing posts, and anchoring the boards to them, the trellis was done in two days. Mr. Donoghue found jasmine plants through Maggie's husband Dan, and planted them while Anna was at market one day. It would take them years to provide the thick, fragrant cover he knew Anna wanted; in the meantime, he would dress the boards with her other dream design, strings of fairy lights intertwined along the posts, interwoven around the top boards. This he did while she attended her monthly ladies meeting at church.

The day after the lights went up, Mr. Donoghue disappeared for several hours with the truck.

"Honest, Mam, I've no idea where he's gone," Niall swore. "He said something about a load of hay, but that can't be right, we've got plenty out in the barn."

He returned just before dinner, with a tarp tied tightly over the back of the truck blocking any view of what the truck held. At dinner, all he would say was, "Remember curiosity's cat."

The next morning, Mr. Donoghue gathered Niall and Aidan together out by the field. "I need you to distract your mam for the day. Take her sightseeing somewhere, or off to a movie, or shopping."

Niall eyed his father with suspicion. "What are you up to, Dad?"

"Be back for dinner. All will be revealed then."

"She'll not be easy to distract a whole day."

"You'll have to find a way. Here, take her into Omagh, to that dress shop she likes." He handed Niall some money.

"Well I'm stumped," Niall told Aidan as they walked back to the house. "He never just hands money over like that."

"Whatever he's up to must mean a lot to him."

"I guess."

"You know it's my laundry day," Mrs. Donoghue protested when Niall and Aidan suggested shopping. "We can go tomorrow."

Aidan sighed, feeling guilty at the deceit he was about to pull. "It would do me good. I don't quite feel up to working today."

She studied his feigned tired look, glanced over at the concern Niall had filled his eyes with, and finally relented. "I'll go for a few hours, but I need to be back in the afternoon so the whole day's not lost."

Omagh held many attractions, though, and Mrs. Donoghue found the time slip by faster than she thought, as they took her to the dress shop, where she found a soft blue sweater Niall insisted matched her beautiful eyes. They treated her to lunch, then distracted her in a home interior shop where she found a reading lamp she thought would fit their living room just right.

"It's so much money though," she lamented, eyeing the price tag.

"My treat, mam." Niall pulled out the money his father had given him.

Aidan put his hand out to stop Niall. "No, let me." To Mrs. Donoghue he said, "You've all been so good to me, letting me stay as long as I have, getting me back on my feet. I'd really be happy if you let me buy this for you."

She protested, but Aidan won out, and they drove home with the lamp nestled between them in the car.

"Look at the time! I've not only lost the day, but dinner will be late and your father will not be happy."

Niall winked at Aidan. "Bet he won't mind when he sees you in that lovely blue sweater."

Niall pulled their car into the yard, Mrs. Donoghue walked out back to let her husband know she'd be starting dinner, and stopped in her tracks, Niall and Aidan frozen behind her.

There Mr. Donoghue stood, fairy lights twinkling over the patio, steaks slowly roasting on a new grill, new table and chairs gleaming in the soft light, and the sound of a fountain splashing off to the side by a cement bench.

"Oh Will." Anna stood, transfixed.

"You'll not be thinking of David Gallagher tonight, will you Anna?" His eyes twinkled as he drew her into his arms.

"I haven't thought of him since the day I married you!"

They all dined on grilled steak and potatoes out on the patio, amused when sparrows found the fountain and splashed about. Niall and Aidan watched as Niall's parents danced to Kenny G music playing on the cd player Mr. Donoghue had brought out. A fleeting vision of his parents standing close, turning slow circles like that flew across Aidan's mind; he let it pass without tracking it further as he once would have.

Then it was Niall's turn to dance with his mother. As they did, Mr. Donoghue watched, eyes bright with pride and love. "You and Niall could not have made our Anna happier with the work you've done here. She's dreamed of this patio all these years, she'll be beaming for months now it's done."

"You did all the hard work. We just followed your directions with the trellis and roses," Aidan pointed out. "Most of the credit goes to you." Then, eyes fixed on the way the small bright lights sparkled in the night, he said, "I'll be going home tomorrow."

Mr. Donoghue studied the boy, how he swallowed hard and kept his hands pressed tight against his knees. He'd come a long way in two weeks' time, but still had far to go. "You're welcome to stay on here."

"Thank you, but it's time I looked after my own place."

"You're family now," Mr. Donoghue stated. "You're welcome any time. Even if our Niall's away, we'd be glad to have you come out."

Aidan nodded, "Thanks."

Wishing he could impart some great words of wisdom that would carry Aidan through once he returned home, Mr. Donoghue repeated the words his own father had always used, "Life doesn't always give us easy roads, but we've plenty of tools at hand to help smooth the way if we think to use them."

To him the words sounded hollow, inadequate; but Aidan promised, "I'll remember that."

11

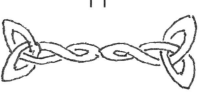

Twelve.

Aidan turned from his side to his back in his bed at home. After so many nights of deep, healing sleep at Niall's house, he thought he'd try his own bed now. At first the soft, familiar blankets felt cozy and comforting; an hour later, they were tangled in a ball as he tossed and turned, unable to relax. His own bed felt foreign and uncomfortable. At the counting of hours chiming from the living room wall clock, he changed positions and tried again to sleep.

One.

The clock's soft chime marked another hour's passing. Aidan turned from his back to his other side, pummeled his pillow into a new shape, and squeezed his eyes shut, demanding sleep to take over.

Two.

Frustrated, Aidan threw his blankets off and stomped his feet on his bedroom's hardwood floor. "Forget this," he announced to the walls, grabbed his pillow, and stormed downstairs. Maybe he'd have better luck on the sofa.

Three.

The late night movie hadn't lulled him to sleep, the sofa was hard and too narrow compared to the bed in the Donoghue's guest room. Noise from occasional cars driving by kept him awake. Or was it the walls closing in on him, suffocating him, sucking all of the air out of the house? Or the weight of the whole house on his shoulders?

This is ridiculous, Aidan thought, sitting up. I might as well get up and do something constructive.

"Malin Head."

The words rang out as clear as if someone had spoken them. Aidan listened hard and heard again, "Malin Head. Sunrise."

Of course. Four or five times over the last two years Aidan and his father had risen early, left his grandmother and sister asleep, and driven up the Inishowen Peninsula to Malin Head, the peninsula's northernmost point, where waves broke in steady procession against rocks, with only shorebirds and a few farm animals to watch as a soft gold sun turned grey dawn to lavender, then orange-pink, then bright daylight. Neither of them spoke, afraid to break the magic spell as a new day was born. On the drive home, they would each discuss their plans for the day, but with subdued voices, awed by the wondrous display they'd seen. Those early morning sunrises were a precious gift, a special bond only the two of them shared.

"Go to Malin Head." The words echoed in his heart now, compelling him to get dressed and start out.

Driving out of Derry, the mist that surrounded his car grew more dense. He drove with caution, following the small glimpse of road visible to him, sure the mist would lift by the time he reached the isolated point where land met sea. When he was sure he'd reached the right spot, he turned left. The fog increased, enclosing him in a thick grey shroud as he advanced over hills and through winding bends in the road.

He'd driven too far, he was sure; too much time had passed. His dashboard clock showed five twenty. He should have reached Malin Head a half hour earlier, even with the slower pace he'd been forced to keep. He peered for any recognizable landmark the mist might reveal. The farther he went, the more lost he felt. He thought to turn back, but found the fog had blocked the road behind as well as ahead.

A loud thud shook his car and the steering became hard. Aidan maneuvered the car to a patch of ground off the road, shut the engine off and stepped outside to find the front right tire flat.

He searched his pockets, came up empty and remembered his phone was still on his dresser. "Too early to wake anyone, even if a house could be found," he told his car. He slid back into the car to wait for daylight.

With the mist closing in around him and nothing to distract, Aidan's mind fell back over the weeks before, the peace of Niall's family's farm, how relaxing the open air and the presence of others had been. He thought back to the beach at Gweebarra, the sea air and constant waves, the beauty of it mixed with emptiness. He saw Fionna again, copper hair shining, smooth skin and delicate jasmine fragrance tantalizing, how they'd reached the deepest need in each other yet even that felt wrong. He wondered where she was now and if she had found peace.

He thought back to Niagara Falls, a moment missed, just as he'd missed the sunrise now. How fast his life had changed, one phone call erasing all the fun and laughter, replacing it with too much sorrow and too much silence, their combined weight as heavy as the mist that surrounded him now, obliterating the calmness he'd known at the Donoghue's farm.

"Maybe Niall's right. Maybe I should spend the summer with him. Maybe I should just sell the house and move out there altogether."

The mist didn't answer.

Tired of silence, Aidan lashed out. "Da, could you give me a clue? Any sign at all?"

Silence echoed around him.

All the anger and hurt that had built up inside Aidan since the accident rose up like a sudden storm, crashing against his inner shore. He exploded, "You promised you'd always be with me, remember? After Mom died, you promised you'd never leave me. You lied! You're gone; you're all gone. Well the hell with you all! I don't need you. I'll figure it all out myself."

Aidan bolted out of the car, slammed the door shut, and strode off. In the mist he had no idea where he headed; he didn't care, he just needed to move. Twice he stumbled over rocks; in his rage he kicked at them and continued his furious pace.

He guessed he'd walked a half hour. By then his anger had eased and the mist had started to lift. Faint shadows appeared, a shrub, a tree, telephone wires, then, at last, a house. He heard voices, man and woman, then they appeared in their driveway as the mist rose another degree.

"Excuse me," he called out. "Could I use your phone? My car's a ways back, she's had a blowout, I've left my phone at home."

The elderly man eyed Aidan head to toe, and glanced at the woman, his wife Aidan thought. She eyed him as well, and nodded back.

"I can lend you more than a phone. Let's drive back to your car and see if we can get her fixed."

With the mist dissipating quickly now, Aidan could see the path he'd walked to find help had been much more crooked and long than it would have been if he'd been able to find and stick to the road.

"That's the way of the mist, isn't it now?" The man, who'd introduced himself as Tadgh, remarked. "Always hides the paths we're meant to take. Sure you wouldn't have suffered a blow out if you'd been able to see clear ahead."

"I'm sure I wouldn't have," Aidan agreed, handing Tadgh the jack they'd located to raise the car up. Tadgh worked with skillful, economical movement, in no time replacing the damaged tire with the healthy spare.

""I don't know how to thank you." Aidan said when Tadgh's work was done, "I've left my money at home, but I'll stop by later to repay you."

Tadgh waived him off, "There's never a charge for helping a fellow being out. You know, entertaining angels unaware and all."

Aidan gave a slight grin, "I'm no angel, just a fool for heading out when I can't see where I'm going."

"Haven't we all at one time or another?" Tadgh shook Aidan's hand. "Safe home to you, boy."

Always hiding the path. As Aidan returned home, he recalled Tadgh's words. To him they reflected more than the mist he'd tried so unsuccessfully to drive through; they described his life, trying to find his way through each day without his family to guide and anchor him. He remembered the angry words he'd shouted to the air around him. A wave of guilt washed over him at their remembrance. "Da, I'm sorry. I know you're there. I shouldn't have said what I did. It's just, sometimes this is such a hard road. I wish I could get an answer back when I talk to you is all."

The next day Mack called, "Just checking in with you, how are you feeling?"

"Fine." Aidan hoped his tiredness didn't come through over the phone. "Paying bills and sorting through paperwork today."

When Patrick called an hour later, Aidan reported, "I'm doing fine. Laundry now, then off to market."

To Michael's query an hour later, he replied, "Cleaning the house."

By the time Niall called Aidan said, "You all need to work out a system. One of you call each day, and report back to the others."

"A little bit much, are we?" Niall laughed.

"Too right!"

Niall spread the word, and a system was set in place. By the time Patrick's turn came a few days later, he noted the strain in Aidan's voice.

"What's going on?" he asked, concerned.

"Nothing," Aidan started, but he could never lie to Patrick. "It's a little hard sleeping, that's all. Honest, everything else is okay."

"You promised to come out for a visit. How about this weekend?" When Aidan hesitated Patrick added, "Conor and Caitlyn won't give me a moment's rest until you come see them."

"As long as Jack and Rita don't mind. I just got home, after all."

"They won't mind, they'll do anything to help you out."

"You're right, they would. Okay, I'll be out Saturday morning."

Two days later, with Conor and Caitlyn both covered in flaming red spots, Patrick had to call the visit off. "Measles," he reported to Aidan. "I'm afraid we'll have to postpone."

Aidan understood, but Patrick still worried. He picked the phone back up and dialed Michael's number. "I wonder if you could do us a favor."

"If I can, sure." Michael listened as Patrick explained his concern, the measles, and the postponed visit. "I've got a friend with a boat," Michael told him. "I'll see if I can borrow it, and talk Aidan into a fishing excursion."

"Thanks. I owe you."

"You do, and I'll keep after you till you've paid up!"

Aidan sat on the bench his grandmother had installed in their backyard and surveyed the garden. What had long been his grandmother's pride and joy was now smothered with weeds and spent blossoms. Where did one even start to create order out of such chaos? He could pull weeds easy enough, if he worked all week, and trim back the honeysuckle, but he was clueless how to rescue her beloved roses, which now showed black spots and some kind of bug bites on their leaves. He knew he was in way over his head on them. He had pulled out the box of garden products his grandmother kept and was trying to make sense of which solution was used for what, and when, when Michael called.

"What are you up to?"

"Trying to save my granny's roses. What do you use for black spot, and what the hell is powdery mildew?"

Michael was clueless. "Damned if I know."

"Fat lot of help you are!" Aidan set the box aside.

214

"Thanks. I hear your trip out to Patrick's was canceled."

"Pretty crafty of him persuading the kiddies to come down with measles just so he wouldn't have to put up with me, wouldn't you say?"

Michael laughed, "That Patrick, he's a smart one. What are you going to do now?"

"You mean aside from killing my gran's gardens?" Aidan asked, attempting humor; but Michael heard the underlying tension in Aidan's voice and understood Patrick's concern.

"Yeah. How would you like a week in Southern France? A friend of mine has a place we can use."

Aidan considered Michael's proposal. "That's a great idea, except for one little thing."

"We don't speak French?"

"That's the one! How do you think we should buy food? Show them pictures?"

Michael laughed along with Aidan. "I think there's a neighbor who speaks English."

Aidan laughed harder. "So we ring the neighbor every time we want a meal?"

"Okay, bad plan," Michael admitted. "How about a week on a boat?"

Now Aidan was intrigued. "Go on."

"Another friend of mine has a boat over in Lough Erne he said we could use."

"Can you manage a boat better than you can speak French?"

"Marginally."

"You realize there's great potential for disaster here."

"I know." Michael heard the sound of adventure in Aidan's voice, and matched it with his own. "Are you game?"

"Beats sitting here watching the roses die!"

The next morning, Michael and Aidan met at the dock in Enniskillen.

"That's my friend, Hugh, standing next to his boat at the end."

Aidan looked where Michael pointed, to a man standing in front of the largest boat Aidan had ever seen. "That boat?" he asked, incredulous. "We're going out on that?"

"Yeah, why?"

"Michael, that's not a boat, that's a wee house!"

"It looks bigger than it actually is," Michael insisted. Upon reaching the boat, though, Aidan was still overwhelmed.

"That's quite a boat," he told Hugh. "Are you sure you want to take a chance lending it to us?"

"Michael's been out on her before." Hugh cast a raised eyebrow to Michael. "If you go slow with her you'll be fine."

Michael saluted Hugh. "Slow. Right, Captain. Got it."

As they stepped below to store their gear away, Aidan poked Michael's back and whispered, with even greater awe, "A whole week on this boat, and we could almost never run into each other."

Aidan chose the front cabin, leaving Michael the more spacious back bedroom. The cruiser's light wood trim and many windows made it feel to Aidan almost as spacious as the outdoors at Niall's farm. As Hugh walked them through various operational and safety steps, Aidan again felt the freedom of openness compared to the closed in house he'd left behind. Hugh left them a map with notes on which places along the upper and lower loughs were best for restocking provisions and anchoring overnight and the best fishing and sightseeing spots he'd discovered, left his phone number with them, wished them luck, and then left them on their own.

Michael backed the boat away from the dock, and guided it with great care along the shoreline of Upper Lough Erne. Through layers of fat white clouds, a soft blue sky covered them. Twice they stopped the engine and drifted with the waves, enjoying the peaceful view and quiet waters. As dusk settled over the water and lights appeared on boats and on homes on shore, they set anchor and sat down to a meal of ham sandwiches and potato salad.

"Tomorrow I'll brave cooking us a hot meal," Michael promised as he opened a bottle of Pinot Grigio.

Aidan took a bite out of his sandwich and watched the lough reflect orange, then purple, then grey as the sun sank lower and lower. "I have to get a better class of friends."

Michael pulled his eyes from the setting sun. "What do you mean?"

"Look at you. A friend with a villa in France, another with a boat on a lough, and not a tiny boat at that; the most my friends can offer is a free pint, and that only once in a while."

Michael didn't recall Aidan ever saying much about the friends he grew up with. "What are your friends doing now?"

"Ben's a loan specialist with a bank, and Brendan and Kieran both work loading freight. Tim's gone into seminary to be a priest."

"A priest?"

"Yeah. Funny, when we were in school he was always the one skipping out on Mass and giving the nuns grief. God only knows what kind of priest he'll be."

"I don't know, but I think you just trumped the French villa and the boat," Michael refilled their wine glasses.

Aidan handed the potato salad dish back to Michael to finish. "Really?"

"You've got an 'in' with God!"

Aidan didn't respond. God was far away anymore, blocked by a wall of anger Aidan felt towards him.

Michael followed Aidan's gaze over the stilled lake to the sun slipping closer to the water. "Ah, friends. Where would we be in life without them?"

Aidan raised his wine glass. "To friends."

They chose to explore Upper Lough Erne first, leaving the lower lough to more experienced boaters better able to navigate its deeper waters. Mornings they would watch the sun paint the lough's blue waters with varying patterns of light and color, listen to terns and grebes call to their mates and offspring, and then study charting maps over tea while they laid out their day's plans.

As they guided the boat through the lough's many secret inlets, swans appeared at almost every turn. Aidan tried not to think of how his granny would love to see them, or how he'd love to explore the coastline by canoe with Jeannie, as he watched canoers drift by, or how grand the peaceful pleasure of fishing these waters with his father would be. Instead, he watched the multiple water skiers and asked Michael, "Have you ever tried that?"

"Do I look suicidal?" Michael responded.

Aidan raised an eyebrow. "No, demented maybe, but suicidal, no."

Michael ate some of the leftover ham and potato salad that served as lunch. "Have you ever gone diving?"

Aidan shook his head, "No."

"What about snorkeling?"

"Nope. I like to stay on top of the water, not below it. What about you?"

"I went snorkeling off Bermuda a few years back. It was amazing, all the colors of the different fishes, all the varieties. I think you'd enjoy it."

Aidan peered into the water surrounding them. "I think all you'd find under here are eels, and I'd just as soon not know about them."

"Good point. Hey, have you ever been to Devenish Island?"

Aidan glanced at the map Michael pointed to, and Hugh's note next to it, "ancient ruins."

"Years ago. I was probably twelve."

"Oh." Michael sounded disappointed.

"I'd go back again. Do you want to check it out tomorrow?"

The next day they steered the boat through the narrow channel that connects Lower and Upper Lough Erne, and reached Trory and the ferry to Devenish Island. The minute Aidan stepped from the ferry onto the island, he felt he did not walk alone. Others accompanied him, not just fellow visitors who followed the paths from priory to cemetery, from cemetery to round tower, and then on to the church. Each step of the way, whispers rose from the ground he walked on and filled the air around him. He could feel the souls of the early Christians who settled on Devenish, and even St. Molaise himself, all trying to reach him with the same message.

"Faith."

One word, whispered over and over, rang in his ears and echoed in his heart. The ornamental high cross spoke it. The cemetery stones called it out. The round tower's highest window, offering gazes across lough and hill, and glimpses across time to an era when Viking raids threatened the monastic community, screamed out "Faith."

Blended in with all those rocks and vistas and souls, Aidan could hear his grandmother's strong, sweet voice. "Faith, boy. Life always comes down to faith."

"Never ceases to amaze me."

Michael's voice beside him made Aidan jump. "What?"

"Scared you, did I?" Michael laughed, then repeated, "It never ceases to amaze me, how old some of these ruins are, how they've survived weather and time." He pointed to the round tower, pencil tip cap pointing skyward as tall and straight as it had for centuries, scarcely a scar or age mark on it.

Aidan studied the fragments of walls that remained of the old priory. "Just like the ruins of Dunluce Castle. They show wear and tear, sure, but they're still standing. I've always wondered what holds the half walls up when the other half of them is gone."

"I've always wondered the same. I once saw the slimmest of ruins, two walls at the corner where they met, just that corner remained, pointing up like a finger in the sky." Michael laughed again. "It looked like that old corner was flipping the bird at any force that tried to defeat it!"

Aidan watched the sun light the interior of the lone remaining arch in the walls. "There's something to these ruins," he agreed. "Some invisible strength."

Invisible strength. The words echoed through Aidan's mind. As they rolled around, he recalled where he'd heard them.

He was four weeks past the accident, past the funerals, deep into trying to find his way through the weight and darkness that had fallen upon his house and his life.

"It's a visit with God you're needing," Rita had told him that morning over tea and scones, seeing the turmoil in his eyes.

"That's just what Gran would say." Rita had sounded so much like his gran he'd been unable to stop the tears rising.

"Listen to her. She was very wise. Go find a quiet place and have a long heart to heart with God."

A quiet place. Aidan had laughed inside at the irony of the statement. He was surrounded by quiet to the point where quiet was smothering him. God didn't seem to be in that quiet place. Still, Aidan followed Rita's advice, and later that day stepped into the church he'd grown up in. The church was weekday empty. Aidan's footsteps on the floor reverberated off the empty pews and walls. Rays of light shining through stained glass windows cast red, blue and purple shafts of dust motes.

His family always sat on the right, five rows from the front. He slid into that pew, and for one brief moment could feel their presence around him. He could see his grandmother stepping forward to receive communion, his father kneeling, head bent, rosary between his hands, deep in prayer. He remembered a dozen times Jeannie had sat next to him, the two of them teasing each other until their grandmother's stern look forced proper behavior upon them.

When he was young, Aidan's faith was as deep as his grandmother's and father's; over the years it continued in varying degrees. But now? God felt as far away as Saturn, as loving and concerned as the stone walls that surrounded Derry. If He was so loving, why had He left Aidan alone? If He was all-powerful, why hadn't He stopped the accident from happening? Faith had been so easy when he was young. Why was it, now when he needed God most, God seemed farthest away?

Aidan studied the colorful windows, oil paintings and marble statues that filled the wall spaces around him. All his life he'd been drawn to their beauty. The vibrant colors of the stained glass windows and the rich oil paintings brought life to ancient Bible stories, made iconic characters and their legendary faith real and had long inspired him to strive for their steadfastness. The life-sized statues of St. Columba and St. Brigid and the altars of Mary and the Sacred Heart of Jesus had done the same.

Now the windows and paintings seemed lifeless and the statues were nothing but cold, hard marble. Even the brilliant painting of Jesus' Ascension over the main altar seemed just that, a flat, lifeless painting, a fairy tale.

Aidan had no idea how long he'd sat there willing the artwork around him to come to life and prove him wrong. After a while a door opened, footsteps approached, and Father Nelligan himself slid into the pew in front of Aidan.

"How are you?"

"Fine," Aidan had lied, knowing he wasn't fooling the priest.

"What brings you here today?"

Aidan chewed his lip, sorting his words with great care. "I don't know where God is. God's supposed to be loving, but I don't feel that love. Why did He take them? Why did He leave me behind?"

Father Nelligan didn't offer the standard, "It was His will," or the equally empty, "It's part of His plan." Instead, he looked Aidan square in the eyes and said, "I don't know."

"So much for comfort from the church," Aidan muttered.

"Aidan, you didn't come here seeking comfort. You came here seeking truth."

In that, Father Nelligan was right.

"I wish I had answers for why life moves as it does, all the twists and turns, all the pain. I'm not God, though. I see one tiny corner of a huge canvas God is painting." Father Nelligan watched to see if his words were sinking in. Relieved to find Aidan listening hard, he continued. "God does love you, and I'm sure He has a reason that you're here without the rest of your family. There are many times in life we can't see the whys and wherefores of the road we're on. All we can do is stay the course until life turns our way again."

"How do we do that?" Aidan tried to keep the edge out of his voice.

"Faith." Aidan cast a blank look his way, and Father Nelligan explained, "Believe that God knows the road you're on and will make things work out somehow in the end. It's what gives us the invisible strength that keeps us going."

Was that the secret Aidan had hoped to find, the key that explained why, after losing his mother, his father still believed in God; why his grandmother, after losing an infant child, after losing her husband, had still moved through life with an air of laughter and an open heart? Is that what kept God alive in a city that had seen so much pain, in a land where famine and emigration had stolen so many descendants? Aidan couldn't answer that question any more after he left than he could before. The church still felt cold with its hard marble and wood, but sunlight seemed to shine a bit brighter through the windows, casting rainbow patterns on the walls.

Michael's poke in his ribs brought Aidan back to Devenish Island. "Are you here?"

"Huh? Oh! I'm sorry. I guess I got caught up in history."

"If you want history, Italy's the place you should go." As they returned to the ferry, and then to their boat, Michael talked of the Colosseum, the Piazza, St. Peter's, the Vatican, and the many intoxicating sights and senses of Rome.

"Do you think you'd ever move to Italy?" Aidan asked that evening, as they watched storm clouds build in the west, while dining on trout they'd caught earlier.

Michael had waited for the right moment to tell Aidan his news, and seized it now. "No, but I'll go there for my honeymoon."

Aidan almost dropped his wine glass. "Your what?"

"Honeymoon. You know, that trip you take after your wedding." He enjoyed watching Aidan's face register shock, then amazement, then joy. "Susannah and I, we're engaged."

"When did that happen?"

"A few weeks ago."

"Do the others know?"

"No. You're the first one I've told." Michael studied the waves that rocked the boat at gentle intervals. "I don't know why I waited to say anything. It's not something I'm trying to hide; I'm happier than I've ever been."

There. The first time he'd said that, and as Michael realized the truth of his words, he could feel the excitement spread through his body, gathering in his heart till he thought he'd explode for joy.

"I don"t know why you're not shouting it from the rooftops. Susannah's gorgeous, real class, although what's she doing with the likes of you I'll never know."

"She's blinded by my charm, of course."

"That must be it." Aidan saw how even Michael's eyes smiled as he spoke of Susannah. "I always thought you'd be the last holdout for marriage. Not that Susannah's not worth throwing in the towel for; I just thought you had years in you before you took that road."

Michael emptied his wine glass and refilled his and Aidan's. "I thought so too. Do you want to know what changed my mind?"

"Sure."

"You and your family."

Aidan eyed Michael, curious. "How did we change your mind?"

"I've always admired, no, been jealous of, the closeness and love I've seen with you and your family. I know it hurts now, but you had something real, something I've always wanted. I want that same closeness and love, and I want it with Susannah."

Don't go down that road, Aidan ordered himself. Don't think about what you've lost.

To Michael, Aidan said, "You and Susannah are a good fit. I can see you both being very happy together."

"Do you really think so?"

"I do."

"What about you?"

Aidan's fork stopped midair. "What? Get married?"

"Of course not. Who would have you?" Michael teased. "No, move away from Ireland. Do you think you ever would?"

He didn't need time to think. "No. Never. It's where my heart beats and my air comes from. I'll always live in Ireland."

Michael raised his wine glass. "To Ireland."

Aidan raised his in response. "To Susannah and Italy. I hope they're both everything you've dreamed of."

It was no good. Aidan knew that after they'd docked the boat at Enniskillen, as gathering storm clouds converged and hard winds rocked the boat side to side, as rain lashed against the boat's frame. As he and Michael both settled on their beds to ride the storm out in sleep, Aidan realized the trip was no good. Oh, the time with Michael was grand; they'd always gotten along well, and the boat, with its rich appointments, smooth handling, sleek lines and spacious cabin, was any man's dream. Still, unlike the time he'd spent at Niall's, where the constant work gave him little time to let his thoughts wander, now he had nothing but time to think. Aidan's mind churned with the same force as the storm that raged outside, fueled by memories Michael's revelation had brought forth. He'd tried so hard, but the black hole that sucked in everything around it was too large. He couldn't escape it, no matter what he tried or where he went. He knew that now.

If he couldn't live without his family, what then?

If they couldn't be with him, could he be with them?

The thought scared him the minute it struck.

Then it drew him in. He examined it like the seashells and sea glass he'd gathered at Gweebarra, studied every angle, every shift of pattern and light. The more he examined it, the more appealing the idea became. The only decision was where, and how?

He'd been to Slieve League once before, two years earlier with his family. While Jeannie and his grandmother were content to stop at the first observation platform and study the cliffs from there, he and his father had ventured farther, climbing the steps alongside the edge. The high cliffs spread out before them, smoky blue with tan and brown markings, rising straight and tall from the rocks and sea below. The wood railing that held him and his father back did not seem strong enough to keep them safe as wind buffeted them, challenging them to hold their ground. They'd gazed at the cliffs from a safe distance, not testing the railing's stability.

Slieve League drew him like a magnet now, and Aidan formed his plan. He would finish the boat trip with Michael, wrap up a few loose ends with Mr. Maloney, leave a note for Jack and Rita, then drive out to Slieve League. From the highest edge he'd let the wind carry him; soon he'd be reunited with his family and his torment would be over.

While Aidan shaped his plans, the boat's rocking and creaking lulled him to sleep. In his dream, he stood at the same observation point at Slieve League as he'd been with his father. Windswept waves met the rocky shore below, mesmerizing him. He would focus on their ebb and flow, then step out to become one with them. As he crouched to duck under the safety railing, a hand on his arm pulled him back.

"Don't do it, boy."

Stunned, Aidan turned to face the person who'd foiled his plan. "How did you know?"

The figure didn't explain, only repeated, "Don't do it. You have much to live for."

"I don't. It's too hard. It hurts too much."

"It's not your time."

Shocked, Aidan suddenly recognized the figure to be that of his father, now fading from sight. As he disappeared, Aidan heard him call out, "Make me proud. Have faith. Follow your heart."

Aidan woke, shaken by how real the dream felt. He felt cold and clammy, trembling in his flesh and spirit. He knew he would never carry his plan out. His father had stopped him.

Follow your heart, his father had said.

What did his heart say?

The storm outside had ended. The rising sun sent faint golden fingers through the windows by his bed, inviting him out. He rose, moving as quiet as he could so he didn't wake Michael who still snored in his sleep. Aidan climbed the stairs to the deck outside. The lough before him shimmered clean silver-blue in the sun.

What did his heart want? Peace? An end to pain? Something to fill his emptiness?

Aidan wanted all of these. More than these, still shaken by his plan and his dream, Aidan knew what his heart wanted most.

"I want to live, Da. But please, don't leave me alone."

Sun streaming in his face and the smell of bacon frying woke Michael. He blinked, yawned, stretched, and yawned again before stumbling into the galley, rubbing his coarse whiskers and his stomach as he walked.

"If you're cooking, I'll take two eggs over easy, potatoes, toast, bacon, and tomatoes," he called out to Aidan as he slid along the table's bench seat.

"Are ye sure that's enough?"

As he watched Aidan fry potatoes and eggs and extra slices of bacon, Michael noticed a difference in his movements that was hard to name. Relaxed? Settled? They carried plates and fresh cups of tea topside and ate in the warm sun. Even Aidan's eyes seemed different, Michael thought, like some shadow had left them.

A heron glided just above the water alongside their boat in search of fish, so close they could hear the swish of its majestic wings and see its feet tucked underneath its large body.

"Wow. That was beautiful," Michael commented, awed.

"It was. My gran always said herons are like a visit from God."

"Did she now?" Michael watched for the narrowing of eyes, or furrowing of brows, or chewing of lips that always accompanied mention of Aidan's family, but none of these signs appeared. In fact, Aidan appeared calm, resigned, and that resolution worried Michael.

"Are you okay?"

"Sure," Aidan nodded, eyes still locked on the heron, now a barely perceptible spot on the horizon.

"We shouldn't have gone to Devenish yesterday."

"Why?"

"It must have stirred up all kinds of memories."

"It did. But it's okay."

The same calm resignation settled over Aidan. Michael stared at him, trying to discern what had changed. "What's going on with you? You're different today."

Aidan studied the docking rope coiled neatly by his feet, and wondered how much of his dream he should reveal. "I didn't sleep much last night," he said at length. "It wasn't just the storm; I had a lot of things on my mind. Then, you know how you can feel somebody telling you something?"

Michael nodded.

"I could feel my father with me, so real I swear I could reach out and touch him." Aidan relished once more the feel of his father's presence, the sound of his words. "He told me to have faith."

"Faith in what?"

"In the future, in finding my way I guess."

Relief washed over Michael. He drew together in his mind everything he could remember about Aidan's father: his infamous love of all kinds of music which he'd passed on to his son, his devotion to his children and hard work in raising them without their mother, his common sense approach to problems Aidan had recounted to them numerous times. What Michael recalled most was Mr. O'Connell's boundless love and support for Aidan.

"Your father was a very wise man." Then, because the contrast was so sharp in his mind, he couldn't help adding, "Not at all like mine."

Aidan watched Michael turn his empty tea mug over and over in his hands. "I don't remember ever meeting your father."

"No, and you're not likely to."

"I've never gotten that about him." Aidan shook his head, puzzled. "You've got so much talent, and you're his only child. I would think he'd be proud of anything you do."

"He's all business," Michael explained, fighting to keep the edge of anger out of his voice. "He doesn't see the sense of music; he thinks I'm wasting my time."

"Your mother's behind you though, isn't she?" Aidan wondered, pretty sure he'd never met her either.

"She follows whatever my father says. She thinks I sing well, but she'll always take his side."

They both watched a family of swans float by and a sailboat raise gold and turquoise sails on the other side of the lough. Michael heated more water and returned with fresh tea. They drank in silence for several minutes, until Aidan asked, "Will you do something for me?"

"Of course, if I can."

"Try to work things out with your father."

Michael looked as if Aidan had asked him to bring St. Patrick back alive.

"He's wrong to not support you," Aidan hurried to explain, "he should be on your side all the way. But he's alive. You still have time with him. I'd give everything for a little more time with my dad."

Michael recalled his last visit home, the acrimony between himself and his father. They could barely stay in the same room for more than ten minutes.

"We'll never have what you and your father did, you know," he pointed out. "He's just not that easy to talk to."

"My dad was one in a million," Aidan agreed. "I know it won't be easy, and I have no right to even ask. But someday it will be too late, and you'll hate yourself for not trying. It's hell when they're gone."

"I'll try." Michael promised, then raised his tea mug. "To our fathers."

Aidan thought of the unfairness of Michael having to live without his father's support, and himself having to live without his father's presence, and the struggle they both faced, and raised his mug in response. "To their sons."

12

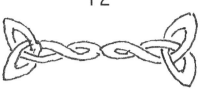

Aidan had just thrown his clothes in the laundry when Patrick called.

"I hear you and Michael had a great trip."

"What do you all do? Keep an open phone line with each other?" Aidan set his suitcase on the stairs to take up later, and reached for the stack of mail on his grandmother's desk. "Just in the door and you're keeping tabs on me already."

"We installed a video surveillance system while you were gone. We can watch everything you do now."

"I don't doubt you would if you thought you could get away with it." Aidan was sure Patrick was kidding; still he caught himself scanning the room for any signs of a camera or other equipment.

"We didn't yet," Patrick admitted. "If our phone calls don't work, though, that might be our next step."

Aidan set the mail aside. "You all shouldn't worry so much." Even as he said it, he knew they were wasted words. If the situation was reversed, he'd be concerned for Patrick, or Michael, or Niall.

"Right. Well, I really called to tell you the measles outbreak is over and we'd love to have you come out for a bit."

Aidan could hear Conor and Caitlyn calling, "Uncle Aidan, hurry," in the background. "Pat, give me a few days, I need to check on the garage and take care of a few things around the house. Then I'll be out."

"He'll be out soon." Patrick told Conor and Caitlyn, both clamoring to know what Aidan had said. "Now, you both have chores to finish. Scoot!"

To Moira Patrick said, "Michael was right, Aidan does sound better."

Moira stirred the chowder she was preparing for dinner. "So, Michael's engaged? Do you know his fiancé?"

"Susannah? I remember meeting her once. Very pretty, very high class." He stole a piece of the shortbread Moira had just pulled from the oven. "She's a good match for Michael."

"Michael's high end. He's so different from the rest of you. I've always wondered that you all fit together so well."

"He's the same as us inside." Patrick pulled Moira to him, hugged her tight and kissed her. "How about you and me go dance in the moonlight tonight after the kiddies are asleep."

"Oh, go on with ye," Moira gave him a gentle push. "I've got dinner to finish."

Niall called just as Aidan finished storing his fishing gear away. "How was the trip?"

"You mean that tin can system you all have with each other hasn't filled you in?" Aidan teased.

"Sure it has. Patrick told me he's already talked to you. I just wanted to hear for myself."

"You all are a hopeless lot!"

Niall laughed, "We are that! Now tell me how the boat trip was."

"It was fantastic. I'm trading you all in for a friend like Michael's, with a boat."

"You would, too, if you thought you could get away with it."

Aidan recounted the grandeur of the boat, the fish they had caught, the beauty of the Lough Erne region, and the stop at Devenish Island. Then he asked, "How does your mom like her new patio?"

"Good heavens, it's like they're on their second honeymoon!"

Aidan could still see the gleam in Niall's parents' eyes as they danced together. "They're really something, aren't they? You heard Michael's news haven't you?"

"Just got off the phone with him. I'm happy for him. Susannah's a lovely lady."

"She is. When are you going to find someone like that for yourself?"

"You sound like my mother." Niall laughed again, but later, when his phone call was done, when his parents had gone to bed and he alone sat watching the fireplace, last cup of tea in his hands and soft country sounds marking the night outside, he wondered the same thing.

"Just wanted to let you know I'm home, boss."

Mack smiled at the term, which Aidan hadn't used since they'd come home. He forced himself to not take it as a sign Aidan was ready to return to the band. "Did you have a good time?"

Aidan poured himself a cup of tea and scanned the bread and pastry box Rita kept well stocked. "What did Michael tell you?"

"Not good that you know our system," Mack sighed. "How will we ever get away with talking about you now?"

235

"You won't." Aidan set his tea and a plate of Rita's sugar cookies on the coffee table, settled himself on the sofa, put his feet up on the coffee table, remembered his granny always got mad when he did that, and swung his feet back to the floor. "Michael and I had a lot of fun."

"I'm glad. What's up for this week?"

"Not much. Taking care of the yard and house a bit. Patrick wants me out for a visit; I think I'll go there this weekend."

"You'd have a good time with Pat and his family." Mack nodded to Kate, who held a bottle of port wine up to ask whether he wanted a refill. He debated whether to ask about Aidan's future plans, and in the end held back. "After Patrick's, you should come out here."

"Yes, that would be good."

Mack smiled at Kate sitting across from him on his patio, fire crackling in the outdoor fireplace. "Aidan really does sound better. He's always said being near water does wonders for him. I think he's right."

"You didn't ask him about the band," Kate observed.

"No, I don't want to press him just yet. When I see him, I'll ask."

Kate read the relief in Mack's eyes. "You've done well with Aidan, helping him through such a terrible time."

Mack shrugged. "I haven't done much. He's done it all, he and the boys. They're a good team."

"They have a wise leader."

Kate shivered as the first chill of evening settled in. She sipped her wine and watched the fire's orange and yellow fingers wrap themselves around the small branch of fuel they'd been fed. Fire rose within her as well, catching her off guard. Once lit, the inner fire flared. She watched Mack feed Kellan and Seamus leftover bits of their dinner steak and bread. The sun had started to slide to the sea, a bright gold ball bathing everything with its warm glow. She should leave now, she knew. She should throw sea water on that inner fire before it consumed her.

Kate thought of the apartment she would return to. For all its lace curtains and rich oriental rugs, it was empty. As empty as her life. The store was successful, but she wanted more. Seeing Mack the last few weeks had reminded her what was missing.

Mack settled back in his chair and smiled at her. His smile had the same effect as a fresh log placed on the fire. If I take the next step, she told herself, there's no going back. I won't hurt him again. It would ruin us both.

A gust of wind sent more shivers down Kate's arms. She stood, crossed over to Mack, removed the wine glass from his hands and drew him to his feet.

"I'm chilly. Let's go get warm."

Mack hesitated. For all that he'd dreamed of Kate's return, now that she stood before him offering herself he was afraid. If he took this step, and hope filled his heart again, he knew he would break if it all fell apart.

Sensing his fear, Kate whispered in his ear, "I love you Mack, and that's not just the wine talking. I know what I'm doing."

Mack and Kate returned to the bed they'd once shared. Mack stayed awake long after their physical reunion, long after Kate had fallen asleep in his arms, watching the rise and fall of her breath. He prayed this wasn't all a dream, that he would not wake up alone in the morning.

Michael unpacked, showered, and called Susannah. "Are you still up for dinner?"

"Of course. Only I have a better choice than Fitzroys."

"What would that be?"

"Your place."

Michael recognized the sensual tone in her voice, and his heart sped double time. "Really now? Alright. We can order in."

Susannah could read Michael's mind and emotions across the phone, thankful they matched her own. "No, I've got all we need."

Later, after her chicken stir fry, wild rice, romaine salad and wine, after their love making, Michael informed her, "I told the boys we're engaged."

"I thought you were going to wait until we had our plans set."

"You're not upset are you?"

Susannah snuggled closer to Michael. "No, just a little surprised."

Michael inhaled her perfume, felt the softness of her skin. "Aidan and I were talking, and I just felt the need to tell him. Then I thought, once he knew I might as well tell the others."

Susannah heard Michael's heart beat in his chest, felt the strength of his arms around her. "What did they all think?"

"For the life of them they can't figure out why you'd want a bloke like me. Now I think on it, neither can I."

"For the life of me, neither can I!" Susannah teased.

The soft sound of Wynton Marsalis music played in the background, moonlight cast a faint blue-white light across their bed and, with Susannah nestled beside him, Michael's world felt more peaceful and perfect than he would ever have dreamed.

"Hey, Suze, why don't you move in here now? Let's not wait till we're married."

"Good idea. It will give me time to clean up the mess you've made of this place."

Michael sat up and looked around him. "I haven't made a mess."

"I know." Susannah gave him a playful push.

They laughed, and made love again.

Jack helped Rita clear the table off and clean the kitchen. She never needed help but sometimes, like tonight, he felt she would like the company, if not the hand.

"That was a lovely roast," he complimented, handing over the platter.

"You don't think it was too dry?"

"No, not dry at all."

"I thought the gravy was a little thin."

Jack shook his head. "I didn't think so. Seemed perfect to me."

"What about the pie? Apples didn't seem tart enough to me."

"No." Jack shook his head again and handed over the roasting pan. "Pie tasted as good as ever."

Rita set the pan down and turned to face Jack. "Now I know you're lying. That pie was one of my worst."

"I wouldn't say worst. Okay, it wasn't your best, but you have a lot on your mind."

Rita pulled Lizzie's letter out of her pocket. "Oh Jack, what is she thinking, divorcing Martin?"

"You know he's not been the best of husbands," Jack reminded her. "Cheated twice on her, he has, and I don't like the mean streak in him."

"I get that part." Rita sank into a kitchen chair. "But what will she and those kiddies do? How will they live?"

Jack sat next to Rita and covered her hands with his own. "She'll be fine. She takes after her mam, has a good head on her shoulders. If worse comes to worst, she can move in with us a wee bit."

Rita smiled through her tears. "You're a good man, Jack MacLaren. Best decision I ever made was to marry you."

"Too right!" Jack's words brought a smile to Rita's face. "Now, if you'll brew some fresh tea I'll see if I can choke down another piece of that pie."

Aidan rose to turn lights out and settle the house for bed. His eyes fell upon a rosary he'd forgotten he had placed on the front window table. Sea glass beads in shades of soft greens and blues shone in the light of the table lamp.

He remembered the day his grandmother had given it to him, the day Macready's Bridge had left for their North America tour.

"You take this with you." She'd pressed it into his hands.

He'd examined the rosary closely, as he did now. "This was my granddad's, wasn't it?"

"Yes." His granny's eyes were lit with memories. "You were named after him, you know."

"I wish he'd lived longer. I would have loved to have known him."

"You have his eyes and his smile."

Aidan shook his head and tried to hand the rosary back. "This is yours. I can't take it."

"I've saved it for you all these years." His grandmother spoke firmly, in a tone Aidan knew was final. "It will keep you safe in your travels."

Aidan thought again of Devenish Island, of his Slieve League dream, of his father's words, and those of Father Nelligan. His grandmother's picture smiled out at him from its place on the table in front of the window. What a tower of strength she was, he thought, and thought again of the faith that had sustained her over the years.

"What would you tell me if you were here?" he asked the woman in the picture.

The rosary his granny had given him now seemed to come to life in his hands. He was sure it was her way of answering his question. God still seemed far away; but maybe tonight, if Aidan took one step in that direction, God would make His presence known. Aidan turned the living room light out, settled into his sofa bed, and recited, "I believe in God, the Father Almighty, Creator of Heaven and Earth..."

13

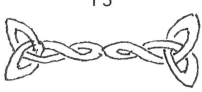

A knock on the front door interrupted Aidan's packing. He opened it to find a stranger, a man he judged to be in his fifties, short, thin, with troubled eyes clouding his face.

"Is this the O'Connell's house?" The man's eyes darted from Aidan to the MacLaren's next door, then back to Aidan. "I'm looking for Daniel O'Connell's family."

"I'm his son." Aidan tried to place the stranger. He wasn't from anywhere in town he could recall, nor did he remember ever seeing the man as a customer in the garage.

The man's eyes grew large. He cleared his throat and introduced himself in a shaky voice, "I'm Malachy Achill."

The name seemed familiar; for a moment Aidan couldn't place it, then it hit him. He saw their bodies again, and the news article with its mangled wreckage photo. Malachy Achill was the lorry driver who'd shattered his world.

Aidan remembered wanting to beat the driver to a bloody pulp. Now the man stood here, smaller than he'd imagined, older, fragile. Thoughts of delivering the beating he deserved flew from Aidan's mind.

"What can I do for you?"

Malachy twisted the brim of the cap in his hands. "I just wanted—" he paused, cleared his throat again, and restarted, "I'm sorry. I came to tell you I'm sorry."

Sorry? The man was sorry? That was it? Aidan wanted to shake the man until he saw the chaos he'd caused. He held his tongue and jammed his hands in his pockets to keep them under control.

"It all happened so fast. One second I pulled my eyes from the road, then they were in front of me, I hit the brakes, but I couldn't stop in time."

"The phone," Aidan interrupted, "you were on your phone."

"My daughter called." He nodded to a woman standing near a car parked by the curb. "She was expecting; she went into labor early." Malachy's eyes became two watery pools. "She lost the baby. A girl. My first granddaughter."

The hatred Aidan had felt for Malachy lessened a degree. "I'm sorry."

"I don't drive anymore. Not even the car. My daughter takes me places. I lost my job, my pension. I have nothing now."

Aidan scanned the man before him once more. Malachy's life was as much a twisted, mangled wreck as his own family's car. "I'm not sure what you want from me. If it's forgiveness you've come for, I can't do that, not yet. I don't hate you. I don't wish any harm on you."

"I just wanted to tell you how sorry I am." Malachy held his hand out. Aidan found his hands frozen to his side, unable to accept the handshake Malachy offered. Malachy slipped his cap back on his head. "I'll be off now."

Aidan watched the man say a word to his daughter, then slide into the passenger seat. His daughter took her place behind the wheel. Aidan watched them drive to the end of his street and turn left, and watched several minutes after they had disappeared from view.

The sound of children's laughter floated through the air as Aidan pulled into the lane that led to Patrick's house. He had dreaded that sound and the memories of Jeannie and himself the sound would call forth; yet now, driving toward the creamy stone cottage with bright blue trim where the Leahy family lived, he found the laughter drew him in instead of pushing him away.

"Uncle Aidan! Uncle Aidan!" Conor and Caitlyn both shouted in unison, racing from the front step where they'd been waiting towards his car.

"Come play with us," Conor begged, grabbing Aidan's arm as soon as his car door was open.

"You promised you'd play football with us," Caitlyn grabbed his other arm.

"Good night in the morning!" Patrick stepped in to rescue his guest. "Give the boy a chance to catch his breath! Tea first, and then he'll play with you," and warned the two crestfallen faces before him, "if you behave yourselves."

Shaking his head, Patrick reached for Aidan's suitcase. "I've forgotten how attached to you those two are, despite what I say to discourage them."

"Darn kids never listen do they?" Aidan handed a small bag to Caitlyn and instructed, "Take these to your mom." To Conor he handed a midsize bag and said, "Take this in but don't open it until later."

As the kids headed off, Patrick told him, "You didn't need to bring anything, just yourself."

"It's just some scones from Rita, and a wee treat for the kids to have fun with." Aidan headed toward the house where Moira had stepped out and stood waiting by the front door. "Patrick, I forgot what a beautiful place this is."

Patrick viewed the house he and Moira had worked hard to restore. The small cottage with gleaming blue door and window shutters shone against the green field that surrounded it and the blue sea spread out behind. Although isolated, with the nearest neighbor ten kilometers down the road, its country setting gave Conor and Caitlyn plenty of room to run and play, and he and Moira a peaceful, quiet place to raise their family.

"It is a grand home isn't it," Patrick agreed.

"Come on, the two of you." Moira held the door open and waved for them to move faster. "Lunch will be cold if you don't get in here now."

As Aidan followed Patrick in, he noticed all over again how the cottage's small outward appearance belied the spacious feel inside. Multiple lace curtained windows, clean, whitewashed walls and a combined cooking, eating and sitting room arrangement made the cottage feel twice as big as it was.

Conor set in pestering Aidan as soon as they started their meal. "What's in the bag? What did you bring us? When can we open it?"

"Conor, you're being rude." Moira sent him a stern look to remind him of proper behavior. To Aidan she apologized, "I'm sorry. He does know his manners, he's just forgotten them."

Aidan winked at Conor. "Ah, they know I'll be bringing them pressies, they can't help that they're excited." He passed a plate of sandwiches to Patrick, and told Conor and Caitlyn, "After lunch, when your mom and dad say it's okay, we'll open that bag up."

Conor said no more, but fidgeted in his seat while the others ate their sandwiches and soup, and some of Moira's oatmeal raisin cookies. Finally, as Aidan drank the last of his tea, Conor asked eagerly, "Now?"

"Yeah, now?" Caitlyn chimed in, as impatient as her brother.

Aidan looked to Patrick and Moira for approval. They both suppressed grins and nodded. "Okay. Let's see what we've got here, only we have to take it outside."

Conor and Caitlyn watched as Aidan drew out rainbow colored paper, thin strips of wood and a large ball of twine and set them on the ground. Last, he pulled out instructions and a picture that revealed a diamond shaped kite. "Think you can put this together?"

Both kids looked apprehensive until Patrick stepped in. "Sure we can."

Within an hour they had the kite assembled. Aidan showed them how to send it airborne, where its rainbow colored body sailed in the steady breeze, dipping and turning as the air changed directions. Conor and Caitlyn laughed and called out advice to each other as the kite played in the wind.

When the kite finally grounded, two tired, excited kids ran to where the adults had stood watching.

"That was fun, Uncle Aidan!" Conor exclaimed.

"Did your daddy fly kites with you?"

Met by immediate silence, Caitlyn turned to Aidan, wide-eyed. "I'm sorry. I wasn't supposed to say anything about your daddy."

Aidan gave her shoulders a light squeeze. "That's okay. Yes, he did fly kites with me, and with my sister."

She viewed him with the open innocence kids have, unafraid to say what's on their minds. "You miss your daddy don't you?"

"Yes." Aidan nodded. "I miss all my family." Then, to shift the suddenly somber mood back to the fun they'd been having, he rolled the kite string back on its spindle and said, "But today we're having fun, right? Do you think you two can get this going on your own, or do you need your daddy's help?"

"Daddy, help," both kids begged, pulling at Patrick's arms until he finally gave in.

As they watched Patrick work at sending the kite airborne again, both kids cheering him on, Moira told Aidan, "I'm sorry. We told the kids you wouldn't want to talk about your family. They forgot that just like they forget manners."

"They're kids. They didn't mean any harm." Aidan fixed his gaze on Patrick guiding Conor and Caitlyn as they took turns holding the string that allowed the kite to soar without flying away. Their laughter caught in his web of memories; in his eyes he saw Jeannie and himself, both children, racing in an open field, rainbow kite sailing high in an overcast sky.

"She's really high, isn't she Gran?" Jeannie's young voice called out.

From a distance, their grandmother called back, "She is, she's a beauty."

As he and his sister continued to fly their kite that day, the wind picked up, yanking at the paper bird. Both kids fought to hang onto the string as the kite soared and dove, soared and dove again. Their father stepped in to help; Aidan could still feel his father's warm hands as he let the memory slip away and focused on Patrick again.

Moira caught Aidan's eyes travel back in time then return. Enough, she thought, that's enough memory for now. As Patrick reeled the kite in, she called out, "It's tea time. Let's have those scones Aidan brought with him."

"Are you sure you don't mind sleeping on the sofa?" Moira asked later while Patrick told the twins a bedtime story.

"Not at all, with that lovely wee fire before me. This will be fine."

"We thought we'd add another room onto the house next year, then our company would have a proper bed."

Aidan took in the thick stone walls, lattice windows, thatched roof and deep hearth of the cottage. "I thought you both wanted to keep this place as close to the original as you could."

"We did."

"I wouldn't change a thing. Company will be happy to sleep anywhere, or they're not worth having over."

"You might be right." Moira set a bottle of wine and three glasses on the coffee table.

Aidan winked. "It happens every so often. Just don't tell anyone; I don't want my image blown!"

"What image is that?" Patrick joined them and sank into the chair by the sofa.

"That I'm the wisest of the group."

"You just keep your fantasies there, boyo." Patrick poured wine for each of them. "Hey, the kids asked to go to Carrowmore tomorrow. I told them I didn't think we would."

Aidan thought of the megalithic tomb site nearby. He'd never been there, but it couldn't be all bad if the kids wanted to go, and he'd not be the one to stand in their way. "I don't mind if we do."

Moira set a tray of cheese and sliced apples next to the wine, and sat at the sofa's open end. "For some reason they're fascinated with the place."

"We'll sleep on it and see how the morning looks." Patrick poured more wine for himself and Aidan. "Things okay back home this week?"

"They are." Then Aidan revealed, "The lorry driver from the accident stopped by just before I came out here."

Moira froze. Patrick almost dropped the wine bottle. "He did? What did he want?"

"Mostly to say he was sorry."

"I'll bet he is." Patrick set the wine bottle down hard.

"He's not a monster." Aidan recalled the sight of the man on his doorstep. "I wanted to hate him, but I can't. He's a broken man. His life's been ruined the same as mine."

Moira placed a hand on Aidan's arm. "Your life isn't ruined. Changed, yes, but you'll build a new life."

Build a new life. The phrase stuck in the back of Aidan's mind as he studied the orange, yellow and white of the fire's flames long after Patrick and Moira went to bed. He heard them settle in, heard their light laughs and knew Patrick would have whispered some intimate joke, heard soft prayers, then silence as sleep carried them off to dreamland.

Dreams. To Aidan it was a double-edged word.

Patrick and Moira had built their dream world in this small corner of land with its wide sea view, strong stone walls, and children's laughter ringing inside and out. Michael was poised to realize his own dreams with Susannah. Mack had lived his dream several times over through the rise and fall of success in the music business. Aidan wasn't sure what Niall's dreams were, but guessed they were somehow tied to his family's farm.

Malachy Achill had dreams, retirement perhaps, and the joy of grandchildren. Those dreams were dashed now. Fionna had dreams, and parents who stood in her way.

His own family's dreams flooded his mind.

"A place by the ocean for you," his father would always insist.

"A boat to go with it," Aidan would add, "and that home studio you've always talked of."

How many hours had they spent researching equipment and locations, figuring costs, and planning how to spread the word to draw other musicians to their new place? That dream was over now.

"Someday my artwork will hang in studios, here, in Dublin, maybe even in London." Jeannie's whole face shone the afternoon she'd shared her dream with him. Aidan pictured them again lunching at the Craft Village in town, inspired by Cafe del Mondo's atmosphere and the high praise her paintings had received in a recent public display. "I can teach art for a living, and draw and paint after work."

"You'll be brilliant," he'd assured her that day. Now the artwork that filled their house was all that remained of Jeannie's dream.

His grandmother's dreams were few and simple. "A large kitchen," she would say, glancing around her small domain where pans, spices and cooking utensils spread over every available surface. "I want a kitchen with room to spread out. And a large, sunny garden to look out on while I work."

Aidan fell asleep contemplating dreams realized and dreams forever lost.

They rose the next morning to a blue sky with cotton ball clouds scattered across it.

"What do you think about Carrowmore?" Patrick asked Moira as she fried sausage and eggs for their breakfast.

Moira set fresh bread to toast. "You said yourself Aidan's come a long way. Unless he's had a bad night, I don't think there's any harm."

The drive to Carrowmore was quick; soon they stood in a field with stones spread throughout grassy, wildflower-flecked fields.

"Conor likes matching up the numbered stone markers with the map," Patrick explained to Aidan as both kids ran ahead. "Caitlyn just likes the fun of running through the fields and naming the wildflowers."

When they all reached the central cairn, Listoghil, though, both of the twins stood silent while their father explained, "This is where people a long time ago buried their family who had died. We need to be quiet while we walk through here."

"We know, Daddy." Conor took Patrick's hand. "You tell us every time."

"This place is older than Jesus, isn't it Daddy?"

Patrick nodded, not correcting her theology. "Yes, Caitlyn, it was here a long time before Jesus was born."

They walked the narrow path through the Listoghil cairn single file. Stones of various sizes rose up around them, held in place by wire mesh. In the center of the cairn, a passage tomb made of large rocks and flat capstone stood the same as it had nearly six thousand years. As they walked through, Aidan marveled at the tomb's longevity and the prehistoric culture that had built such elaborate sites to honor their dead.

Honoring the dead. He wondered, for all his grief how had he honored his family?

After Carrowmore, Conor and Caitlyn called out in unison, "Daddy, let's go to the beach!"

"You do indulge those kiddies." Aidan teased so only Patrick could hear as they drove toward Strandhill.

"What's the good having them if we can't spoil them a bit?" Patrick saw in the rearview mirror where the twins sat with Moira in the back seat. "Look at their faces, aren't they a grand sight?"

"They sure are." Aidan watched the twins, faces lit as bright as the sun outside, smiles animated as they told their mom, "We're going to find some shells, aren't we?" "I want to run into the waves." "Can we eat our lunch on the beach?"

Unlike Gweebarra, Strandhill Beach filled Aidan with a sense of peace. Maybe it was the sun shining down on the water, causing the sea to shine like a field of diamonds spread out before him. It could have been the sight of Conor and Caitlyn running to the edge of the waves, tempting them to catch the twins, and them dashing back when the waves touched the edges of their shoes, or maybe it was their laughter ringing out as they played the wave chase game.

Whatever the cause, Aidan strolled along the beach soaking up the feel of sand beneath his feet and the sun on his face and arms, and felt good inside. No, happy, he realized, I really feel happy right now. He waited for the guilt that followed any moments of fun anymore, and smiled when no guilt rose up in him.

"Now there's a sight I've been waiting to see."

Aidan turned to Patrick who had just caught up with him. "What's that?"

"That sunny smile of yours. I knew if we came down to the beach we'd find it."

"You did, did you?" Aidan's smile grew as he watched a beginner class of students try their hand at surfing at the other end of the beach. "What made you so sure?"

"The sea, more than anything else, is the water of life to you."

"It is." Aidan thought back to Gweebarra, the rain, the loneliness, and his encounter with Fionna. His Gweebarra stay was light years away from what this visit to Strandhill was like. "I think it's more than that, though. I'm learning I'm better off when I'm around people. It's not good for me to live alone. Or maybe I'm starting to accept the fact that they're gone."

A sailboat appeared on the horizon. They both watched it, crisp white canvas stretched out stark against the blue sky, floating on the breeze as if on wings. Patrick asked, "Have you ever sailed? I know you've fished a lot, and had a few boat trips on the loughs around, but have you ever been very far out on the great sea?"

Aidan shook his head. "My father and I always talked of doing that, but we ran out of time..." Aidan's words trailed off.

"Do something for me, will you?"

"If I can." Aidan was a bit afraid of what Patrick would ask.

"Someday take yourself out sailing anyway. You, of all people I know, would love it."

Aidan didn't respond right away. He remembered the fishing trip and every other activity he'd tried since he'd come home. At last he said, "I don't know. It wouldn't be the same without my dad."

Patrick watched the waves flow steadily in and out. "You know, my dad and I spent hours walking this beach, year after year, gathering shells, driftwood, sea glass, watching the boats and birds breeze by." For a moment, collected memories filled Patrick's mind and he couldn't speak. He let them play out, savoring the richness they brought to him. At last he cleared them away. "After he passed on, I tried walking here alone, but it was never the same. I hated it, truth be told."

Aidan nodded. "That's how it was when I tried fishing a few weeks ago. With Michael it was fun; on my own it wasn't."

"No, it wouldn't be," Patrick agreed. "I did learn, though, to do things different. Now I walk the beach with Conor and Caitlyn and teach them all the things my father taught me."

"Maybe someday I'll have kids of my own to take fishing and sailing," Aidan mused.

"Maybe. In the meantime, why don't you buy one of those sailboats, and we'll go out with you. In fact, why don't you just move out here. We'd love to have you around."

Move out there. That night, while the rest of the house slept, Aidan considered Patrick's words. He remembered his failed sunrise drive, and the first time he thought of moving. He had passed the thought off then, but now it held more appeal. He could go anywhere in the world, he realized. He could sell the garage and the house and start fresh, leave all the painful memories behind, carry with him only what he wanted most, what he couldn't live without. It could work, he thought. Why not? It could be fun.

The whole world stretched out before him as he debated where he would go. France, he thought. No, Spain, Barcelona. Or Germany, Hamburg, Bonn. Hell, he could go to Tahiti! Live in a grass hut with a girl in a bikini! Yeah! He drifted to sleep with thoughts of a tropical beach, a girl, and drumbeats pounding in the background.

The last day of his visit turned stormy, rain pounding against roof, tapping a steady beat against windows, yet inside the Leahy's cottage warmth rose from the hearth fire and stew simmering on the stove. They played cards and games all day. After dinner, both kids called out, "Daddy, is it music time?"

Patrick knew the request was coming, as every rainy night became music night. "Go ahead, bring me our instruments." As he said this, he kept one eye on Aidan. Sure enough, the smile had gone out of Aidan's eyes, replaced by a guarded look. Patrick weighed changing music night to story night, but the kids came out carrying flute and guitar, faces glowing with excitement, and he didn't have the heart to let them down.

First, Patrick played "Cockles and Mussels" on his fiddle, with Moira singing along. Then Caitlyn played "Annie Laurie" on flute, and Conor demonstrated his progress on his father's guitar in "Danny Boy." They all played together on "Wild Irish Rose," Patrick slowing his beat to match his kids' pace. As rain continued to pelt the outside, the Leahy cottage glowed inside.

After "Wild Irish Rose" was finished, Conor handed the guitar to Aidan. "Now you play."

"Yes, please Uncle Aidan?" Caitlyn echoed.

Patrick watched as momentary hesitation flashed across Aidan's face. He held the guitar in his hands, the feel of the wood smooth and inviting, strings tempting, then handed it back with a smile. "Tonight's your family's music and I'd rather enjoy that. I'll play for you another time, okay?" Then, to counter their disappointment he promised, "When your music's done, and you're bathed and ready for bed, I'll tell you a story."

Aidan's stories were always a treat to the twins, even more exciting than his music. Both kids ran off to get ready for bed, while Moira returned to the kitchen, clearing dishes she'd abandoned while music was playing.

As Patrick stored the various instruments in their cases, he eyed Aidan. "You know, you can't avoid it forever."

"I know, I'm just not ready yet."

"You've come a long way these last few weeks."

"You've all helped me along."

"You won't be complete until you get back to your music."

Aidan looked Patrick square in the eye. "I don't think so, Pat. It's like you and your dad at the beach. What used to make you complete is different now."

Freshly bathed and in their pajamas, Conor and Caitlyn returned to their mom and dad, and the warm fire, and settled on the sofa.

"Once upon a time," Aidan started, "there was a boy," he looked over to Conor who called out, "Conor!"

"and a girl," Aidan looked to the sofa, where Caitlyn, snuggled against her mom, called out, "Caitlyn!"

"and a kite. The boy and girl loved that kite. Every day they would fly it, after school, after dinner, whether it was sunny or rainy. They loved playing with their kite.

"One day, they decided to fly their kite even though their mom and dad were both busy and had asked them to wait. They let the kite rise up in the air, and were busy admiring its beautiful rainbow colors, when a strong wind came up and grabbed the kite out of their hands.

"They didn't think to call their parents. Instead, Conor and Caitlyn chased after the kite, calling it, hoping to catch it. Before long, they found themselves at a strange beach.

"'What should we do?' Caitlyn asked her brother, near tears.

"Conor, trying to be brave, thought hard and said, 'Look, there's a boat. Maybe they can take us home.'

"Caitlyn looked where Conor was pointing. There in the water before them was a sailboat with a rainbow sail.

"'Ahoy there mateys,' the man behind the wheel of the boat called out. 'You look like ye'r needing a ride.'

"'We are,' Conor called back, even as Caitlyn whispered, 'We're not supposed to talk to strangers.'

"'Come aboard.' The skipper brought his boat in close to shore, and Conor and Caitlyn scrambled on board.

"'Where is it ye'r wanting to go?'

"'Home.' Caitlyn answered.

"'And which way is home?'

"'That way.' Caitlyn pointed left.

"'That way.' Conor pointed right.

"The skipper smiled. 'So we're lost, are we?' Both twins nodded. 'There's only one thing for it then.' He spun the boat's wheel hard.

"Around and around the wheel spun. Around and around the boat spun. When it stopped spinning, the skipper steered the boat in the direction it faced, which was away from the beach.

"In just a few minutes, they were far away from any sign of land. The skipper stopped the boat's engine, lowered her sails, and anchored the boat. 'Let's see what the ocean has for us today.'

"Seven dolphins swam by, very close to the boat, so close Conor could see their eyes. They jumped high, and fell back in the water, splashing Conor, Caitlyn and the skipper in the process.

"Three gulls flew overhead. The skipper reached into a bucket, pulled out a small fish, and tossed it high in the air. The first gull caught it. He handed a fish to Conor, who threw it as high as he could. The second gull caught it. Caitlyn took the third fish, but didn't throw it out. Instead, she held it high in her hand. The third gull swooped down and took it right from her.

"'Pretty tricky of ye!' the skipper laughed.

"A mother whale and her baby swam close ahead. 'Watch carefully,' the skipper instructed. The twins stared hard. Soon the mother whale jumped out of the water, and then back in. The baby repeated its mother's actions.

"They all clapped and cheered.

"The sun started to sink low by now, and Caitlyn was afraid. 'Please, can you take us home now?'

"'And which way would that be?'

258

"Conor and Caitlyn both sighed. Instead of guessing, this time Conor admitted, 'We don't know.'

"'There's only one thing for it then,' the skipper told them, and spun the wheel hard. The boat spun around fast. When it stopped, the skipper steered the boat in the direction it faced. Soon they were back to the beach, and there, waiting for them, were their mom and dad.

"'Thank you. That was fun!' The twins turned to the skipper, but the boat and the skipper were gone. Behind them stood a man, with a rainbow kite in his hands."

"It was you!" Conor jumped off the sofa. "You were the skipper!"

"That was fun!" Caitlyn cried out. "Can we have another story?"

"Time for bed for you both," Moira announced. "Say goodnight to Uncle Aidan and your dad."

"Goodnight Uncle Aidan. Thanks for the story. It was great." Conor hugged him, then hugged his dad, and headed down the short hall to the bedroom he shared with his sister.

"Goodnight Uncle Aidan," Caitlyn repeated, and hugged him tight. "You don't have to go home tomorrow do you? Can't you stay longer?"

"Yeah, can't you stay longer?" Patrick asked as Caitlyn followed her brother.

Aidan shook his head. "No. I have a few things to take care of. But I promise I'll come back another time."

"I think Aidan's leaving the group," Patrick confided to Moira later that night.

Moira read the fear in Patrick's eyes. "You could be wrong. If that's his choice, though, you can't force him to stay."

"I know." Patrick watched Moira step out of her slippers, fold her sweater and leave it at the foot of their bed, then slide next to him under the sheets. He kissed her, and clasped her left hand in his. "Let's pray."

The next morning, Aidan gathered his belongings into his car and took one last look at the cottage gleaming in the early sun.

"Listen, what I said about your music last night," Patrick started as he handed over a thermos of tea and a bag of sandwiches, "you do what's best for you. If you never play music again a day in your life, we'll still be friends. You'll always be a part of our family here."

"Thanks. For everything." Aidan nodded towards the cottage, and Patrick's family standing on the front step. "You've got it all right here; everything anyone could ever want. You're very lucky."

"I am that," Patrick agreed. He watched Aidan back out the driveway and drive over the hill, and then turned to his kids. "Let's see if we can set that kite to flying."

14

Aidan knew what he had to do as he pulled away from Patrick's home. At the top of the hill he pulled his car into a dirt road that led to an abandoned cottage and dialed Mack's number. When Mack answered he asked, "Are you going to be home for a bit? I thought I'd stop by."

"I'll be here. I've got some steaks, you can join me for lunch."

Aidan rang off and gazed at the cottage before him. Weeds grew tall near the house, along the road, and in the fields that surrounded the property. No fresh laundry hung out to dry, no sounds of children playing or dogs barking rose from inside. Downhill from the cottage Aidan could see Patrick's house, and Conor and Caitlyn flying their kite while Patrick and Moira watched nearby.

Fresh from his visit with Patrick and his family, with his heart still warmed by the laughter and love that filled their home, the emptiness and neglect this cottage suffered shouted out, cutting a fresh wound in Aidan's heart as it mirrored his own life.

"This house should be filled with that kind of love." Aidan wondered if it, like he, would ever have the life that Patrick had. "Someone should buy this house, fix it up, give it new life."

New life. For the first time in months he could feel the pull to give his life a fresh start. The first step, and the hardest, would be what he had to work out now with Mack.

As Aidan drove up to Mack's home, he was impressed anew with how the grey stone manor house rose up from the grassy field as if it were one with the ground, had been born in the land the same as the trees and hills and rocks, solid and eternal. Its arched doorway, curved entrance steps and rounded central wall lent a delicate air to the stone structure, giving it a welcoming rather than imposing feel, while its numerous windows, in the day's bright sun, reflected its surrounding green trees and fields and brilliant blue sea.

Aidan entered through the iron gate set in the stone wall that defined the estate's borders. Kellan and Seamus, Mack's Irish Setter companions, ran up, red coats gleaming, noses lifted to test the scent of this new visitor.

"Hello boys." Aidan patted their heads; they waved their tails in familiar response.

"You look better than last time I saw you," Mack remarked, coming up behind his dogs.

"That wouldn't take much."

"Still, I'm glad to see it. Come on around back. You can tell me what you've been up to while I grill our steaks."

Aidan followed Mack to the grand patio Mack had built years earlier, field stone pad adorned with teak benches and chairs, a marble-top table that seated twelve, and an open fireplace, all overlooking the sea.

"Medium rare isn't it?" Mack placed two steaks on the grill.

"Good memory!" Aidan sat on a bench.

"Tell me about your visit with Patrick."

Aidan recounted his latest vacation while Mack turned steaks, set out salad, produced baked potatoes smothered with butter, and warm garlic bread, and two Guinness bottles to go with their meal.

"Filling me in on your travels isn't what you stopped by for is it?" Mack questioned when Aidan was through.

"No." Aidan downed some Guinness and eyed Mack. "It's time I moved forward with a number of things. I'm going to sell my father's garage. I think I'll sell the house, as well. It's time for me to make a fresh start in a place that doesn't drag me down."

"Those are two very wise decisions." Mack took in Aidan's calm demeanor, impressed by the mantle of maturity the young man now wore. Still, there was one more thing to resolve. "You could have phoned me about that. There's something more, isn't there?"

Aidan studied the view, seawater afternoon blue, two boats cruising back and forth, while he chose his next words.

"I want you and the boys to go on without me."

There. He'd said it. His decision was out now, no more battle inside him as two sides waged war. He'd made his choice.

Mack weighed his approach. If he pushed too hard, he risked pushing Aidan away. If he didn't push at all, he'd be letting Aidan and all of them down.

"When's the last time you played your guitar?"

"New York. Our last show."

Mack suspected as much, but was still stunned that Aidan, who had not gone a day without picking at his guitar in all the time Mack had known him, could so completely abandon it now.

"What would you do, if not music?"

Aidan fell back on the answer he'd always given whenever he and the rest of the band had discussed what they'd do if Macready's Bridge failed. "I could always be a bin man."

This time Mack didn't laugh. "If I thought picking up other people's refuse would make you happy I'd say go for it. Or stocking shelves, or selling veggies in a market stall, or cleaning tables; if it was what you really wanted, we'd all be happy for you. But I don't think that's what you really want."

"What I really want doesn't matter." Aidan watched Kellan and Seamus nose the air as some new scent wafted their way.

"Of course it matters." Mack set his fork and knife down. "You've come through the worst of it, Aidan. Now it's your future you have to take care of. And I think music is the life you want, the life you were made for."

"You and everyone else."

"But not you?"

Aidan focused on his Guinness glass, turning it different angles. How far could he tilt the glass without the liquid spilling out? At length he asked Mack, "Do you know why I went into music in the first place?"

Mack thought he knew, but wanted to hear Aidan say it. "Why?"

"I remember, I was nine." Aidan looked past Mack to the sea, and allowed his mind to travel back across the years. "My father was playing his guitar. I was used to that, he played all the time. For as long as I can remember, he'd sing to us, lullabies when we were babies; then, when we were older, after dinner, after my granny had finished washing the dishes, after Jeannie and I had completed our homework, all kinds of songs, traditional ones and more contemporary tunes. Sometimes I'd wake up in the middle of the night and I'd hear him strumming away, something soft and pretty. I always imagined that was him playing a song for my mom.

"One day, just after my ninth birthday, my father called me over to him, had me sit down, and placed his guitar in my hands. I was terrified, to be honest. I had no clue what to do with it and I sure didn't want to look dumb in my father's eyes. You knew how he was, though, always so patient; he taught me where to place my hands, how to set my fingers on a string, how to play a note. He showed me the A chord, and G, and D. I learned from him how to pick the notes, and how to strum.

"Every night from then on my daddy and I found time to play music together. He'd teach me new chords and new songs. I looked forward to our lessons every night, treasured the time I spent learning from him and being so close with him.

"I was ten when he bought me my first guitar. I still have it at home. One night not much later than that I got to see him perform with the guys from Rosie's Ring. It was an outdoor festival, I remember, and when they played everyone was glued to the stage. Some people danced, some cried, some sang along, some just stood there frozen by the beauty of their music. They had complete power to move the hearts of everyone there.

"That's when the music bug bit me. That's when I knew I wanted to be just like my daddy when I grew up. I wanted to play something that would move people the way he did."

Aidan pulled his mind back to the present, and was surprised to see tears in Mack's eyes. He brushed away tears of his own. "That's what my father and I did, the way some fathers and sons play ball or watch sports together. We played music.

"I don't know how to face music without him."

Mack thought back to the New York hotel, to the phone call that changed everything for Aidan, for them all. He had wondered, that morning, how Aidan would survive the loss of his family. He couldn't predict, no one could, how Aidan would cope. Now he sat before Mack, strong, mature, ready to move forward.

"You didn't know how you'd ever make it this far," Mack reminded Aidan, "yet you have. You've overcome all the challenges life has thrown at you. Now it's time to face this last one."

Aidan stayed silent.

"You're still afraid," Mack observed.

Aidan knew he'd come here to level with Mack, to make it clear they had to get back to work without him. In true Mack fashion, his manager had cut to the heart of the matter. Aidan had to answer; Mack deserved that.

"Fishing without him was hard enough. There's no way I can go back to singing or playing guitar."

Mack understood, but he wouldn't let Aidan give up without one more push. "Do you remember the rope bridge you boys made me cross last year?"

"Carrick-a-Rede?" Aidan couldn't help laughing. "Oh yeah! We really had to talk you into that little adventure."

"Did you know I was afraid of heights?"

"No! Seriously? No way!"

"Yep. Can't stand 'em. But I wasn't about to let you guys know that. I just pushed on, praying all the way."

Aidan digested Mack's words as he finished his stout.

"What if I try and still can't do it? I don't want the pressure of all of you waiting on me."

"Why don't I book rehearsals in a couple of weeks, and recording, say, a month from now. See what you can do in the next two weeks. If you're not ready at the end of that, we'll find someone else to step in. Will that work for you?"

Aidan eyed the man who had led them through so much. He tried to think what it would be like to step away from Mack and the rest of Macready's Bridge. Was it harder to face a life without music, or a life without them?

"Sure, that's fair," he told Mack.

They finished their meal, then walked Mack's property line along the sea, talked of trees, and land, how the water changed colors as evening approached, and the roof Mack knew needed repairs. Mack said no more about music of any kind. When Aidan left to return home, Mack prayed he'd given the boy the right advice, and that Aidan would find his way through the next hard decision.

Aidan sat on the sofa staring at Annie, who still kept her silent vigil in the living room corner. Mack's words rang in his ears as they had the past two hours since he'd arrived home. Studying her blond wood body and rosewood neck, he recalled every time his father had set Annie to dancing, waltzes, quicksteps, reels, jigs, and quiet slow dances, music that brought parties to life or set a crowd to silence to hear the musician's magic. Daniel

O'Connell had brought Annie to life the way no one else, even Aidan, ever could.

Still she called to him, begging him to remove her from her banished cell, bring her out into the air and light, and give her back her voice. When her begging became a clamor that echoed in his heart, he stood up, walked over to where she stood, and held his hand out, inviting her to dance.

How smooth she felt in his arms, and how light. Her excitement fairly leapt out through her strings as Aidan cautiously turned her tuning keys and restored her harmony. His fingers trembled, but she held the notes steady, encouraging him to continue. Finally she was tuned.

Aidan sat back. The dance was calling; he recalled the tunes, but was unsure he could follow the steps.

This was it, the fork in the road, the place to decide which way his future would go. Play a song and move forward, break with the memories that haunted him, leave them behind. Or stay frozen in time, and still the music that had always driven his heart.

At last he drew Annie close, wrapped his right arm around her, held his left arm out to support her, and stepped into the dance, his favorite, "Red Admiral Butterfly", slow at first, hesitant, feeling the weight of aloneness, hearing each note bounce off the walls in the empty room around him. He followed that with other songs his father had taught him. As he played, old feelings returned, notes echoing in his heart, bouncing off his bones, electrifying his cells, carrying through at last to his vocal chords, forcing them to step out into the dance floor and join in the fun.

"It's grand to hear you sing and play your guitar again," Jack remarked as he and Rita shared dinner with Aidan two nights later.

"It feels good." Aidan passed the mashed potato dish to Jack. "You all were right. I needed to get back to music." He set his fork down and looked at them both. "There's something else I've realized I need to do."

Rita glanced at Jack, both of them anticipating Aidan's next words. "What's that?"

"You know I'm selling my father's garage. I think Terry Reilly will buy it, if he can work the financing out." He watched for their reactions. "I'm going to sell the house too. It's too hard to live there alone. Do you think that would be wrong?"

"No, boy, not wrong at all," Jack reassured him. "Where would you go?"

"I'm not sure yet. I came across an intriguing abandoned cottage out by Patrick; it's just crying out for someone to move in and restore it. It's up the road from Pat and his family, which would be fun, and it's close to the sea."

Then he said, and had no idea why he said it, "There's also this huge house out by Niall's, an old estate; it needs tons of work but it would be right by Niall and his family. The house and grounds are large, I could do almost anything with that place."

Rita thought the gleam in Aidan's eyes looked much like his father's eyes shining whenever Daniel had a new venture in mind. "You've turned a fine corner, Aidan. Whichever house you choose, you'll do well."

"I wouldn't have turned a corner at all without you two." The first phone call from Jack and all the moments after ran through Aidan's mind. "I don't know how I'll ever repay you for all the help you've given me."

"I can think of one way."

Rita looked at Jack, puzzled; Aidan looked at Jack, curious.

"Give us first crack at buying your house."

Rita's eyes grew large at Jack's request. "I haven't talked this over with you yet," he told her, "but the time is right."

To Aidan Jack explained, "Our daughter, Lizzie, she's getting a divorce. We've discussed her moving in with us; if we bought your place she could live there with her kids, and we'd be right next door to help her out."

"I'll make sure you're first in line."

As he left at the end of the evening Aidan noted, "It will feel so strange to not live next to you both."

"Aye, but that's the way of life, isn't it? Always some kind of change coming at us. The trick is to find our way when we can't see the road ahead." Jack placed a firm hand on Aidan's shoulder. "You've done well, Aidan. You've done your family proud."

"It would be nice to hear them say that."

Aidan still thought that later, as he turned lights out and stretched out on the sofa to sleep. His mind churned with thoughts of moving, the decisions ahead, leaving Jack and Rita and the house he'd grown up in behind. He remembered the failed sunrise drive, and his anger that'd he'd had no signs from his father when he needed it most. He longed again to hear their voices, now falling away from memory no matter how hard he fought to preserve them. Without looking at photos, even their faces were softening around the edges, losing their clarity.

"Follow your heart."

"What?" Aidan sat up and glanced around the unlit room, sure he'd heard a voice.

"Don't be afraid to reach for your dreams. Follow your heart."

Now he knew the voice, his grandmother's, was real.

"Gran?" He called out loud. Then, even though no light was on, his grandmother stood clear as day before him. "Gran! Is that really you?"

"Go for the house you want. Follow your dreams. Let your heart lead."

"Gran! Where are you? Where's my dad and Jeannie? Are you okay? Is my mom there?" Before he could call the questions out, she was gone; but peace filled the room, a peace he couldn't explain, the same peace that filled his heart as he eventually lay back down. Instead of sleep, he weighed the words his grandmother had spoken. By the time the morning sun's rays lit his granny's curtains in the living room window, his decisions were clear.

Aidan sat in Mr. Maloney's office, signing the last of a series of forms.

"MacLarens will have first crack at the house, right?"

"Yes, as long as their finances allow, it should be a simple process."

"The same with the garage? Terry Reilly's still set to buy it?"

James Maloney glanced through another form. "Yes, we've got confirmation on that, he will be able to buy the garage."

"So we're just about done. The estate's almost wrapped up." Aidan felt a mixture of relief and finality.

Mr. Maloney rose and offered his hand. "Aidan, you've handled all of this very well. Your father would be most proud of everything you've done."

"Thank you." Aidan left, hoping the solicitor's words were right.

Flaherty's was packed with its usual Friday night crowd; Aidan was grateful Kieran and Brendan had arrived early to save a table for them all. He ordered a round of pints for the three of them, and added a fourth when he saw Ben was also there.

"I didn't expect to see you," he remarked as he set a pint in front of Ben.

Ben shrugged. "The layoff is complete, I'm living home again for a bit."

"I'm so sorry. Hey, you're smart and you work hard, I'm sure you'll find something soon."

"I'll have to move away, I'm sure."

"What about you?" Kieran asked, "I see you've got the house for sale."

Aidan nodded, "I think I've got a buyer, I'll know in a day or two."

"That fast?" Brendan asked, stunned.

"Yep. Everything's falling into place just right." Aidan drank some Guinness before asking Kieran and Brendan, "Are you two okay on your jobs?"

Brendan pulled some papers out of his jacket pocket. "I think so, but we're not counting on that lasting forever." He pushed the papers towards Ben, "We're drawing up plans for our game arcade."

Ben surveyed the plans and whistled, impressed. "Very good start, boys. Why don't we meet tomorrow to go over what you've got so far."

Kieran looked sad instead of excited. "Aidan, I can't believe you're moving away. It won't be the same here without you."

Aidan took in his three friends, remembering good times, and times they'd helped each other out of various scrapes. "I know, it will be odd all the way around. I won't be far away though; we'll see each other again."

Music rose from the music corner, familiar to all of Flaherty's patrons, especially Aidan. Charlie, Sean and Tommy sounded in fine form, running through three fast paced songs before stopping. Aidan watched Charlie cast his eyes over the crowd, and suspected what was coming. This time, he was ready.

"Aidan O'Connell, will ye give us a wee tune tonight?"

As the eyes of everyone in the pub turned his way, Aidan nodded and rose.

"Auld Lang Syne?" he suggested to his father's bandmates. They agreed, he picked up Charlie's spare guitar, and they sang, slow and sweet, just the way Daniel O'Connell had taught them.

Before Aidan left, Charlie pulled him aside and handed him a paper bag, "I think this was your father's. Didn't realize I'd had it all these months. I'm so sorry."

Aidan opened the bag to find his father's favorite wool cap. "My dad was sure he lost this! Thanks. I'm so glad to have it back."

Charlie winked and wrapped Aidan in a bear hug. "You're a fine lad, young Aidan. Stay in touch."

"That sounds great!" Mack exclaimed as they finished afternoon rehearsals. Three weeks had passed since Aidan's visit. "Aidan, a wee bit louder on that last refrain. Patrick, you're tripping over your notes again. Niall, could be just a bit stronger on the first lines." He turned to Michael. "Michael, perfect as usual."

"Perfect as usual," the others mimicked, teasing their mate. He just beamed, "When you've got it, you've got it!" Then he turned to Aidan. "It's good to have you back."

"It's good to be back." Aidan glanced around the room at them all. "I know the past few months have been hard on all of you. Thanks for standing by me."

"Ah, before we all break for the weekend can I make an announcement?"

They all looked at Michael.

"Susannah and I have set our wedding date, third Saturday in November. You're all invited."

Cheers of "fair play," "well done," and "congratulations" rang through the room.

Mack spoke next, "The next time you call the house, if a woman answers the phone you haven't rung a wrong number." He enjoyed their looks of shock for a moment, then explained, "Kate's moved in with me."

"Way to go boss," "Good for you," and "It's about time she came to her senses" echoed all around.

Patrick and Niall rose and started packing their instruments.

"There's something else," Aidan called out. When they turned to him he said, "You know I've had the house and garage listed for sale. Things are all finished now, the garage and house are both sold. I'll be moving next weekend."

"Where to?" Patrick beat the others in asking.

"I'll give you all the address once the papers are signed. Think there might be a party involved as soon as I'm settled!"

As they broke for the weekend, Aidan drew Niall aside. "If it's okay, I thought I'd drive out and visit you and your folks for a bit."

"They'd love to see you. Why don't you ride home with me? You can leave your car here."

"I've got to take care of a few things first. Might take a couple of hours. I thought maybe I'd stop by for dinner, if you all don't mind eating a bit late."

"Fine. You'll stay over, won't you?"

"Sure."

Aidan stood in the front room of his house with Jack and Rita. "Are you sure you don't mind me not moving all my stuff out till next weekend?"

"Of course not, Aidan," Jack assured him. "We'll make sure nothing happens to it till you and your friends come by."

"And you'll both come out to see the new place in a few weeks?"

"I can't wait!" Rita's eyes lit with excitement. "You couldn't have picked a more perfect new home."

Aidan pressed the keys into Jack's hand. "I'm glad it's both of you buying this place. I think my dad and gran would be happy."

"I think they would be too." Rita smiled.

Aidan hugged them both, then asked, "Do you mind if I take a minute or two alone here? I'll close the door tight behind me."

"Of course. Take all the time you need."

"Well, it's done," Aidan announced to the empty house. "I've done the best I could." He walked through the house, upstairs and down, now filled with packed boxes to be moved to his new home, clothes to be donated to church and other charities, pictures taken down from walls, furniture tagged for new owners or marked for moving. Downstairs, he walked through the empty dining room where they'd taken so many meals, the kitchen his grandmother had always called her domain and threatened anyone she thought would intrude, the front room his father had always filled with music. He stepped out in the garden and noticed, on the fence, two magpies calling to each other. He had to smile. "Two for joy. Right, Gran, I've got your message."

He slipped his father's cap on his head, picked up the box of special items he didn't want to leave behind, and Annie and his own guitar in their traveling cases. Taking one last look around, he whispered "goodbye" and pulled the door closed behind him.

An hour later, Aidan pulled up to Niall's home, and handed Niall a bottle of champagne when he greeted him.

"What's this for?"

"We're celebrating." Then, to answer Niall's puzzled look he explained, "I've closed the deal on my new house."

"That was fast."

"I found the perfect place and didn't want to lose it."

"Can't wait to hear about it."

They leaned against Aidan's car as he described his new home. "It's big. Plenty of room, too much maybe but I can see me building a studio there, and someday, a long way off mind you, raising a family. It's an old place, needs a fair amount of work, but, well, I'm following my heart on this one."

Niall smiled. "It must be the right move. Your face lights up in talking of it. Where is this house? By the ocean I'm guessing."

Aidan shook his head. "No, it's out in the country. Backs up to a pond though, so it should suit me fine."

"What town is it near? I hope it's not too far away."

Aidan made a show of considering distance and location, then said, "No, not too far at all."

"Really?" Niall cast about in his mind, trying to think of any properties he'd heard were for sale.

"Yeah. There's lots of land to it, too. Who knows, maybe I'll raise me some sheep."

Niall still drew a blank. "Which town is it in?"

"Same as yours." Aidan decided to end his friend's agony. "In fact, I think you can see my new place from here."

Niall followed the direction Aidan was pointing, and studied the landscape hard before saying, "There's only the Gallagher estate out—" He stared at Aidan. "That's not it, is it?"

Aidan smiled wide in reply.

Niall stared at Aidan, stunned, then shouted out, "Mam! Dad! Quick! You've got to hear this!" When they came running, Niall exclaimed, "Wait till you hear! Aidan's bought the Gallagher place!"

Will Donoghue eyed the large estate on the other side of their lough. "The place needs a lot of work," he cautioned, then smiled at Aidan's excitement. "It is a house of dreams, though. I'll wager you already have your head full of plans."

Anna Donoghue's eyes shone as bright as Aidan's. "Now that you own it, maybe someday I can see it inside."

Aidan held up a ring with two keys jingling down. "How about now?"

The large house echoed back their footsteps and voices as they walked through, pointing out cracks and holes, broken windows, water stains from a leaky roof, and marveled over slate floors, marble mantles, and the intricate carvings on wood trim that framed doorways and lined ceilings.

"My granny would love this kitchen." Aidan's arms swept the spacious kitchen around them. "And Jeannie's artwork can hang in the library. And out there, that large building off to the right?"

"That was the carriage house," Mrs. Donoghue informed them.

"Don't you think that would make a perfect music studio?"

"O'Connell Studios. And we can call the house O'Connell Estate now."

Aidan shook his head. "Niall, I don't care what the house is called; but the studio, that will be Roisin Studios, after my mom. That was my mom and dad's dream."

"At night you'll be able to see our lights." Niall pointed out from the large master bedroom windows to where his family's farm stood. "And we'll be able to see yours."

"You don't think I'm moving too close to you, do you? I promise I won't be a pain."

Niall eyed his best friend, grateful he was still his band mate as well. "Not at all. I've told you before, you're family now."

As they continued through the house, the peace Aidan had felt the night his grandmother appeared returned, and grew stronger as they secured the front door and drove back to the Donoghue's farm, as they drank champagne and dined on Mrs. Donoghue's shepherd's pie, and discussions of his new home continued. As they dined and talked, he could feel his granny's presence again, and Jeannie's, and his father's, and even his mother's, and he knew he'd crossed from the past to the future, and the future was bright.

Acknowledgements

Turning a dream into a reality is never accomplished alone. I could not have completed Aidan's story without the support and encouragement of a very special group of people. Ann Crisafulli, you read the story first, your faith in me and encouragement in going forward was crucial and enabled me to stay on my path when the going got rough. Joyce Grinewich, Charlene Rosati, Tanya Rosati, Susan Hermiston, Joan Cross, Deb Scott, Kim Krajewski, Kelley Galyen, my wonderful readers, I am deeply indebted to you for your comments and encouragement throughout this journey.

Beth Ostrowski, my artist friend and fellow traveler, sharing Ireland with you was an incredible, unforgettable experience; I know you will recall so many locations we visited as you read this story. Research was never so fun! Half the success of any book is what readers find between the covers; without a good cover, a reader may never look inside. Thank you for creating such a beautiful cover design!

Oonagh Robinson at Long Tower Church in Derry, Northern Ireland, thank you for answering my many questions. Pauline McClenaghan and Finola Faller, thank you for your input at critical moments. Pam Stucky, thank you for traveling the writing path ahead of me and lighting my way.

I have many friends and family members who encouraged me throughout my work on this book, I will not try to name you all for fear of leaving

leaving someone out, but special thanks go to Karen, Angela, Linda, Mary, Joanne, Bob and Joyce, Lisa, Stacey, Jennifer, Gretchen, and Phyllis. My wonderful Western New York poetry friends, connecting with you all was the first step in my being brave enough to get to this point, you freed my creative mind!

Finally, and most importantly, thank you God for guiding me from start to finish. This is your story, not mine; thank you for trusting that I would tell it in the right way.

About the Author

Sinéad Tyrone lives in Western New York. Her poetry has appeared in The Buffalo News, The Empty Chair and Beyond Bones III. She is an avid photographer, reader, and student of Irish history, music and culture. Walking Through The Mist is her first novel.

Visit Sinéad's website at www.sineadtyrone.com.

Made in the USA
Charleston, SC
25 July 2014